Praise for Nicole Hurley

The McCalister Legacy
'Engaging and heart-warming, this is a great read
for a chilly night.' —Canberra Weekly

Lawson's Bend
'Nicole Hurley-Moore has once again proved to me that she is
a trusted figure in the world of Australian rural fiction. *Lawson's
Bend* delivers on all fronts, providing readers with the ideal mix
of small town intricacies, mystery and a hearty romance.'
—Mrs B's Book Reviews

White Gum Creek
'The perfect summer read.' —Noveltea Corner

Country Roads
'A heartwarming tale of taking chances, facing your
fears and opening yourself up to new experiences.'
—Beauty and Lace

Hartley's Grange
'. . . lives are put back together, lessons are learned, and old
friends resurface in a timeless story of life, love and living.
A wonderful read for a lazy Sunday afternoon which will
leave you with a total dose of that "feelgood" feeling!'
—Blue Wolf Reviews

McKellan's Run
'So very readable—you won't be able to put it down.'
—Newcastle Herald

Nicole Hurley-Moore grew up in Melbourne and has travelled extensively whilst living through the romance of books. Her first passion in life has always been her family, but since doing her Honours in Medieval Literature she has devoted much of her time to writing historical romance. Nicole is a full-time writer who lives in the Central Highlands of Victoria with her family in the peaceful surrounds of a semi-rural town. She is the author of the immensely popular novels *McKellan's Run*, *Hartley's Grange*, *Country Roads*, *White Gum Creek*, *Lawson's Bend* and *The McCalister Legacy*. *Summer at Kangaroo Ridge* is her seventh novel published by Allen & Unwin.

Summer at Kangaroo Ridge

NICOLE
HURLEY-MOORE

ALLEN&UNWIN
SYDNEY·MELBOURNE·AUCKLAND·LONDON

First published in 2022

Copyright © Nicole Hurley-Moore 2022

All rights reserved. No part of this book may be reproduced or transmitted in any form or by any means, electronic or mechanical, including photocopying, recording or by any information storage and retrieval system, without prior permission in writing from the publisher. The Australian *Copyright Act 1968* (the Act) allows a maximum of one chapter or 10 per cent of this book, whichever is the greater, to be photocopied by any educational institution for its educational purposes provided that the educational institution (or body that administers it) has given a remuneration notice to the Copyright Agency (Australia) under the Act.

Allen & Unwin
83 Alexander Street
Crows Nest NSW 2065
Australia
Phone: (61 2) 8425 0100
Email: info@allenandunwin.com
Web: www.allenandunwin.com

 A catalogue record for this book is available from the National Library of Australia

ISBN 978 1 76087 555 8

Internal design by Mika Tabata
Set in 12/16 pt Fairfield LH by Midland Typesetters, Australia
Printed in Australia by McPherson's Printing Group

10 9 8 7 6 5 4 3 2 1

 The paper in this book is FSC® certified. FSC® promotes environmentally responsible, socially beneficial and economically viable management of the world's forests.

Thanks to Chris, Ciandra, Conor and Alannah for all their love, support and sometimes questionable suggestions.

One

Christmas was a big deal for the Carringtons and the one thing they never took for granted. The entire family always made a point of being together on this precious day.

Tamara looked fondly at the people gathered around the long wooden table. The old kitchen was filled with delicious scents—like cloves, ginger and cinnamon—that she always associated with Christmas. It was noisy as her family chatted, laughed and, in the case of her two younger brothers, squabbled. The Carringtons all shared similar physical characteristics, from their dark hair, oval faces and light-coloured eyes, which ranged from a bluey grey to Felix's almost green.

It had taken a lot for her family to get to this point and Tam had had her doubts that they would ever be happy again. Her fingers fiddled with the small gold compass that hung around her neck.

'You all right?' Seb asked as he gave her a gentle nudge with his shoulder. 'You're a bit quiet.'

Tam smiled at her twin as she pushed a lock of her dark brown hair behind her ear.

'I'm just enjoying the scene.'

Seb glanced around the table. 'Yeah. It's good, isn't it?'

Tamara nodded but before she could answer one of her other brothers interrupted.

'Tam, can you pass up the potato salad?' Lix called out from the opposite end of the table.

'Felix, you don't have to shout.' Aunt Maddie gave him a mock frown, picked up the salad and handed it to her little daughter, Rori, to pass up.

'Sorry,' Lix replied sheepishly as he waited for the salad to reach him. 'Thanks.'

Seb turned to Tam with a grin. 'Some things never change. So, after the Christmas Day cricket match, it's time to find out which film is next in our top five Chrissy movies, right?'

Tam gave him a shrug. 'I don't think I can hang around that long tonight. I've got somewhere to be.'

Seb studied her. 'Really?' He gave her a penetrating look from his pale blue eyes. He was tall with a well-built physique and a sharply defined jawline. When he smiled, small dimples appeared in his cheeks; which was known to have a devastating effect on a portion of Kangaroo Ridge's female inhabitants. But he wasn't smiling now. The Christmas movie tradition had started years ago. Each year they would have a heated discussion on which movies should be included. Then for five days they would watch one each night, finishing the marathon on Boxing Day.

'This is a special family thing. We always watch the movies together,' Seb said.

'You can't guilt me into staying,' Tam answered.

'But don't you think—'

She didn't let him finish. 'Just because I have to leave doesn't mean that I don't love you all. I need a bit of time alone this year—I deserve that, don't you think?'

Seb was silent for a moment. 'I thought that we said we'd do everything we could.'

Annoyance sparked in her blue eyes. 'I did—I do.'

Aunt Maddie reached over and laid her hand over Tam's. 'Is everything all right, sweetheart?'

Tam nodded. 'Yes, nothing to worry about.'

Seb looked at his aunt. 'She says that she has to go out later. Won't be here for the movie.'

'There's plenty of us here, Seb,' Maddie said evenly. 'One person missing isn't going to ruin the evening.'

'I guess.' He moved back in his chair.

Tam loved him, she did. But sometimes he drove her insane. She picked up her glass and had a sip of the crisp white wine. Christmas fare for the Carringtons was a cold offering of meats, salmon, salads, cheeses, vegetables and dips. It had taken her, Aunt Maddie and Lix nearly all morning to put the food together and decorate the table but it was worth it. She sat back now and admired all their hard work. The most important thing was the chocolate cake surrounded by miniature gingerbread houses, which her younger siblings Gray and Lucy had made yesterday. It had become a tradition that those two would make the cake and Tam had to admit they were getting better at it with every passing year—this one was fantastic. Seb had been in charge of the bakery, snack and drink run, he got the easy job because he was still working at the pub until late last night.

'I took a call from a frantic bride yesterday.' Tam glanced at her aunt. 'She wants to know if there's any chance we could schedule a tiny wedding next month.'

Maddie blew out a breath. 'Geez, I don't know. We're booked right up until April, aren't we?'

Almost six years ago, Maddie and Tam had come up with the idea to turn the old farm into a wedding venue. Maddie had been desperate to find something that could sustain the family and keep it together. The farm was on one hundred and fifty acres, with a weed-filled garden, one barn, some broken-down sheds, a few grapevines and a dam as big as a lake. Tam had been only nineteen at the time but she had thrown herself into the project without hesitation. All the years of hard work had paid off and now Carrington Farm was a much sought-after venue and they were generally booked out months in advance.

'I feel really sorry for this girl though,' Tam continued. 'She had her dream wedding planned but right before the big day the venue she'd booked went under and she lost her deposit. Then the next venue she booked cancelled and now everywhere else is booked up.'

Maddie nodded sympathetically. 'Let me think about it,' she said. 'How tiny is tiny?'

'They've cut it down to their immediate family—her mum, her best friend and the groom's brother. She said that it didn't need to be big or special, they just want to get married.'

'Well, every wedding is special, no matter the size. Let's have a look at the bookings after lunch and see what we can do.'

'Okay.' Tam nudged her brother in the shoulder. 'Don't worry, it'll be done before the cricket starts.'

'I'll hold you to that,' Seb said with a nod.

* * *

After lunch Tam and Maddie headed to the office to look at the bookings while the rest of the family cleared away the remnants of lunch. Then they all assembled on the flat green lawn at the front of the house for the Christmas cricket match.

The day was warm and Tam sat with Rori in her lap under the dappled shade of the large peppercorn. Gray bowled and

Seb swung his bat, missing the ball entirely as it sailed past and slammed into the wickets.

Seb sank to his knees dramatically and shouted, 'Noooooooooo.' Rori laughed while Gray and Lix whooped in victory. Tam smiled—Seb was good at nearly everything . . . except cricket.

The day and the match wore on with laughter and lemonade. After dinner, Tam picked up her keys from the bowl on the kitchen bench. Her sister, Lucy, peered up from the fridge.

'Not staying for the movie?'

Tam shook her head. 'Nah, I wanted to catch up with some friends.'

'Your loss, you'll be missing the most quintessential Christmas movie,' Lucy said as she grabbed the orange juice.

'Okay, which one?'

'Your favourite—*Die Hard*.'

'Damn.'

'Told ya.' Lucy laughed. 'See you later, then.'

'Don't overdo the popcorn. Remember what happened last time,' Tam called as she shrugged into her leather jacket and headed to the back door. Her red motorbike, an original 1969 Triumph Bonneville, was parked in the backyard underneath a shady willow.

Tam settled on the seat, turned the key and slowly rode out the driveway. The sun had set behind the hills but the sky was still filled with the afterglow of orange, yellow and pink. Tam turned left at the gate and headed further out of town; the gums that lined the uneven bitumen road were bathed in a rosy light.

Not far from Turpin Hill, she turned down a dirt track and kept going, passing the No Through Road sign. Tam rode past an open rusty metal gate and followed the dirt driveway that snaked through the clumps of eucalypts until the small cottage came into view.

She parked in the front garden and walked to the blue front door. It opened before she had a chance to knock.

'I was beginning to think that you weren't going to make it,' a deep voice said from the shadowed doorway.

Tam smiled. 'I said that I was coming,' she said and she stepped into his waiting arms and kissed him.

Two

Eight years ago

'Sorry, Gemma, I don't think I can make it,' Tam said as she stepped outside so her parents wouldn't hear her phone call. It was a couple of days before Christmas and her best friend, Gemma Allen, was trying to persuade her to go to a party the next day—Christmas Eve.

'What do you mean you can't come? Look, your dad will be working and your mum is super busy, so she won't even miss you.'

'Yeah right,' Tam responded. She looked back at the house with all its Christmas decorations, and through the window she could see the beautiful tree that her parents had set up.

'No, seriously, she won't. Besides, it starts in the afternoon and we could be back before it gets dark. No one would ever know.'

'Have you even met my parents?' Tam wrinkled her nose and shook her head. 'If they found out that we were going to the Hendersons' place, they'd chuck a fit.'

'Oh come on, Tam, everyone is going,' Gemma cajoled.

'Who's everyone?'

'Most of our class, even some of the Year Twelves—you know, *everyone*.'

'I still don't think I can go,' Tam replied. She wandered through the front garden, with its little shrubs and ornamental bushes, scattered haphazardly among the garden beds, where all Mum's flowers grew.

'I need you,' Gemma pleaded. 'Will Griffith will be there—this could be the chance I've been waiting for.'

Tam sighed. 'Gem, you've had all year.'

'You can't just blurt these things out. What if he says no?'

'But why this party? It's not as if you won't run into him over summer—you'll even be working together.'

'I can't ask him at work,' Gemma said.

'I just don't understand why you're making such a big thing about this party. Blake Henderson's okay but his older brother is scary.' Tam sat down on the bench outside her house, under the old peppercorn tree. 'I really don't think we should go.'

'You don't even know that Taylor will be there.'

'It's his house, Gem—where else would he be?'

'Tam, I'm begging you. Please come with me. I promise we won't stay late and we'll be back before our parents miss us.'

'I don't—'

Gemma didn't let her finish. 'Please, Tam?'

Tam felt like she was being torn in two. She knew that her parents wouldn't want her to go out to the Hendersons' place but Gem was her best friend and she'd never asked for anything before. And, she had to admit, part of her was excited about the idea of going. The Henderson parties had a raucous reputation.

'What time does it start?'

'About one, apparently there's a barbecue,' Gemma answered with a hopeful tone.

'How are we supposed to get there and back? It's miles from nowhere.'

'I've talked my brother into driving us,' Gemma said.

'He agreed?' Tam's voice was tinged with astonishment. Jace never went out of his way to help his sister.

'Let's just say he agreed almost straight away.'

'You blackmailed him, didn't you?'

'Well, I kind of pointed out how angry Dad would be if he knew that Jace had been out the back paddock with a couple of his mates, smoking something other than cigarettes.'

'Really?'

'Yep, I caught him last week.' Then she added, 'Don't get judgey. It's survival of the fittest at my place and he would do the same if the situation had been reversed.'

'I'm not judging,' Tam said quickly. Gem's parents had always played Gem and her brother off against each other. Everything was a competition about who could do better at school, at sport and at life in general. The pressure on them to succeed and outdo each other was phenomenal. Tam had always thought it was a pretty messed-up way to treat your kids. It meant Gemma always saw Jace as her main rival rather than someone she could count on, and it was obvious that Jace felt the same. Tam knew her friend couldn't wait until she finished school so she could move out.

'So will you come?' Gemma asked again. 'Please.'

Tam let out a sigh. 'As long as we're back before it gets dark.'

'I promise,' Gemma replied with a laugh. 'Thanks, Tam, I really owe you one.'

'No, you don't,' she assured her. 'Just don't let Taylor anywhere near me.'

'Don't worry, there'll be so many people there I doubt he'll notice you,' Gem said, before adding, 'but even if he does, I've got your back. It'll be fun.'

'Okay,' Tam said, but she didn't feel convinced.

Three

Dylan Petersen walked into the Kangaroo Ridge Hotel around ten in the morning. He slipped in the side door that was usually left open during the day.

'Seb, are you decent?' he called out as he walked down the hallway.

There was a surprised shout before Seb yelled back, 'Geez, you scared me! I'm in the kitchen.'

Dylan stuck his head around the corner of the door and laughed at his best friend. 'Sorry.'

Seb waved him in. 'Want some coffee?'

'I wouldn't say no.' Dylan sat down on a tall stool next to a large stainless steel island. 'So how did yesterday go?'

'I think everyone had a great time.'

'Did your grandfather turn up?'

Seb shook his head as he made the coffee. 'Nope, not that any of us expected him to. He's got his life and we have ours; it's better that way. You know what he's like.'

'You'd think he'd want to make an effort,' Dylan replied.

'It's not his style.' Seb shrugged before changing the subject. 'You should have come around, there was plenty of food. Shouldn't have spent Christmas by yourself.'

'Thanks, but I wanted a quiet day to catch up on a couple of things.'

Seb studied him for a moment. 'What sort of things?'

'Nothing special.'

'You're not going to tell me, are you?'

'Nope,' Dylan answered with a smile.

Seb let out a laugh before saying, 'Come out for dinner later, that is if you aren't doing anything.'

'Thanks, I might do that.'

Seb poured the coffee into a blue mug. 'I'm thinking about closing the pub like this over the Christmas period every year.'

Dylan nodded. The pub was only closed for three days over Christmas but it was the first time he could remember it ever being shut. He knew it had been in the Carrington family ever since it opened its doors back in 1882 but there had been a chance it would close about eight years ago. With luck, and a lot of support from Aunt Maddie and the community—who didn't want to see the town's only pub close—Seb had managed to turn the hotel's fortune around and make it a viable concern. Dylan knew it had been a lot of hard work for his friend though.

'Seems fair enough,' he said, 'the town tends to grind to a halt now anyway.'

'That's what I thought. Besides, it gives the staff a nice little break.'

Dylan accepted the coffee mug from Seb. 'So what are you doing today?'

'Nothing much. I'll probably watch some of the Test match,' Seb replied. 'I have to make up a couple of meal boxes too.'

Dylan looked surprised as he put the mug down on the island. 'Who for?'

'George and Phil. I figured they might need some supplies.'

George and Phil were two of the pub's oldest regulars, and could be found at the bar every evening around six.

'They've got a carer, a cleaner and I think even meals on wheels,' Seb continued, 'but I'm not sure if that comes with a beer. They come in every night for a meal and a beer.'

'But the pub doesn't do meals every night,' Dylan said.

'We always make sure that there's something for them, even if it's only a turkey roll or a pie.'

Dylan looked at Seb for a while. 'I didn't know that.'

'They've been coming to the pub since well before either of us were born—I figure it's the least we can do,' Seb said. 'So, coming to the house tonight? There's some pretty tempting chocolate cake.'

Dylan sighed. 'Well, you know that is one of my weaknesses.'

He and Seb had been best friends for longer than he could remember. They had been through a lot, mostly good but there had been some really dark days too. He remembered when they were kids how they used to go swimming in the Carrington's dam on hot summer days, and the time when Seb came out with a couple of leeches on his leg, screaming like he'd been attacked by a crocodile. And all the times they were yelled at by annoyed people about the two of them causing mayhem on their bikes in the town. They had both lost their parents, although Dylan had felt the loss of Seb's parents more than that of his own father who had slowly drunk himself to death. Those awful days had bonded them together so now they felt like family, like brothers.

Dylan ran his hand through his slightly shaggy blond hair. 'Dinner at your place then.'

'It'll be simple,' Seb warned.

'Just the way I like it.'

* * *

'Do you think we can pull this off?' Tam asked.

Maddie studied the booking schedule for the tenth time. 'I think we can. As long as the bride is willing to compromise a bit.'

'She said she was desperate and willing to do anything,' Tam replied. 'Let's see if she really meant it.'

They decided to go over and inspect the space they had in mind for the wedding to see if they could swing it before they rang the bride. They left the house and walked through the garden, past the lush and vibrant vegetable patch and onto the path through the adjoining field. They could see the barn on their right, and up ahead the magnificent trees that surrounded the lake.

'So we can't use the barn because it's solidly booked out for the next few months. And the same goes for the orangery,' Tam said as they headed to the lake. They passed the barn, which had been converted into a beautiful space and could seat up to one hundred guests. It even had a small dance floor. Tam had used the old wood of the building as a feature and offset it with white linen, festoon lights and an abundance of summer flowers planted in garden beds and pots. There was an automatic watering system from a pump over at the water tanks, which kept the blooms fresh and vibrant. The entire effect was a rustic elegance with more than a hint of romance—an integral part of any wedding.

Beyond the barn was a raised platform on the edge of the lake. It was used to perform the actual ceremonies and was a popular option for couples during late spring and summer. The orangery was in the opposite direction and was used for smaller affairs, and for the brides who wanted their ceremonies inside and away from any unexpected rainstorms.

Tam and Maddie kept walking all the way around the lake, until they reached almost the farthest bank. Here, under the shade of a couple of old willows, was the hexagonal summer house. It was made of wood with a shingle roof and three of its sides were filled in with lattice. It had been built back in 1923 and was one of Tam's favourite places on the property.

Tam looked at the structure before glancing at Maddie. 'It wouldn't take much to spruce it up.'

Maddie nodded. 'Maybe a fresh coat of paint.'

Tam walked a few steps away in the direction of the water. 'You know, I reckon we could build a small deck in front. If we held the ceremony on the deck then the summer house could be used for the reception. It's only five people, it's not like we need a ballroom.'

'That's a brilliant idea,' Maddie said. 'Even if this bride doesn't want it, we should still do it. It'll add a lot of value.'

Tam grinned. 'It's such a lovely spot. I can see myself settling down here with a book and perhaps even a picnic.'

Maddie leant against one of the posts and stared out across the lake. 'I'll give Dylan a ring and see if he can fit us in.'

'I'll hold off calling the bride until we have his answer,' Tam said.

Maddie pulled out her phone from the back pocket of her shorts while Tam walked down to the edge of the water. From here all you could see was the reeds around the bank and the overhanging branches from the trees. A dragonfly darted past her before dipping down and almost skimming the lake's surface as it flew away. A breeze fluttered the hem of her red sundress and the tranquillity of the spot was only broken by the sound of a dozen tiny wrens in the undergrowth. It was a pretty place, a special place, and one that Tam was willing to share with a desperate bride, if only for a few hours.

* * *

Dylan's phone sounded in his jeans' pocket as he was getting out of the car. He'd helped Seb deliver the food box to George and Phil and then they had stayed for a coffee and a chat, so the task had taken a little longer than either of them had anticipated.

'Hey, Maddie,' he said as he answered the phone. 'Everything all right?'

'Hi, Dylan. Tam and I were wondering if you had time to squeeze a project in,' Maddie replied.

'How big of a project?' Dylan's building business was going from strength to strength but he'd decided to take a few weeks off this summer for a much-needed holiday.

'A small deck in front of the summer house,' Maddie said with a hopeful tone in her voice.

'Hmmm, maybe,' Dylan replied. 'Seb's invited me over for dinner. How about I check it out then?'

'That would be fabulous,' Maddie said. 'We'll see you later then. And thanks, Dylan, I really appreciate it.'

'No worries, see you tonight.'

'What was that about?' Seb asked as they walked back into the pub.

'Looks like I'm being roped in to build a deck for Maddie and Tam.'

'Whereabouts?'

'The summer house. Apparently they have plans for it.'

'Last time they *had plans*, we ended up stripping the floor in the barn and hanging a million festoon lights.' Seb laughed.

Dylan chuckled. 'I remember, and I have to admit I'm scared.'

'Well, it's too late now. You didn't really want a break from building, did you?' Seb asked with a wink.

'Nah, it's all right. I mean how big can the deck be?'

Seb raised an eyebrow.

'Oh, come on,' Dylan said with a laugh. 'It can't be that involved. It's just a summer house.'

'Famous last words, mate.' Seb laughed again. 'Famous last words.'

Four

Dylan stood next to Tam as the entire Carrington family studied the summer house and the ground around it. It was later than it felt as the sun hadn't set yet behind the hills. Summer was in full swing, along with daylight saving. The air was still warm and a small breeze drifted over the lake, rippling the water as it went. The same breeze swirled around him and brought the scents of water, dry grass and a hint of Tam's perfume. The latter was sweet, light and had a touch of something floral. It wrapped around him and for a crazy moment he almost took a step towards her. As if she read his thoughts, she turned her head and gave him a fleeting smile.

Damn, being around Tam was always problematic.

'So, what do you think?'

He snapped his head up in Maddie's direction. She was staring at him with an expectant look upon her face.

'Um . . .'

She shook her head and let out a sigh. 'You zoned out, didn't you?'

'Sorry, Maddie, I guess I did.'

'You know, this is one of my favourite places.' Tam smiled at Dylan.

'Yeah, me too,' he said as he returned her smile.

Seb walked over and slung an arm around his aunt. 'Don't be too hard on Dylan, Maddie,' he said. 'You know how distracted he gets if he doesn't eat.'

Dylan let out a breath, at least no one seemed to notice his preoccupation with Tam. 'So the deck goes there, in front of the summer house?' he asked as he pointed to a patch of ground.

Tam nodded. 'We were thinking it could go from where you're standing to about here.' She stepped away from him and walked towards the water's edge. 'That way, there'd be plenty of room to hold the ceremony on the deck.'

'So that's all you want—a plain deck?'

'Well, Maddie and I were thinking . . .'

'Oh, here we go.' Lix nudged Dylan's shoulder. 'You're in for it now.'

Dylan gave him a grin. '*We're* in for it now.'

Lix took a step back. 'What? I didn't say . . .'

Maddie's eyes shone with amusement. 'Oh, sorry, sweetheart, didn't I tell you? We're all going to pitch in.'

Lix closed his eyes for a moment before letting out an exaggerated sigh. 'Fine, no worries—I'll help with the deck.'

'Don't worry,' Rori said as she gave him a hug, 'I'll help you.'

Lix knelt down and tapped his little cousin's nose with his finger. 'I'm counting on you, baby bear.'

'I'll do my best,' Rori whispered back.

Lix gave her a hug before looking back to Dylan. 'Looks like you've got your construction crew,' he said.

'Excellent and with Rori's help, we'll get this knocked off in no time.' Dylan winked at Rori.

'Are you sure it's okay?' Tam caught Dylan's gaze. 'I mean, it's actually your holiday and we're railroading you to make the deck.'

He gave her a smile. 'It's fine. Plus I get to hang out with all of you,' he replied but his eyes never left hers.

'I don't want to force you into anything,' Maddie said.

Dylan shook his head and grinned back at her. 'Don't worry about it, it'll only take a couple or so days once we get going.'

'We all appreciate it,' Seb said. 'And don't worry, we'll all pitch in.'

'I'll come around tomorrow and start measuring up and make a list of what will be needed.' He looked over at the summer house. 'So, are you fixing this up for yourselves or will you be doing weddings here too?'

'Mainly for us,' Tam said. 'But there's a bride with a tiny wedding party and we thought that maybe this spot would be ideal for her.'

'If we spruce the place up a bit, it would give us options,' Maddie added.

'Sounds like a pretty good plan,' Dylan replied. 'I suppose you'll be painting it as well?'

'Yep, Gray and I are the chief painters,' Lucy said from where she was standing near the summer house. Gray looked up and smiled. He had a mischievous face with just a hint of dimples in his cheeks. His pale eyes glowed through the wisps of hair that had fallen cheekily down over his forehead, and you could tell that this was a guy who would charm the pants off anyone.

'Once it's painted,' Maddie said, 'Tam will work her magic on the decor and pull it all together.'

'She's good at making things pretty,' Dylan said before he realised that Tam was watching him. Prickles of heat flamed his cheeks so he quickly walked off, pretending to take a second look at where the deck was meant to go. 'How far did you want it from the water?' he called out without turning around.

Maddie bit back a smile. 'Just about where you are now,' she called back.

'Right, no worries—I reckon that'll work.' Dylan nodded and tried to regain his composure before heading back to the family.

'Well, if that's everything,' Maddie said, 'how about we all go back and get some dinner?'

'Thank God,' Gray said as he slung an arm around his aunt. 'I'm starving.'

'You're always starving,' Lucy replied, nudging him as they started back to the house.

Dylan fell into step with Seb at the back of the group. His friend slowed down his pace until the others had moved on a bit and Dylan hung back with him.

'Hey, don't tell me you've still got a thing for Tam,' Seb said quietly. 'I thought you got over that back in Year Eleven.'

'I don't know what you mean,' Dylan replied as he tried to walk a fraction faster.

Seb put his hand on Dylan's shoulder and stopped him. 'Seriously, mate, do you still like Tam?'

Dylan turned around and faced his friend. He knew he should just laugh it off but the words tumbled out before he could stop them. 'Would it be so bad if I did? Am I that bad?'

A frown creased Seb's brow. 'That's not it and you know it. It's complicated, that's all. The family is our first priority. It's not as if I don't think you're good enough to be with her—you're my best friend.'

Dylan closed his eyes as he tried to find the right words. 'I know that you, Tam and Maddie all sacrificed things to keep the family together after the accident, and I admire you for doing it. You've been amazing, Seb, but at some time you have to start thinking about the future.'

Seb rubbed his neck with one hand as he looked out across the lake. 'Yeah, I know. But we've spent almost eight years trying to hold it together, we can't just stop now.'

'When was the last time you went on a date?' Dylan asked.

'Oh, I don't know. A couple of months back?'

'It was almost seven months ago and you didn't follow it through with a second date,' Dylan said. 'Don't you think that you should start to live a little? All of you?'

'There's plenty of time for that, once the kids are more established.'

'Lix is twenty-two, Gray is at uni and Lucy is sixteen. I'm not saying you have to abandon the family but they're not little kids anymore.'

'Yeah but—'

'People grow up. Things change. Don't let your life slip by because you're too busy looking after everyone else.'

'Dylan, we weren't talking about me—we were talking about you and my sister. I just don't want you to get hurt—you know how she is.'

'What do you mean?'

'She's driven and sometimes she takes too many risks.' Seb turned his head and looked at Dylan. 'Like buying that damn motorbike.'

'And the skydiving,' Dylan said.

'Exactly. I've tried to talk to her but she keeps telling me to mind my own business.'

'She does have a point. I understand that you worry about her but you can't lord it over her.'

Seb shrugged. 'Maybe I am too hard on her. It's only because I care about her.'

'If you hold on to something too tightly, it will end up slipping through your fingers.' Dylan hoped his words wouldn't come back to haunt him.

'Is that your quote?'

'Nah, I think it's from *Star Wars*,' he said with a laugh.

This wasn't the first time that he'd felt as if he was caught in the middle. He understood Seb's concerns, he really did, but he could also see why Tamara felt caged. Both of the twins had given up years of their own lives to ensure their younger siblings had a stable family. It had been hard—awful at times—and neverending. Tam and Seb had just finished Year Eleven and were seventeen when their parents died. They'd gone from teenagers about to start their own lives to shouldering the responsibility of keeping their family together—a feat neither could have done without the support of their aunt.

'Tam needs space sometimes, that's all,' Dylan said. 'Loosen up a bit, the family is doing fine.'

Seb glanced at his friend. 'They are, aren't they?'

'Yep, nothing to worry about,' Dylan replied. 'So what about dinner? I'm starving.'

'You sound like Gray. Come on then, let's see what we can rustle up.'

They started back towards the house.

Five

Christmas Eve, eight years ago

Tam walked downstairs and into the open-plan living room. Her plan had been to write a note on the whiteboard in the kitchen and sneak out of the house without anyone knowing but that quickly fizzled when her mum, Estella, appeared from the kitchen.

'Hi, darling,' her mum said. 'Are you off somewhere?' Her sandy-coloured hair was up in her obligatory messy bun and she was wearing a black singlet top paired with a vibrant sarong, which was wrapped around her waist. She wasn't that much into jewellery but she always wore her emerald engagement ring and the diamond studs that had been a ten-year anniversary present from Tam's dad.

Tam bit her bottom lip. How did her mum always know what she was intending to do? It was like she had some weird psychic ability.

'I'm just going to Gemma's for a while,' Tam said.

Her mum nodded. 'Okay, just make sure that you're home before dark. It's Christmas Eve and we still have another movie to watch.'

'I'll be home, promise.'

'Do you need a lift to Gemma's? I have to take Lucy into town to get a few last-minute things.'

'I'm okay. I thought we were all set for Christmas though?' Tam replied.

Her mother rolled her pale grey eyes. 'So did I, but apparently not. Most of the food is ready for tomorrow's lunch but there's still a bit to do.'

'I can help you later tonight, if you like?' Tam offered.

'That would be nice. What time will you be back?'

'I don't know, maybe somewhere between six and seven.'

'That'll work. Oh and Grandad will be here by midday tomorrow. You and Seb may have to occupy him so I can get the lunch out.'

'Not a problem,' Tam said. She loved her grandad and it would be great to see him again, although she wasn't as close to him as she'd been with Nanny. Since her grandmother's death he'd moved into a retirement village one town over. 'I miss him not being here.'

Her mum laid her hand on the side of Tam's face. 'Me too. But I think this house reminds him too much of Nanny.'

Tam nodded. She understood. 'He said that he's made a load of friends in the new place.'

'I was worried at first but it seems like it's turning out perfectly.' Her mum leant against the dining table. 'Hopefully your dad will be able to close the pub earlier today since people will be preparing for tomorrow.'

'That's great. Is Aunt Maddie coming?'

Her mum shrugged. 'She's snowed under with work and she's not sure if she can get the time off.'

'That sucks.' Tam loved her aunt, she was always so much fun, even Tam's dad loosened up a bit when she was around.

Maddie worked in events at a luxury hotel in the city, and last year Tam had spent a few days of the school holidays with her. She had a tiny flat, not far away from the hotel and all the hustle and bustle of the city. Melbourne was so different from the slower, more laidback vibe of Kangaroo Ridge. Tam had loved it in the city and made a promise to herself that one day she'd move down, even if it was just while she attended uni. Kangaroo Ridge was her home and she couldn't envision being anywhere else permanently, but that didn't mean she couldn't shake things up and have a bit of an adventure.

Tam gave her mum a quick smile. 'I should go—Gemma will be waiting for me.'

'See you later then,' her mum said. 'Have you got your phone?'

'Of course.'

'Call me if you need to get picked up or anything.' Her mum made eye contact. 'Seriously, if you need me then ring. Promise?'

Tam nodded. 'I promise.' She took a couple of steps towards the back door.

'Hey, not so fast.' Her mum gestured to her to come back.

A worried look crossed Tam's face. Maybe her mum knew more than she let on? She turned back, 'What?'

'Since when do you go out the door without a hug?'

'Sorry, Mum.' Tam chuckled as she wrapped her arm about her mother and gave her a quick hug.

'Much better,' her mum said before she broke contact and stepped back. 'Have a good time.'

'Thanks, Mum. Love you,' Tam said and hurried to the door.

'I love you too,' her mum called back to her.

* * *

Tam made it to the end of the driveway before the weight of her guilt landed on her. She'd lied to her mum and she hated it. She should turn around and go back inside. But Gemma was counting on her. She couldn't back out now. Still, the whole thing didn't sit right.

With one more look back at the house, Tam made her way to Gemma's place.

* * *

When Seb wandered into the kitchen, he caught his mum staring out the window.

'Everything okay?' he asked.

She turned her head and gave him a smile. 'I was just watching Tam go.'

'She's going somewhere?'

'Gem's place.'

'Yeah right,' Seb said under his breath as he yanked the fridge door open and surveyed its contents.

'What do you mean?' his mum asked.

Seb shrugged as he poked around the fridge. 'Can I have some of this cheese or is it for tomorrow?'

'You can have some.' His mum sounded a bit frustrated. 'So where is Tam going?'

'Maybe she is going to Gem's, but I know the Hendersons are having their yearly Christmas bash. There's a lot of people going.'

'But you're not?'

'I can't stand Taylor Henderson. Why would I go anywhere near his place?' Seb replied with a shake of his head.

'He's a bit of a handful,' his mum agreed.

'That's a nice way of putting it. Look, I might be wrong. I shouldn't have ratted Tam out.' Seb grabbed some hommus and a handful of grapes.

'So it's a big party?' his mum asked.

He nodded. 'Yeah, there's talk that all the Year Elevens are going, as well as most of the Year Twelves.'

'I don't know why she didn't tell me if she was planning to go.'

Seb gave his mum a look. 'Seriously, would you or Dad have let her go?'

His mum didn't answer straight away.

'Look,' Seb added, 'maybe I should go and bring Tam and Gem back?'

'No, it's fine. I'll discuss it with your dad and then work out what to do. We're not even sure that Tam's gone out there anyway.'

'Okay, but if you want me to get her I will.' Seb locked eyes with his mum.

She took a step closer and ruffled his dark hair. 'I know that I can always count on you to look after your brothers and sisters. Thanks, darling,' she said. 'Now, off you go with your snack. I've got to pop out with Lucy to grab a couple of last-minute things.'

Six

There was a chorus of goodbyes from the Carringtons as Dylan got into his blue ute. 'Thanks for dinner,' he called out and then, with one final wave, he gave them all a grin before driving off.

'I might head off as well,' Seb said as everyone started to wander back into the house. 'I have a couple of movies calling my name.'

'I like the sound of that,' Lix said. 'You don't mind if I tag along and crash at the pub, do you?'

'Course not—I'd love the company.'

'Okay, give me a sec. I just want to grab a couple of things and raid the kitchen for snacks.'

Maddie put her hand on Lix's shoulder. 'Leave us some,' she said with a laugh.

'You got it, Maddie,' Lix said before disappearing inside.

Maddie waited for the others to move inside before she looked back at Seb. 'So, just between us, has Dylan still got a thing for Tam?'

Seb's eyes widened at the question. 'How did you know?'

'It's pretty damn obvious,' Maddie replied. 'He's been carrying a candle for her since high school.'

Seb walked over to the seat swing on the porch and sat down. 'I reckon he still does. Although I wish he didn't.'

A frown flickered across Maddie's face. 'I thought you'd be all for it. Dylan's a great guy.'

'But I don't think Tam is the right person for him.' Seb blew out a breath. 'That came out wrong. What I'm trying to say is that they're not suited.'

Maddie sat down next to him. 'I think they'd make a great couple.'

Seb shook his head. 'Tam doesn't take anything seriously. It might work out for a while but she'd lose interest and move on.'

'That's a bit harsh,' Maddie replied as she searched Seb's face.

'No, it's not. Don't get me wrong, I love her and she and Dylan are two of my favourite people but . . .'

'Don't you want Tam to be happy?'

Seb shot her a hurt look. 'Of course I do but Tam has a wild streak and I don't think Dylan could handle it.'

'She doesn't have a wild streak,' Maddie said. 'She's just making up for lost time.'

'Maybe.' But something in Seb's eyes told her that he didn't believe her.

'You've both had to give up so many things—hanging out with friends, partying and being teenagers. And I wasn't as much help as I should have been in the beginning,' Maddie said quietly.

Seb took her hand and gave it a squeeze. 'Don't ever say that, Mads. We all leant on you, even though you had no one to lean on yourself.'

Maddie gave him a smile. 'I don't regret a minute of it. But I was an adult, you guys were just kids. You two bore the brunt of the responsibility, and Felix did too—maybe not quite to the same extent but he was always there, doing what he could. You and Tam may be twins but you're very different people. Tam's just kicking over the traces and having a bit of fun. She deserves it.' Maddie looked Seb in the eye. 'And so do you.'

Seb closed his eyes as memories flooded over him. Trying to hold a business and a family together when it had been ripped apart. It had been hard, and at times he wasn't sure that they would make it, but against all the odds they had. But they hadn't done it alone, many people had helped, like Michael Chen, who they all called Uncle Mick as he was one of Dad's best friends. He had stepped up and managed the pub until Seb was old enough and confident enough to take over the reins. Without Mick's help, the family would have lost their only stream of income.

'Perhaps you're right,' he said.

Maddie gave him a nudge with her shoulder. 'Of course I am. You've taken on a lot of responsibility, Seb, and that's a credit to you but sometimes you tend to treat Tam like a daughter rather than your twin. It drives her.'

Seb nodded. 'Yeah, I know I can be—'

'A bit of a control freak?' she butted in with a laugh.

'Wow . . . okay,' Seb said quietly. 'I guess I am.'

'Only sometimes, darling,' Maddie said. 'All I'm saying is Tam deserves some happiness and if that comes in the form of Dylan, well, all the better—he's practically family already.'

'I just don't think it's a good match,' Seb said again, before adding, 'and I don't want either of them to get hurt.'

'I understand but that isn't your call. We love who we love and no one, no matter how well intentioned, can tell us otherwise. And even if it gets messy, Tam will always be your sister and Dylan your friend.'

Seb nodded. 'I'll try to step back and learn to hold my tongue.'

'Exactly, let them work it out for themselves,' Maddie replied. She was quiet for a moment. 'Has Tam ever taken an interest in Dylan?'

Seb shrugged. 'Not that I know of, although she doesn't share her secrets with me. All I know is Dylan was besotted with her when we were younger.'

'*Besotted*, really?'

'Oh yeah.' Seb nodded. 'He used to be teased about it a lot.'

Maddie gave him a look that had him holding up his hand in a sign of denial. 'Oh God, not by me . . . what do you take me for? He's my best friend. No, all I'm saying is it was pretty obvious that he liked her and the other guys gave him a bit of flak over it.'

'Does Tam know?'

'I doubt it. As far as I know she's never seen him as anything other than my friend and now a damn good builder.'

'If other people could see that Dylan liked her, I would imagine Tam would have known too—she's pretty perceptive.'

'You'd have to ask Lix—the two of them have always been close,' Seb said.

* * *

It was about 10 p.m. when Lix carried two mugs into the office and set one down in front of Tam.

'Hey,' she said, 'I thought you were hanging out with Seb tonight. Wasn't there something about a movie marathon?'

'He didn't make it to the end of the first one,' Lix replied. 'He fell asleep before the climax. So I figured I might as well come back here and catch whatever horror fest Lucy and Gray were watching.'

'And Seb?'

'I chucked a blanket over him and left him snoring on the couch,' Felix said with a grin.

'So what's this?' Tam gestured to the mug.

'Mocha with a heap of whipped cream.' Lix pulled out a chair and sat down opposite her.

'You spoil me,' Tam said as she reached for the mug.

'So whatcha doing?' Lix looked at the laptop and the stack of papers that were strewn across the office table.

'I'm playing around with the decor for the summer house.'

'It seems like a lot of work for one bride,' Lix said. 'I mean, it's going to cost quite a bit and we've only got one possible wedding.'

'But once it's fixed up we can offer it as an option for other couples,' Tam said. 'Even if it's only used a few times a year, it's better than it sitting there doing nothing.'

Lix pointed to several sketches. 'What's that?'

Tam gave him a smile. 'Some ideas. I was thinking about this sort of thing for the main focal light.' She pushed one photo forward so he could get a better look.

'So is it going to have the same sort of vibe as the barn?'

'Yes and no. I want all three venues to look cohesive but for each to have its own distinct style too.'

'I might take a few pictures tomorrow before Dylan gets here. You know, we can do the whole before-and-after photos as well as some construction shots. They might be fun to add to our website.' Lix took a sip of his mocha. He glanced at Tam and grinned. 'I'm quite talented, you know?'

'You really are. There's no way I could have made the website look so beautiful and inviting. Your photos are always stunning,' Tam said earnestly. It was true. Lix had a gift. Which is why she and Maddie had enticed him into running the social and advertising side of the business.

'Thanks, sis, but I meant the mocha.' He laughed and his green eyes twinkled with amusement.

'That goes without saying,' she said as she started to gather up her things.

'Calling it a night?'

Tam was silent for a moment. 'I might go out for a bit.'

Lix gave her a nod as he stood up, taking his drink with him. 'I thought you might. Have a good night.'

'Yeah, see you tomorrow,' Tam said as she closed her laptop. 'Love you.'

'Love you too,' Lix said before he disappeared out the door.

Tam sat there for a little while longer. Out of all her siblings, Lix was the one who really understood her. He had always been her friend, her sounding board, cheer squad and keeper of her secrets. She was so grateful to have him.

She stood up and placed her laptop and papers on the old sideboard before heading upstairs to grab her handbag and jacket. She made her way back downstairs and through the house towards the back door. In the darkened kitchen she grabbed her keys out of the bowl on the bench. Light came from the lounge room where Gray and Lucy were watching some terrifying movie with a lot of screaming and jump scares. Quietly she slipped out the back door. Within minutes she was heading towards Turpin Hill, the motorbike's headlight illuminating the old bitumen road as she went. Above, the clear night sky was dusted with a thousand stars and Tam felt anticipation begin to flare inside of her as she turned down the dirt track towards the hidden cottage in the middle of the night-shadowed bush.

Seven
Christmas Eve, eight years ago

Gemma's brother pulled the car over and parked on the opposite side of the road from the Henderson place.

'Are you sure about this?' he asked as he turned his head and looked at Gemma.

'Why?' Gem responded defensively.

'It's just . . .' Jace looked back out the window. 'Never mind.'

Tam grabbed her bag but remained seated. She was getting a little apprehensive because everyone seemed to think they shouldn't be going. Maybe she should stay in the car and get Jace to drive her back home.

Gem flipped down the mirror behind the sun visor, checked her makeup and fiddled with her blonde bangs. She was pretty and had an almost otherworldly, elfin look about her.

Gemma looked over into the back seat at Tam. 'You ready?' She scrunched her nose when she saw that Tam looked far from excited. 'Oh come on, it'll be fun.'

'Just remember I don't want to stay late,' Tam reminded her. 'I told Mum that I'd be back around six or seven.'

Jace looked at her in the rear-vision mirror. 'You told your mum that you're going to the party?'

Tam shook her head. 'No, I told her that I was hanging out with Gem at your place.'

'Right.' Jace turned his attention back to his sister. 'Listen, you're not going to tell Dad about the other day, are you?'

Gemma shook her head as she looked over at the Henderson place. 'No, I don't break my word.'

Tam noted that Jace stared at Gemma for a moment too long as if he was seeing her for the first time.

'Thanks,' he said. 'I don't mind driving you and Tam out here. But I really don't think it's a great idea.'

Gemma's head snapped back to look at him. 'What do you mean?'

Jace's hands tightened on the steering wheel. 'They're trouble, Gem. Maybe not all of them—but Taylor . . .'

'I know,' Gemma replied quickly. 'But that's not Blake's fault.'

'No one said it was,' Jace continued. 'But I really don't think that you should be hanging out here. Besides, you said that a heap of people are going but I don't see many people, do you?'

'Maybe Jace is right, Gem. Perhaps we should go back home.' Tam leant forward from her seat. 'We can catch up with the others after Christmas.'

For a moment Tam thought Gemma was wavering and that maybe she was beginning to see sense, but then two cars rolled up and parked outside the house. Half a dozen of their school friends piled out of the cars and headed inside.

'See, we were just a bit early,' Gem said triumphantly. 'There's nothing to worry about. Honestly, you two.'

Jace nodded. 'All right, but I'm going to Bendigo with Matt and Jenny, I can't pick you up until later tonight. If you need to get home earlier, you'll have to work something else out.'

'How late do you mean?' Tam asked before Gem even had a chance to open her mouth.

'We're spending all afternoon there so probably not until six or something like that,' Jace said.

'We'll be fine,' Gem said. 'I'll give you a call around then, okay?'

'All right,' Jace said.

'Come on, Tam—let's go.'

Reluctantly Tam started to get out of the car. 'Thanks, Jace,' she said before she closed the back door. She had also just shut off her only route of escape.

Jace called out to his sister, 'I'll see you later, Gem. Don't do anything stupid.'

Gem frowned at the word but stopped long enough to give him a wave goodbye.

'Can you believe him?' she exclaimed as she linked arms with Tam. 'Just because he's older, he thinks that he can boss me around.'

'I think he's looking out for you,' Tam answered as they crossed the dusty dirt road towards the house.

Gemma looked surprised at the idea. 'No,' she said with a tone of disbelief. 'You don't really think that, do you?'

'Actually, I do,' Tam said.

Gem was silent as she tried to digest what Tam had said. They walked until they were by the old fence where a scraggly rose vine clung and wound itself through the broken wire. There was a dilapidated iron gate which opened onto the paddock next to the side of the house. The grass was beginning to dry off and the only shade came from a stunted peppercorn that stood by a rusting shed down the back of the block. Several cars in various stages of disrepair were scattered around the shed's perimeter, along with a stack of tyres and assorted doors, panels and engines.

The party was set up in the middle of the paddock. The scent of cooking onion filled the air as the summer sun warmed Tam's back. She scanned the people to see if there was anyone she knew. A group milled around a small gas barbecue next to a couple of trestle tables and several eskies. Music thumped out of a small speaker as two girls she didn't know danced not far from the barbecue. She strained her ears but she couldn't place the song.

Tam glanced at Gemma. She tried with all her might to push down the panicky feeling that had started to bubble within her. She only recognised a handful of people, which was a much smaller number than what Gem had promised.

Another car pulled up nearby and several more people got out of it.

Gemma grinned and waved at Dylan Petersen and Will Griffith, before she leant in close to Tam and whispered, 'See, I told you that Will would be here.'

Tam nodded, relieved that Dylan and Will had arrived. Dylan was Seb's best friend and something about that made her feel better. Even so, she still couldn't shake the feeling that she shouldn't be here.

'Yeah. Now you can tell him that you like him and ask him out, so we can go home.'

'Shhh,' Gem bit back. 'God, Tam—he'll hear you.'

Unless Will possessed exceptional hearing, she doubted it. It took another minute before the new group walked up to where they were standing.

'Hey, Tam,' Dylan said with a nod. 'Didn't realise you'd be coming. Gemma.'

'A last-minute thing,' Tamara replied. 'Seb didn't come.'

Dylan leant against the fence, the bright sun shining down on his golden head, illuminating the different shades of blond and gold. It wasn't until that moment that Tam realised just how pretty his hair was.

'I didn't think he would. You know how he feels about Taylor,' Dylan said.

'I thought you felt the same.' Tam looked into his blue eyes.

'I thought I'd stop by anyway.'

Another car pulled up. 'See,' Gemma said to Tam, 'I told you that heaps of people were coming.'

'So, why are we hanging around here?' Will asked as he flashed a smile at Gemma and held out his hand. 'I'm starving, let's get something to eat.'

Gem shot a look at Tam before stepping forward and taking his hand. 'Yeah, let's go in.'

Dylan stood back to let Tam walk through the gate before falling into step beside her.

Eight

From his bed, Dylan could see the sun inching its way over the hill in the distance. The pale morning sky silhouetted the gums on the ridge and for a moment he was content. He looked down to where Tamara was sleeping by his side and wished that things could stay like this forever. He closed his eyes, he could pretend that this was enough for her . . . but somehow he knew it wasn't.

She stirred next to him and he was torn between letting her sleep and holding on to the moment a little longer or waking her up, like she'd asked him to do. He hesitated as the cool morning air fluttered through the old lace curtains and over to where he was lying. It was fresh, almost bracing against the warmth of his skin.

He was caught in a charade, not of his choosing. They had been seeing each other for almost a year. Tam wanted to keep it a secret, so no one knew—not even their closest friends or family. At first it had been almost exciting to have a secret and keep it. The thrill of hidden meetings in secluded spots was heightened by the threat of discovery. But as time passed the feeling diminished; not how he felt about Tam—the love, the wanting and the longing only intensified—but the sneaking around part.

Every now and again he'd suggest or hint, and once he'd almost begged, that they act like a proper couple. Yet each time Tam said that their relationship was fine as it was and people knowing would only complicate things. Maybe she was right—he could only guess how Seb would react when he found out that his best friend was in a relationship with his sister.

And each time he'd mentioned it, Tam had pulled away. He'd loved her ever since they were seventeen but he was frightened that maybe she didn't feel the same way. And yet the idea of not having her in his life terrified him more.

Tam stretched and let out a sigh.

'Good morning,' Dylan said as he leant over and kissed her forehead.

She looked up at him with her pale blue eyes and smiled. 'Hey, did you sleep okay?'

Dylan nodded. 'Yeah, how about you?'

'I could stay here all morning,' Tam said with a yawn as she sat up.

'So stay.' Dylan kissed her. 'We could just take the whole day off.'

Tam shot him a grin before throwing back the covers. 'Tempting as that is, we've got stuff to do, remember?'

'Nothing that we couldn't put off for a day,' Dylan said hopefully. He watched her get out of bed and start searching for her clothes.

'I seem to remember that you promised to do some building around the summer house,' Tam said as she glanced out the window and saw the rising sun. 'Damn, it's getting late, I'd better get moving.'

Dylan propped his head on his hands as he leant back against the rustic wooden bedhead. 'It's barely dawn, Tam—how can you possibly be late?'

'I've got a lot on today. Besides, I thought I'd get home before everyone else gets up.'

'You're a grown woman, you can come and go as you like,' Dylan reminded her.

'That's true—but if no one knows then they won't comment. You know that I hate speculation, especially when I'm the point of interest.'

'I don't know why we can't just tell people that we're together.'

'Because it's no one's business but ours.' Tam shrugged into her leather jacket.

'But I hate all this hiding about. I don't want some sort of grand gesture in the middle of town but can't we at least make it official by telling Seb and the rest of the family?'

'Why muck up a good thing?' Tam replied as she leant across the bed and dropped a quick kiss on his mouth. She pulled back before he could wrap her in his arms. She was already picking up her bag which was sitting on an old, scuffed rocking chair in the corner of the room. 'I'm off. Apparently, I've got a hot builder turning up later to build a deck.'

'You're dodging the question again,' Dylan said as she headed for the door.

She yanked open the door before looking over her shoulder. 'I love you, Dylan—isn't that enough?' Then she disappeared.

Dylan sat up and ran a hand through his blond hair before grabbing a pillow and tossing it towards the foot of the bed.

God, she could be infuriating sometimes.

Moments later he heard her motorbike kicking into action. He got out of bed and wandered over to the window, in time to see Tam ride off. He waited until she'd vanished from view as she followed the winding dirt track back to the front gate. Her words danced around his head: *I love you, Dylan—isn't that enough?*

He stared out the window at the bush that surrounded the cottage as he thought about what she'd said.

Maybe it wasn't enough, perhaps this time he actually needed more.

Dylan sighed as he rubbed his hand over his face. He needed coffee, with any luck it might clear his thoughts. He took one last glance at the empty driveway before turning on his heels and walking towards the kitchen.

* * *

Tam rode down the winding track but she didn't see the beauty of the bush in the morning light because her mind was stuck on what Dylan had said.

In high school, Tam always had the sneaking suspicion that he liked her but she didn't see him that way back then. And she'd never had a chance to. When her parents died, there was no more time for parties, fun or even boys. She had to step up and look after Lix, Gray and Lucy. She'd made a promise and she intended to keep it. Because of that promise, she had worked hard and did her best to always make the right decisions for her family.

She remembered the night she, Seb, Lix and Maddie had sat around the old kitchen table and made a list of what they had, what was owed and how they could generate enough money to keep the family going. What they had was a pub that neither Seb or Tam could run, a broken-down farm that hadn't been worked in decades and a rambling old house that, even though it could house everyone, was in need of repairs. A small inheritance from their parents and Maddie's savings were enough to keep them afloat for a while, if they were careful. But along with her money, Maddie had brought a surprise that none of the Carringtons saw coming—she had been about six months pregnant when she'd arrived.

At first, Tam had thrown herself into keeping the family together. If she worked as hard as she could then maybe she'd be able to forget the pain of her parents' death, even if it was only for a moment or two.

She kicked over the traces whenever she could. Perhaps it was another form of escape but she partied hard anytime she was able to snatch a little time for herself. She became unpredictable and even reckless when she allowed herself to and because of it lost most of her friends, except for Gemma. Even though they weren't together back then, Dylan had always been around and he had brought her back from the edge numerous times. She was lucky to have him in her life. It hadn't been a lie what she'd said this morning, she did love him but she knew that he wanted more. He wanted the whole damn fairy tale even down to the picket fence and the happily ever after. The problem was that she didn't know if she was ready for that. Hell, she probably didn't even deserve it.

Maybe she should walk away and let him find a future with someone else, someone who could actually make him happy? She didn't want to let him go but perhaps it would be for the best.

No, she told herself, everything would be fine. Dylan would drop the subject like he always did. All she had to do was let it blow over.

Tam drove up the driveway of Carrington Farm and parked her bike behind the house.

'Hey,' Lix said as she walked into the kitchen.

'You're up early,' she said as she walked over and picked up the kettle.

'I just boiled it,' Lix told her. 'There should be enough in there for you.'

'Thanks.' Tam went about making a cup of tea.

'Everything all right?'

She paused. 'Yeah, everything's fine.'

'You're really not good at that,' Lix said as he sat on the bench and sipped a steaming mug of coffee.

'What are you talking about?'

'You've never been a good liar. I can see through the bullshit, what's up? Did you have a fight with Dylan?'

Tam shook her head as she poured the water into her cup. 'No, I didn't. It's just . . .'

Before she could finish, Maddie walked into the kitchen. 'Good morning!' she said happily. 'Gosh, you two are up early. Shall we have breakfast together?'

Tam shot Felix a glance before turning to Maddie. 'That would be nice.'

'Good idea,' Lix added. 'How about I make pancakes?'

Nine

Tam glanced out the office window when she heard the sound of tyres on the gravel drive at the front of the house. Dylan's ute pulled up by the small rose garden that had been planted by her grandmother decades ago. She was about to go out when she saw that her brothers were already there.

'Call this an early start?' Gray laughed as Dylan clambered out of the ute. 'It's nearly ten o'clock.'

'Yeah, well I'm on holidays,' Dylan called back. 'You two ready to get your hands dirty?'

'Sure thing,' Lix said. 'Meet you at the summer house?'

'No worries.' Dylan got back in the ute. 'I can drive down that little track that comes out behind the summer house, can't I?'

Lix gave a nod.

Gray gestured to the ute. 'I'll go with Dylan.'

'I'll catch up with you in a minute,' Lix said and headed back into the house.

A few moments later he stuck his head around the office door. 'Dylan's here.'

Tam looked over from the window and smiled. 'I figured. So what's happening?'

Lix shrugged. 'I'm not one hundred per cent sure as I've never built a platform before. Are you coming down?'

'Soon. I've got a couple of things to do here first.'

Lix gave her a big smile. 'Right, see you later then,' he said before he disappeared.

Tam sat down at her desk and looked blankly at her computer screen. This thing with Dylan was problematic. Things were great as they were and she really wished that he'd stop rocking the boat because if he was set on taking their relationship to the next level then maybe they couldn't be together.

She blew out a breath and sat back in her chair before leaning forward again to pick up her phone. First, she had a bride that needed rescuing.

'Hi Angie, it's Tamara Carrington. Just wondering what you thought about our alternative idea for your wedding? I have a few more details, if you're interested.'

Tam spent the majority of the morning in the office and it wasn't until sometime after lunch that she walked down to the summer house. By that time all her family were already down there working alongside Dylan. The footings for the deck had been put in and Dylan and her brothers were cutting and carrying wood, while Maddie, Lucy and Rori were painting the outside of the summer house.

'How's it going?' Tamara called out as she walked over to Dylan and Seb.

Dylan gave her a bright smile. 'Pretty good.'

'Not bad,' Seb replied with a nod. 'You took your time getting down here.'

'Well, you might be building the deck but the whole summer house has to be redone too. I was going over the design and ordering the materials,' Tam shot back. Sometimes Seb really got under her skin and it made her prickly. She rarely questioned him, so why did he think it was his place to do the same to her?

Seb glanced at her. 'Sorry, did that sound like a criticism?'

Tam took in a breath before answering, 'Yeah, it did.'

'It wasn't meant to be,' he said. 'Anyway, did you get some nice stuff?'

Tam gave him a nod and then a smile. He might drive her insane sometimes but she did love him . . . well, most of the time. 'I think so.'

'Great.' He had a look of relief on his face. 'Maybe you can show it to me later?'

'Sure if you like.' Tam turned her attention to Dylan but before she could say anything Rori came running up to her carrying a dripping paintbrush.

'Tam, Tam, you've got to come and help,' Rori said as white globs of paint dripped off the brush and onto the grass.

'Woah, steady on there.' Tam laughed as she held up her hands and studied her paint-covered cousin. 'It looks as if you've got more paint on you than on the wall.'

'You've got to come,' Rori said. 'I told Lucy that I could paint the whole wall but I can't reach the high bit.'

'So you want me to help?'

Rori vigorously nodded her head, sending her long dark locks bouncing about. 'Yes, but we can't tell Lucy, it's a secret.'

'You don't think she'll notice?'

'Not if we don't tell her,' Rori said before grabbing Tam's hand and tugging her towards the back of the summer house.

Tam felt the squish of wet paint between their hands but it was too late to do anything about it. She glanced over her shoulder to Dylan as she was dragged away.

'Looks like I'm off to paint,' she said.

He chuckled. 'I'll see you later then.'

After almost an hour, Tam and Rori stood back and admired their freshly painted pale lavender wall. The day was so hot, the paint dried within minutes, so they had been able to put on an undercoat and the coloured top coat. The summer sun blazed down but the house was somewhat protected by the tall gum trees at the back that gave dappled shade. A bank of several rhododendrons also almost ringed the back of the structure. Tam's grandparents had planted them years ago and now they were around six feet high and about to burst with purple and pink flowers, which would offset the pale, almost barely there lavender of the paint very well.

'I think we did pretty good, don't you?' Tam asked as she turned and looked at her paint-splattered cousin.

Rori nodded. 'Sure did and I bet we beat Lucy.'

'What was up for grabs?'

'She said if I could finish the whole wall she'd buy me a tub of my favourite ice-cream,' Rori explained.

'Really?'

'Yep and you can have some since you helped.'

'I might just take you up on that. So what flavour are you going to get?' Tam asked.

'Strawberry,' Rori answered with a bright smile.

At that moment Lucy walked around the corner. 'Oh wow, you've finished. That's a pretty good job, Rori!'

Rori looked pleased but then a frown flitted across her face. 'Tam helped, I couldn't reach the high bits.'

Lucy squatted down in front of her. 'That's why I came to see if you needed a hand,' she said. 'Either way, I think we should talk Lix into driving us into town to pick up some ice-cream.'

'Really?' Rori replied with a look of happiness on her face.

'Absolutely. Come on, let's see what Lix is up to,' Lucy said as she held out her hand.

Tam opened her mouth to warn her about the amount of wet paint on Rori's hand but it was too late. It didn't appear that Lucy minded though as they started walking away. Rori glanced over her shoulder. 'Are you coming too?'

Tam shook her head. 'Nah, I'd better stay here and help the others. Especially now we've lost our best workers.'

Rori let out a laugh before turning around and skipping alongside Lucy.

Tam followed behind and watched with some amusement as Lucy managed to convince Lix that he really wanted to drive them to the supermarket. He finally put down his nail gun and sighed in defeat.

'Oh all right, Luce,' he said

'Great! We'll clean up and be at the car in five minutes,' Lucy said brightly. 'Come on, Rori, I'll race you to the house.'

'Thanks, Lix,' Tam said.

He gave her a half-hearted shrug. 'We all know that those two run circles around me.'

'Around all of us,' Tam replied.

'Including me,' Dylan said as he sauntered over and joined them. 'Last time Rori roped me in to getting my nails painted.'

Lix laughed. 'I remember,' he said as he handed his nail gun to Tam. 'You'd better take this.'

Tam raised her eyebrow. 'Really?'

'Yep, you'll do great—I have faith in you.' He started to back away. 'Besides, Dylan will help you out,' he added with a wink.

'Wait, where's everyone else?'

'In the summer house. They're putting up some scaffolding so Gray can paint the ceiling,' Lix explained before he gave her a wave and headed back to the main house.

'You've used one of those before?' Dylan asked as he stood close to her.

'Of course.' Tam turned around and studied the partially made platform. 'So you want to show me what Lix was working on?'

'Sure.' He reached out and placed his hand on the small of her back.

Tam felt the heat of his hand through the light cotton of her singlet top. She glanced up at him to find him staring back at her. The already warm air seemed to sizzle around them. Her heart beat a little harder and when he momentarily bit his bottom lip a rush of desire coursed through her. For a brief moment she wanted to throw caution to the wind and throw herself on him

The whole thing lasted only a few seconds before they broke apart. Tam was sure that no one had seen them as everyone else was still in the summer house helping Maddie.

* * *

Seb had just stepped into the doorway when he saw Tam and Dylan together. A frown creased his brow as he looked at his sister and best friend standing close together. There was clearly a connection between them. Deep down he always thought this could happen as it was obvious that Dylan was attracted to her. What he hadn't realised was that Tam might feel the same way.

He took a step back inside the summer house. It wasn't any of his business, at least that's what he kept telling himself. But how could he stand back and watch two people who he loved crash and burn?

It wasn't that Seb thought there was anything wrong with his sister, he even admired her in a lot of ways, especially the way that she was never afraid to be herself. More than once, he'd wished that he could be more like Tamara and get a dose of her confidence. What worried him about the possible relationship was that they were opposites and would be behind the eight ball before they'd even started. Maybe he should have a word with Tam and put a stop to it before anyone got hurt.

He took one more look outside. Tam and Dylan were measuring and cutting the boards for the deck. They were working closely together in the dappled sunlight and, even from where he was standing, Seb could see the way they were looking at each other.

He sighed. How was he going to nip this in the bud? And, more importantly, should he even try?

Ten

Christmas Eve, eight years ago

Tamara followed her friends down to the party. She noticed that they were all dressed to impress in their trendiest casual clothes. They had spruced themselves up so much that they hardly looked like the friends she knew so well.

Most of the other people at the party didn't go to her school, and the ones she did recognise were several years older. They must have been Taylor's friends rather than Blake's, or so she imagined. She was a little surprised and disappointed as she had heard that all the Year Elevens and Twelves were going. The uncomfortable feeling deep in her stomach didn't fade away, no matter how hard she pretended it wasn't there. Maybe it was guilt. She knew her parents would flip if they found out she was here—especially her dad.

'Hey, Blake,' Dylan called out as a guy about Dylan's height ambled over. Blake's light brown hair seemed to match his eyes and, when he smiled, Tam noted that he had a dimple in his left cheek. Up until that moment she'd never noticed it before.

'Hey,' Blake said with a grin. 'I'm really glad that you all made it.'

'Thanks for inviting us,' Dylan responded. 'Anyone else from our class coming?'

'I hope so, but it's Christmas Eve and some of them wouldn't have been able to get away,' Blake replied.

'You're right,' Gemma said. 'Tam and I can only stay for a while because we have to be back. Mum would never forgive me if I was out late.'

Blake nodded. 'I really appreciate you coming . . . I mean a lot of people wouldn't because . . . well, you know, thanks.'

Will Griffith let go of Gemma's hand and gave Blake a playful thump on the shoulder. 'Happy to be here,' he said as he looked towards the barbecue. 'Can I get in on that?'

'Sure thing,' Blake said. 'Help yourself.'

'Should we have brought something?' Tam asked.

'Oh no, not at all. I think there's enough sausages to feed us for a whole week,' he answered. 'Come on, let's grab some.'

They followed Blake down to the barbecue. The grill was filled with sausages and there was a pile of onion on the side. On a table close by there was about a dozen loaves of bread, several bottles of tomato sauce, a roll of kitchen paper and a large bowl of coleslaw. Blake and Dylan stepped forward and started grabbing bread to make sausage sandwiches for the rest of them.

Gemma edged closer to Tam. 'There's nothing but sausages,' she whispered so no one else could hear.

Tam gave her a gentle poke in the ribs. 'You don't want to embarrass Blake.'

Dylan glanced over his shoulder. 'Hey, Tam, do you want everything on yours?'

She smiled and gave him a nod. 'Oh yes please—that'd be great.' She turned back to Gemma, whispering. 'You know that Blake's family struggles a bit, so suck it up.'

Gemma let out an exaggerated sigh. 'Oh all right,' she said before calling out to Will. 'Will, could you please get me one with everything too?'

'Sure, Gem,' he replied.

She looked back at Tam. 'Happy now?'

Tam grinned at her. 'Yes, I think I am.' She glanced over at Blake who was laughing at something Dylan had said. Taylor was certainly the more handsome of the two brothers. He was taller with high cheekbones, a well-defined jaw and hazel-coloured eyes but those eyes could turn as cold as stone in an instant. There was something about him that scared Tam and yet she couldn't put her finger on what it was exactly.

The guys returned with the sausage sandwiches and all of them wandered over to sit in the shade of the lonely, stunted peppercorn tree. It wasn't much protection from the summer sun but it helped a little. Dylan sat down next to her as they listened to the music and watched as more people arrived. Tam was keenly aware of Dylan, they weren't touching but she was sure that she could almost feel his body heat. She tried to damp down the surge of butterflies that pirouetted inside her.

Dylan had always been around. He and Seb played footy together, hung out all the time and basically lived in each other's pockets. Tam had always been in the same grade as them at school. Even the same class, except when they had started travelling to Bendigo to go to the high school. There she chose different electives and didn't see either of them quite as much. But they all still hung out after school and her mum even set a place for Dylan at the table most nights. For years she'd found Seb and Dylan annoying but something had shifted last winter; the change was so minuscule Tam didn't even realise it at the time. But it was as if she was actually seeing Dylan for the first time and he'd gone from that goofy friend of Seb's to something more. He still teased her every now and again but she'd noted that he kept looking at her whenever they were together. How did she know? Because she found herself looking at him too.

Nothing had happened but she couldn't deny there was a little buzz of excitement every time he walked through the door. It was dumb and Seb would freak if he ever suspected but she couldn't help herself. Tam was realising she had a full-blown crush on that boy and there was nothing she could do about it.

No one knew, except for Gemma, who told her time and time again to go for it because Seb would eventually get over it. It wasn't bad advice but Tam was worried about how it would affect her relationship with her brother. People thought that because they were twins they would be like an extension of each other, but it wasn't the case. In fact, they seemed to be polar opposites. And Seb always acted as if he'd been born five years before her rather than twenty-five minutes.

Now, at the party, Tam wiggled back so she could rest against the tree trunk, and as she moved, her hand brushed Dylan's. She stilled for a moment, unsure of what to do. She should pull her hand away but the seconds ticked by and she didn't. She finally willed herself to pull away but in that moment Dylan closed his hand over hers.

The world seemed to fade away. All she could focus on was the touch of his hand and the warmth that emanated from it. She sucked in a breath before daring to turn her head and catch a peek of Dylan. As soon as she raised her head she saw that he was already staring back at her. Her stomach did a flip.

He gave her a small smile and pulled her hand a little closer. Tam was conscious of the beat of her heart. She glanced at

Gemma and Will but neither of them appeared to notice. Tam let herself lean against Dylan's side, their hands still locked together.

It was weird in a good way. A flush of excitement tingled across her cheeks. The party continued on in front of her but Tam wasn't seeing it, all her attention was directed on Dylan and how it felt to hold his hand. The only lucid thought that went through her head was . . . *Oh God, I'm in trouble now.*

Eleven

That evening after the day's work at the summer house, Seb walked into the farmhouse kitchen and saw Felix staring at Rori as she finished off a bowl of strawberry ice-cream.

'Hey, what's up?' Seb asked.

Lix turned at the sound of Seb's voice. 'Oh, nothing—just perplexed how someone so tiny can demolish a huge bowl of ice-cream so fast.'

'Rori, have you had dinner yet?' Seb asked.

Rori shook her head. There was a smear of ice-cream across her mouth as well as several drops down the front of her dress.

Seb looked back to Lix. 'Oh, you're in such trouble,' he said with a grin.

Lix raised both his eyebrows. 'What do you mean?'

'Maddie will chuck a fit if Rori doesn't eat dinner. How much of that stuff did you give her?'

'Relax, it was only one bowl.'

'Yeah, but didn't she already have one when you got back from the shops?'

'That was hours ago,' Lix replied.

'I'm still going to have dinner,' Rori said. 'I already promised Lix I would.'

'You did?' Seb asked as he sat down opposite her.

'I had to, otherwise he wouldn't give me the whipped cream and sprinkles on top,' she explained.

Seb shot Lix a look, who in turn gave him a shrug.

'Why don't you go and wash up? You've got some ice-cream on your chin,' Seb said to Rori. 'I've got to talk to Lix for a minute.'

Rori scooted off the chair but stopped and turned back to him. 'Lixie isn't going to get in trouble really, is he? Because I asked for the ice-cream.'

Seb chuckled. 'Nope, he's not—I was only joking with him.'

Rori nodded. 'All right then,' she said before she ran over to Felix and gave him a hug. 'Thanks for the ice-cream.'

He ruffled the top of her head with his hand. 'Anytime, you're my favourite cousin.'

'I'm your only cousin!' Rori said, laughing.

'Exactly.'

Rori ran off. Both Seb and Felix watched her go before they turned back to each other.

'So, what's up?' Lix asked.

'I was wondering if you know anything about Tam and Dylan?'

Lix stared at him for a while before walking over and leaning on the bench. 'That's none of my business,' he replied. Felix had piercing green eyes, dark hair and a finely shaped face. He was showing a two-day old stubble on his chin which accentuated the family jawline, and gave him a deep, sensuous look.

Seb studied him. 'You and Tam are practically joined at the hip. She must have told you something about Dylan.'

'Why are you asking?'

Seb drew in a breath before continuing. 'Because there seemed to be something going on between the two of them earlier this afternoon.'

Lix wandered over to the fridge and opened it. 'If you want to know if anything is going on, you'd better ask Tam,' he said as he grabbed a bottle of water.

'Oh come on, she won't tell me,' Seb said.

'Look, I don't know what you thought you saw but the two of them are friends. Dylan has been hanging around this place for as long as I can remember. He may be your best friend but we all tend to look at him as another brother.' Lix opened the water and took a swig.

'So there's nothing going on between them?'

'Again, not my business. Ask Tam.'

Seb held up his hands. 'Okay, okay—there's no need to get annoyed.'

Lix frowned. 'Really? Because I kind of think there is. It's like you're going behind her back instead of being straight up. And what does it even matter if they're interested in each other? Dylan's a good guy, why wouldn't you want them to be together?'

Seb leant back against the island bench. 'I didn't mean it to sound like that. I only wondered if I was actually seeing what I thought I did, that's all,' he answered with a smile as if he was trying to defuse the conversation. 'You're right, I should ask Tam.'

Lix nodded.

'It's just that sometimes Tam and I don't . . . well, you know,' Seb said.

Lix opened his mouth and then closed it again. The gesture wasn't lost on Seb.

'What were you going to say?' he asked.

Felix shook his head. 'It doesn't matter. Listen, I've got to add a few photos to the website.'

'Hang on, what were you going to say?' Seb pressed on. He realised how awkward this had become but he really wanted to know what was on his brother's mind, even if it was less than positive.

Lix's shoulders slumped a little and he sighed. 'It's just . . .'

'What?'

'You always take on the authoritative role. I know with everything that happened to our family, you had to. But we've all grown up now. We have our own ideas and thoughts about what's best—not just for ourselves but as a family. And sometimes it's really hard to talk to you. You treat us like you're our dad not our brother. You have to control everything and it doesn't make it easy sometimes.'

Seb was quiet for a moment as the words seeped in. 'I'm sorry, I don't mean to act like that.'

'I know that you love us and you've sacrificed a lot but . . .'

'But what?' Seb asked.

'You see how hard it is for Tam, don't you?'

'What do you mean?'

'It's hard enough when you tend to be overbearing with the rest of us but with Tam it's even worse.'

Seb frowned. 'We just butt heads, that's all.'

Lix shook his head. 'No, it's more than that. You haven't forgiven her yet, not really.'

'What the hell are you talking about?' Seb gasped as he stared at his brother.

'You know exactly what I'm saying. You both need to sit down and talk it out—you should have done it years ago.' Lix started to back away. 'I've got work to do. I'll see you later.'

Seb wasn't sure how long he sat in the kitchen. Lix's words spun around in his head and, no matter how much he wanted to dismiss them and tell himself that his brother was talking out of his arse, there was a niggling thought that maybe, just maybe, some of what he said was true. He had always put his and Tam's relationship down as feisty sibling stuff but perhaps there was more to it than a brother and sister who occasionally didn't get on.

* * *

Tam tried to push her thoughts aside as she rode up to Dylan's cottage. She knew what he wanted but sometimes she was unsure she could give it to him. It wasn't that she didn't love him, she did. And it wasn't that she didn't want to be with him, she did. But they were happy at the moment, no one knew about them except Lix and she knew he'd never say anything. So why not carry on as they had been? Why did Dylan want to change things now?

As she rode down the dirt track, she saw that he'd left the cottage lights on for her, like a beacon in the darkness. She pulled up in front of the house and Dylan walked out to greet her.

'I wasn't sure if you could make it tonight,' he said.

'I didn't want to stay away,' she answered with a smile.

He bent down and kissed her and Tam wrapped her arms around him and kissed him back. It was the type of kiss that was long and warm and beguiling. His fingers began to trail over her body, leaving instant fires in their wake.

When the kiss ended, it took Tam a moment to recover and catch her breath. It was always the same, Dylan's touch had an extraordinary effect on her. Like a guilty pleasure, once was never enough.

'It was so hard not to kiss you today at the summer house,' he murmured against her neck. 'You looked so beautiful in the sun by the lake.'

'It was hard for me too,' she admitted as she moved her head so he'd have better access.

'When can we tell them, babe?'

'Soon,' she promised. 'We'll tell them soon.'

Placated by her words, Dylan gently tugged her inside and shut the door.

Twelve

Christmas Eve, eight years ago

Tam looked at her watch, they had been at the party for about three hours and she was getting anxious.

'Will you quit that?'

She glanced over at Gemma. 'Sorry, I was checking the time.'

'You did that five minutes ago and five minutes before that,' Gemma said as she sat up from where she'd been resting against the tree. 'I know that you want to go home but our ride won't be here for another couple of hours, so just relax.'

'I can't,' Tam replied. 'It's stupid but I've got this feeling that I can't shake.'

Gemma sighed. 'That's your conscience, you're feeling guilty because you didn't tell your mum that you were coming.'

'Maybe, but I also don't feel very comfortable here. This party is more Taylor's friends than Blake's.' She looked around at the various groups who were milling around. There was a large group around the barbecue area, and another, smaller group dancing to the music. Scattered around were other small gatherings who were laughing and drinking, and being very noisy about it.

'True but Dylan and Will are here. It's not like we're the only ones from school,' Gemma said.

'I know but still . . .'

'Everything is going to be okay. We'll stay a bit longer and then Jace will pick us up around six. We'll be home before your parents can even miss you.'

Tam sighed. There was only one way back home and it was with Gem's brother, so she would have to wait. She was silently trying to resign herself to that fact when another idea popped into her head.

'How are Will and Dylan getting back to town?'

Gemma shrugged. 'I don't know.'

'Perhaps they're going back earlier.'

'I don't understand why you're so set on this,' Gemma replied with a wave of her hand.

'Because I want to go home. Come on, Gem, it's Christmas Eve and I want to share it with everyone back at the house. Besides, I came along today for you and it looks like it worked because I've seen the way you and Will have been looking at each other.'

A smile spread across Gemma's face. 'I know, right. Yeah, now if you and Dylan . . .'

Tam shook her head. 'Nothing there,' she said, lying through her teeth. 'Dylan was just being nice because of Seb.'

'Sure,' Gemma replied as she narrowed her eyes. 'Just keep telling yourself that.'

Tam didn't say anything, instead she looked in the direction that Dylan had walked a couple of minutes before.

Gemma paused. 'Okay, if you want to go, we'll go. I know I sort of pushed you into this.' She leant over and touched Tam's arm. 'But mission accomplished, I got Will's attention and we're meeting up in a couple of days. I appreciate that you came even though you didn't want to.'

'It's all right,' Tam said with a smile. 'I figured it was my turn to be best friend material.'

'We just have to work out who we can get a ride with,' Gemma said.

'I'll go and ask Dylan how he's going to get back,' Tam replied. 'Maybe, they wouldn't mind leaving early.' She stood up. 'Will you be all right here?'

Gemma gave her a look. 'What do you think is going to happen to me—in broad daylight in front of fifty people?'

'I was just checking,' Tam answered.

'Will only went off to grab us a couple of drinks. I doubt he'll be long,' Gemma said.

'Okay, I think Dylan went behind the back of the house,' Tam said. 'I'll go and check.'

With one last glance over her shoulder at Gemma, Tam walked away from the tree and towards the party. The closer she got to the barbecue the more people there were. The music was loud and she still couldn't place the artist. The couple of girls that had been dancing on and off, ever since Tam arrived had now been joined by a handful of others. Several guys who she didn't know were standing together watching the girls, among them was Blake's older brother, Taylor. Seeing this, Tam changed her course and walked around the impromptu dance floor. She kept going, hoping that Taylor was too preoccupied to notice her.

She hadn't told anyone, not even Gemma, but whenever she'd seen him in town she'd caught him looking at her and it always creeped her out. And it wasn't just a glance, his stare always lingered up and down the full length of her body before coming to rest on her face. It made her feel uncomfortable and uneasy and she went out of her way to avoid him, whenever possible.

Yeah, she felt bad about lying to her mum about where she was going, and her dad would be angry if he found out she was at the Hendersons', but it was Taylor who unnerved her.

There was something about him that made the potential of her father's anger pale into insignificance. She just wanted to get the hell out of there and go back home.

She glanced at her watch again as she made her way behind the old weatherboard farmhouse. It looked as if it needed a little love—the original white had bubbled under the hot summer sun and in some places had flaked off altogether. Beside the back door there was a tub of geraniums that looked as if they were in desperate need of some water. The flyscreen door was closed but the door itself was open. Tam wondered if Dylan was in there and if she should go in. As she hesitated, the flyscreen door opened and a middle-aged lady came out, carrying a couple of large bowls.

'Oh, let me get that,' Tam said as she held open the door.

'Thanks, love, I appreciate it,' the woman replied with a bright smile. 'Looks like they've been through one coleslaw already and nearly all of the sausages.'

'I can carry those, if you like?' Tam offered as she held out her hands.

'That would be wonderful. You're one of Blake's friends, aren't you?' the woman asked as she handed the bowls to Tam. 'I'm his mum, Alice.'

'I'm Tamara Carrington and yes, I go to school with Blake.'

'Oh, your Estella's girl?'

'One of them, I have a little sister—Lucy.'

'Yes, I remember. Your mum and I went to school together,' she said with a faraway look in her eyes. After a moment, she shook her head as if she was trying to dispel a dream or a memory. 'Ah, but that was a lifetime ago, before we all had to grow up,' she added with a small smile.

'I didn't know you went to school with Mum.'

'Yes, I did. If you're right with the bowls, I'll grab the other things,' Alice Henderson said as she disappeared back into the house.

Tam stood by the back door, holding the two large bowls and waited for Blake's mum to return. Alice Henderson appeared older than her mum. She had a slender figure but there were deep lines around her eyes and forehead that the bangs from her long bob couldn't hide. It wasn't that Mrs Henderson wasn't pretty, she was—especially when she smiled and her eyes lit up. Tam could see the mother in the son, Blake had the same shaped face and warm light-brown eyes.

After a minute or two, Alice Henderson appeared carrying a large tray with a stack of what looked like homemade hamburgers and a pile of sausages.

'Right, well this is the last of it,' she said with a laugh as she joined Tam. 'After this is cooked up, everyone will have to resort to Vegemite sandwiches.'

Tam gave her a smile. 'I'm sure everyone will have had enough.'

'Hope so because they're not getting our Christmas ham. Come on, love, let's go.'

Tam followed Mrs Henderson back towards the barbecue, winding her way through the crowd. One of the girls who was dancing bumped into her but Tam managed to keep a hold of the bowls. The girl with russet-coloured hair gave her a dirty look but stepped back when she saw that Mrs Henderson had glanced over her shoulder.

'Is everything all right, love?'

Tam gave a nod. 'Yes, it's fine,' she answered as she walked forward to catch up.

'Good.' Alice Henderson gave a pointed look to the girl with the russet hair.

Tam hurried over to the trestle table next to the barbecue and put down the bowl of salads. Mrs Henderson gave her a pat on the shoulder. 'Thanks, Tamara, for helping,' she said in a slightly raised voice, so she could be heard over the music.

'Not a problem,' Tam replied. 'I don't suppose you've seen Dylan?'

'Jack Petersen's boy? I did see him earlier, you could try the other side of the house—there was a group of kids there,' she said.

'Thanks,' Tam said with a smile. 'I'll try there.' She turned around and headed back the way she'd come. It took her a couple of minutes to navigate her way as the biggest crush of people were in that area. After a minute or two Tam had made it to the back door. She paused before following the cracked cement path around the far side of the house. She strained her ears and listened if there were any voices coming from ahead but all she could hear was the *doof doof* beat of the music.

There was a lemon tree around the corner along with a small veggie patch and tiny garden shed. Tam walked over to the tree and inspected the area but there was no one in sight. With a sigh, she turned around to head back to Gemma but she stopped dead in her tracks as Taylor Henderson loomed in front of her.

Thirteen

Maddie looked up from her desk when Tam walked into their office.

'Is everything okay?' she asked. Now that New Year's Eve had passed, everything was getting back to normal again.

Tam nodded as she sat down at her own desk. 'Yep, the deck and the painting inside the summer house are almost finished. If all goes well, we should be able to stain the deck tomorrow, or at least that's what Dylan said.'

'Then we're on track,' Maddie answered with a smile. 'Which is just as well because if everything pans out like it should we're going to be super busy all the way up until winter.'

Tam laughed as she crossed her fingers. 'Hey, don't jinx us.'

'No need to worry,' Maddie said. 'As long as we've got each other, everything else will fall into place.'

Tam looked down at the papers on her desk. She was still tweaking the final elements for the summer house. Maddie always put a positive spin on things, or at least she tried to. Ever since she'd moved into the farmhouse, she'd done her best to keep everyone together and tried to give them a glimmer of hope for the future. It hadn't always worked and she and Tam had had a couple of big arguments in the beginning. Tam wasn't proud of it, even now she still felt a twinge of guilt whenever she replayed them in her head.

To her credit, Maddie had never once held those times against her or harboured a grudge. She seemed to accept that Tam was a troubled teen who was still trying to process her grief from losing her parents. Tam had always appreciated the fact that Maddie never tried to replace their parents, she was just there in her own capacity as a beloved aunt. Her kindness and patience had guided all of the Carrington children through the darkest period of their lives and eventually out the other side. At the end of the day, Maddie had sacrificed her own life to try to save theirs. Of course she would never admit it, and whenever Tam had brought the subject up, Maddie just waved her hand as if she were shooing a fly away and changed the topic of conversation.

'Tam, can I ask you something?' Maddie added now. 'I know it's none of my business, but I'm kind of curious.'

'This doesn't sound good,' Tam answered with a nervous laugh.

Maddie carried on. 'Are you seeing Dylan?'

Tam picked up the closest pen and fiddled with it. 'Why do you ask?'

'Just a vibe I've been getting off the two of you,' Maddie said. 'That, and the fact he couldn't seem to keep his hands off you the other day.'

Tam sat back in her chair and stared at her aunt. 'No one else saw that, did they?'

'I'm not sure,' Maddie said. Then she added, almost as an afterthought, 'Although, Seb has brought the subject up.'

'Damn.' Tam slumped in her chair. 'I thought we were being careful.'

'So there is something between you?'

Tam nodded.

'I thought so. I've seen the way you both look at each other when you think no one else is about. It's a good thing, isn't it?'

'Yes . . . maybe,' Tam replied.

'Oh dear, that doesn't sound promising.'

'Oh, it's not like that,' Tam reassured her. 'We've been keeping it quiet for the past year.'

'A year!' Maddie's eyebrows shot up in surprise. 'I didn't realise it had been going on for so long.'

'Yeah.'

'But you don't seem . . . happy?' Maddie replied.

'Oh no, I love Dylan, I really do, but I'm not sure everyone will be ecstatic that we're together,' Tam explained.

Maddie regarded her. 'You mean Seb.'

Tam nodded her head. 'Dylan is his best friend, so yeah, it complicates things.' She took in a deep breath before she continued. 'Because, let's face it, Seb and I rarely agree on anything these days.'

'And that's why it's a secret?'

'Partly.'

'And the other part?' Maddie asked.

Tam shrugged. 'I don't know, maybe I didn't want to jinx it.'

The look in Maddie's eyes seemed to say that she wasn't buying it. 'So no one knows?'

Tam looked back down at her desk. 'Lix knows.'

'He hasn't said a word.'

The edges of Tam's mouth curled up into a slight smile. 'Felix always has my back—he's my rock. I can tell him anything and he won't judge me. He'll give me his opinion and I'll listen, most of the time,' she said with a hint of laughter in her voice.

'And you don't feel that with Seb?' Maddie asked.

Tam shook her head. She wanted to have a close relationship with Seb but it never panned out. He would always treat her like a child rather than his equal, his twin. 'No, not in a long time.

It's like he has to control us all, so we don't get hurt. Problem is that we're all adults, or almost adults, now.'

'Yes, it's infuriating. I've had a word with him about him being a little over the top. He knows, he even agrees that he doesn't handle things well, especially when it comes to you,' Maddie explained. 'We have to give him time to readjust or be prepared to call him out on it.'

'I do,' Tam replied. She let out a deep sigh as she leant forward on the desk. 'But he doesn't listen. I love him but the distance between us widens with each passing year. I don't know how to fix it.'

'That shouldn't all be on your shoulders, darling,' Maddie said as she reached over and picked up her teacup. 'You both need to sit down and talk—and really listen to what the other one is saying. It might be uncomfortable but it's the only way that the two of you are going to get on the same page.'

'I've tried to talk to him, Maddie—you know that.'

'Yes, but that's usually during or right after a spat.'

'You make us sound like children,' Tam quipped.

'Neither of you are, which is why you have to do the adult thing and work this out.' Maddie took a sip of her favourite vanilla tea. 'Even though you've both grown up there can still be traces of the wounded teenager lingering inside each of you.'

Tam nodded. If she was honest with herself, she knew that in the middle of an argument both of them could be petty and bring up things that happened years ago.

'Just try and rein it in while you're talking to Seb,' Maddie said.

'When did you get to be so clever?' Tam asked with a grin.

'Natural ability,' Maddie said with a straight face before breaking into a laugh.

'All right, I'll give it a go and talk to him,' Tam replied.

'Good, but before you do, let me chat with Seb first.'

'Why?'

'Because I want to tell him the same thing that I've told you. Remind him to give you a chance to say your piece and listen.'

'Do you think it will help?'

'Maybe, at least it'll be in his mind when the two of you sit down.' Maddie placed her empty cup back on its orange saucer. 'So what are you going to do about Dylan?'

'I don't know. Maybe I should tell Seb. Dylan was all for telling him as soon as we started seeing each other.'

'So why the reluctance now?'

Tam shrugged her shoulders. 'I think that Dylan wants more than I can give him.'

'Can or will?' Maddie asked.

'I don't know,' she replied in a soft voice. 'It's kind of complicated and I haven't worked it out yet.'

'Tam, you have so much to give.'

Tam glanced up at her aunt. 'Maybe, but sometimes it doesn't feel like that.'

Fourteen

Christmas Eve, eight years ago

Tam froze as Taylor Henderson remained in front of her. A flicker of fear ignited within her. She had been so careful to avoid him today and now here he was. She took in her surroundings, they were standing on the opposite side of the house from the party with no one else in sight.

'What are you doing here, all by yourself?' he asked as he took a step closer.

Tam stepped back as the knot in her stomach started to tighten. 'I'm looking for Dylan,' she said. 'Have you seen him?'

Taylor shook his head and took another step forward. 'Nope, it looks like it's just us here.'

Again Tam clocked her surroundings. She looked behind her, thinking that there might be a way out, but the path stopped by another flowerbed and access to the front of the house was cut off by a high wire fence. The only way she could get back to the party was to get past Taylor.

'Why would you want to hang around someone like Dylan Petersen?' Taylor asked. A smile spread across his face. 'There are better options.'

Tam gave him a nervous smile. 'That's not it—I want to know when he's going back to town.' She tried to walk around him.

Taylor stepped in her path. 'You don't have to run off, do you?'

'Gemma will be wondering where I am,' Tam said quickly.

'It's a party, Tim Tam—no one will be wondering where you are.'

Tamara winced at the nickname. Her grandad called her that sometimes, and he always told her that it was because she was as sweet as the biscuit. But hearing it roll off Taylor's tongue made her shudder. He'd taken something innocent and sweet and made it . . . well, *off*.

'We're leaving soon,' she tried again, 'so I'd better get back. Gemma will worry.'

'Oh come on, Tam, don't run off.'

She doubled back and tried to walk around him again, this time she thought she'd been successful but then his hand shot out and grabbed her around the wrist.

'Don't run off,' he said.

Tam tried to wrench her arm from his grasp but she couldn't. 'Let go, Taylor,' she said as evenly as she could. 'I want to leave.'

'Stay,' he said with a smile as he pulled her towards him.

'I don't want to.' She tried harder to wriggle out of his grasp.

'Yes, you do,' he said. 'I've seen how you look at me.'

Tam shook her head. 'No, you've got that wrong. I don't look at you in any *way*. Please, let me go.'

He released her arm and relief ran through her entire body. Perhaps her words had actually got through to him. She rubbed her wrist where his fingers had been, the skin was red and it was stinging. Once again she tried to move past him but this time he grabbed her by the shoulders and propelled her back towards the old garden shed. She fought back but he was stronger and Tam only came to a halt when her back was slammed up against the old, corrugated iron.

'Aargh,' Tam gasped as pain radiated across her shoulders. She pushed back but he batted her hands away, stepped in close and pressed his entire body against hers, pinning her to the wall. 'Get off me!'

She didn't get to say anything else as Taylor bent down and slanted his mouth over hers. The kiss was hard and mean and it terrified her. She scratched at his face and pulled his hair but the assault didn't end. One of his hands clamped over her breast and she struggled to push him away. She tried to scream but her voice was muffled and the panic rose like a tsunami inside her.

'Tamara, are you okay?' came a voice from somewhere behind Taylor.

Taylor stopped kissing her and looked over his shoulder. She saw that Blake was standing by the lemon tree. She'd never been so happy to see someone in her life.

'Get the hell out of here, can't you see I'm busy?' Taylor growled at his brother.

'Don't go,' Tam managed to say in a small voice.

Blake was turning away but hesitated once he heard her. 'No, Taylor, I'm not going anywhere—at least not until Tam says she's okay.'

Taylor partially turned to confront his brother, Tam could feel the anger emanating from him. As he stared down Blake, his grip loosened and Tam took the chance. She drew back her hand and slashed at his face with her nails before shoving him as hard as she could then running towards Blake.

Taylor staggered a couple of steps back. 'You bitch,' he called out as he held his hand up to his bleeding cheek.

'Go find Dylan,' Blake said quickly when she reached his side. 'He's back with Gem and Will. Get out of here as fast as you can.'

Hot, burning tears were blurring her eyes but she managed to reach out and squeeze Blake's hand before turning and running as fast as she could. She headed back behind the house and around the other side, hurrying through the crowd around the barbecue. Several people stared at her and she saw Blake's mum look at her with concern. But Tam didn't stop.

She could see her friends standing together not far ahead. Tears coursed down her face as she pushed herself to run faster. She didn't stop until she barrelled into Dylan, who automatically opened up his arms to catch her.

'Tam!' Gemma called out as she rushed over to her. 'What's the matter?'

Tam buried her head against Dylan's shoulder. She didn't answer for a moment because she was trying to catch her breath.

'It's all right,' he said softly. 'Whatever has happened—everything will be okay.'

She looked up. 'I . . . we've got to go. I can't stay here,' she said between sobs.

Dylan nodded. 'Okay, we'll go.'

Gemma gave her a hug, even though she was still in Dylan's arms. 'We'll go,' she said quickly. 'But it's too early for my brother to pick us up.'

'I don't care if I have to walk back to town, I can't stay here,' Tam whispered.

'It's all right, we'll start walking and work out a ride as we go.' Dylan guided her towards the old iron gate. 'Will, grab our stuff and ring your mum to meet us on the way.'

The four of them walked through the gate and started heading down the dirt road which led back to town.

Gemma was walking close to Tam and holding her hand, while Dylan still had his arm around her.

'Tam, are you going to tell us what happened?' Gem asked gently.

'I just really wanted to leave,' she answered with her eyes downcast.

'My mum's not answering,' Will said. 'She's probably busy at work or something. Dylan, can your dad . . . ' Will trailed off when he saw the look on Dylan's face.

'I suppose that means we don't have a ride,' Gemma said quietly. By car, the journey to the Hendersons' took under fifteen minutes but walking would take considerably longer. 'You look pale, Tam,' Gem said, 'do you want to sit down?'

'No, let's keep going,' Tam said. She began to sob, 'I want to go home.'

'We'll get you home, don't worry,' Dylan said. 'Do you think you should ring your mum? It might be the only way we can get back to town.'

Tam wiped her tears away and took a deep breath. He was right. Even if it meant that she'd get in trouble for going to the party at least she'd be home. She pulled out her phone and speed-dialled her mum. Tam sniffed back her tears, determined to be calm for her mother. It rang a couple of times before her mum answered, Tam could make out Lix's voice in the background. As soon as she heard her mother's voice, all her fear came rushing back.

'Mum, I need you. I'm sorry . . . I,' Tam stammered out. 'He tried to . . . he touched me and tried to . . . ' She tried to get the words out but a lump formed in her throat and she could barely breathe as she gasped for air.

Her mum was telling her to calm down, talk slowly but she couldn't talk.

Dylan took the phone. 'Mrs Carrington, it's Dylan. Tam's okay, Gemma, Will and I are with her. We've left the Henderson place and are walking back towards town. Can you come and get us?'

Fifteen

Tam sat on the bench beneath the wisteria, which overlooked the lake. She always enjoyed sitting there as it was a peaceful place where she could gather her thoughts. For better or worse, her relationship with Dylan had been outed. Tam wasn't sure what that would mean for them but she knew that she'd have to tell Seb before someone else did.

It took a couple of rings before Dylan answered his phone.

'Hey, what's up, babe?' Dylan asked. 'Everything okay?'

'Yes and no,' Tam responded. 'Apparently we were seen at the summer house and Maddie put two and two together.'

'Ah, so what do you want to do about it?' he asked.

'I don't know, I should probably tell Seb before he hears from someone else.'

'I could talk to him, if you want.'

Tam was silent while she mulled over his offer. 'No, but thanks. I know you're his best friend but I should talk to him first.'

'If that's what you want.' Then he added, 'Tam, this is a good thing. We've kept it under wraps long enough.'

She drew in a breath. 'Yeah, it's a good thing,' she said. 'Listen, I'm going to see Seb now—so this is a heads-up. I'm hoping his reaction will be positive but I can't remember the last time that the two of us agreed on anything.'

Dylan laughed. 'I'm sure it'll be fine. You're his sister, I'm his best friend and he loves us both.'

'I guess we'll know soon enough. I'll give you a ring after I talk to him.'

'It'll be all right,' Dylan said. 'You worry too much.'

'We'll see,' Tam replied. 'I'll talk to you soon.'

'Okay, love you.'

'You too. I'll see you later,' Tam said before she ended the call.

* * *

Dylan sat back against his chair and looked out the kitchen window onto the bush that bordered two sides of the house. Relief swept through him, finally after all this time he could stand up and say that Tam was his girlfriend. He'd wanted to do that for so long but she was always so hesitant. In the beginning, he'd thought that maybe she didn't want to tell anyone because she didn't think their relationship was going anywhere. It was a bitter thought, and he'd begun to believe that he was way more into her than she was into him.

A large ginger cat jumped up onto the table, walked over to Dylan and butted his head against his hand, trying to force a pat.

'Hey, Red, you know you're not meant to be on the table, don't you?' Dylan said as he gave in and patted the cat.

The cat ignored his words, settled down on the table and let out a rumbly purr as Dylan continued to pet him.

The idea that Tam wasn't serious circled in his brain for weeks during that early period of their relationship. He tried to forget it, to move past it but he couldn't. Once the seed of doubt had been sown, it grew with abandon. Finally, after they had been together for six months, he worked up the courage to ask her straight out.

He should have done it earlier but a little voice in his head kept telling him that if he brought the topic up there was a chance that he could lose her forever. To his relief, she said that it wasn't like that. She wanted to keep their relationship quiet so there weren't any outside pressures—like how Seb would react when he found out. Dylan believed her and had to admit there might be some truth in what she said about Seb. It was true that he was his best friend, but sleeping with his sister was bound to change things.

So they went on the same as they had been; meeting up every few nights in his cottage. It was good, it was fine . . . until it wasn't. He wanted some sort of commitment, a public signal that they actually gave a damn about each other.

Red rolled on his back expecting Dylan to rub his tummy. The cat batted his hand when he wasn't quick enough on the uptake.

'Demanding, aren't you?' Dylan chuckled as he complied.

Now they could finally quit acting like friends and be honest, not only to the people around them but also themselves. He loved her, it was as simple as that. Dylan wanted the whole shebang—commitment, marriage, family—and he wasn't ashamed to admit it.

Yeah, Seb may have a few things to say but they'd talk it out and get past it. At least that's what he hoped.

* * *

Tam rode her bike down the narrow drive that led to the side entrance of the pub. She parked it close to the door and took off her helmet but stayed on the bike for a couple of moments while she tried to gather her thoughts. She was going to follow Maddie's advice but had to admit she was a bit apprehensive. It seemed stupid—she hadn't done anything wrong, falling in love wasn't wrong especially since they weren't hurting anyone—but that was the way she felt. She swung off the bike and walked through the open door.

It was the middle of the afternoon and the pub was open but there were only a couple of people sitting around. She wasn't surprised, things were still a bit slow at this time of year, especially in Kangaroo Ridge.

'Hey,' she said when she saw Seb behind the bar.

'Tam, I didn't know that you were coming. Is everything all right?'

'Yeah, everything is fine.' She leant against the well-worn bar. 'I just wondered if we could have a chat.'

'Now?'

Tam nodded.

'Why don't we go and have a seat in the lounge?'

Tam gestured with her head towards the two customers at the bar and raised an eyebrow. 'Will they be all right?'

'Sure thing.' Seb called out, 'Hey, George, I have to talk to Tam for a minute. Will you be right?'

The old man looked up from his glass and gave a wave. 'Seb—Phil and I aren't going anywhere.'

Seb walked out from behind the bar. 'We'll be in the lounge if you need anything.'

'No worries, son,' George said with a crinkly smile.

Tam led the way into the lounge, it wasn't a big room but there were about a dozen tables in varying sizes. It was where the counter meals were served from Thursday through to Sunday each week. She sat down and waited for Seb to do the same.

'Pretty quiet in here today,' Tam said.

'Yep, I expected it,' Seb replied. 'It's really dead. I reckon next year I might as well close for the entire time. I gave the staff time off, so I'm the only one rattling around here.'

'How are George and Phil?' Tam asked.

'I made them some turkey rolls to take home with them tonight.'

'George's son didn't come up for a visit?' Tam asked.

'No, did you really expect him to?'

'It's so sad. He's always talking about his son but I don't think I've ever seen him in Kangaroo Ridge.'

'At least he's got Phil for a bit of company,' Seb said. 'So, what's up?'

Tam wriggled in her chair for a second before she sat up straight and looked her brother in the eye. 'I've got something to tell you and I'm not sure how you'll be with it.'

'Geez, that sounds ominous,' Seb said. 'You haven't killed anyone have you?' He added, trying to lighten the sudden change in mood.

Tam smiled and shook her head. 'Not yet.'

'Well, that's a relief.'

Tam paused as she gathered courage. 'I've been seeing someone for a while now. It's been low-key but a couple of people have suspected what's happening and I thought I'd tell you before you heard it from someone else.'

Seb sat back and studied her for a moment. It made her uncomfortable but she stared right back at him.

Eventually Seb leant back against the chair. 'So who's the lucky guy?'

'Dylan,' Tam said simply.

Seb's eyes widened in surprise. 'Dylan?'

'Dylan and I have been seeing each other,' Tam said quickly. 'It's not really anyone else's business but I thought I should give you a heads-up.'

'Of course it's my business—you're my sister,' Seb said, raising his voice.

'But I'm also an adult and the same age as you. I'm only telling you because he's your best friend and he's been wanting to tell you.'

'So why didn't he?' Seb asked with a harsh tone.

'Because I asked him not to,' she replied. 'Really, Seb, I don't see what the big thing is. Dylan and I are together and that's that.'

Seb stared at her for another moment. 'I don't think it's a good idea.'

Tamara crossed her arms. 'Like I said, it really doesn't have anything to do with you but since we're here, tell me why.'

'Look . . . Dylan is family, you know? I mean he's like our brother. Why would you want to mess with that? It could ruin everything. I mean, how many great friendships are ruined by getting intimate? Why can't you just let him be one of the family, and find someone else to go out with? And anyway, I don't think either of you are suited. You're too different.'

Tam raised an eyebrow. 'Too different? We've known each other for years, it's not like I'm dating a stranger.'

'Dylan wants to settle down some day and you're . . . you're . . .' Seb trailed off.

'What are you trying to say?'

'You're impetuous and I don't want either of you making a mistake and getting hurt.'

Tam nodded. 'I could get mad at you for what you're implying but I get it. You love both of us. But it seems that you're more worried about your relationship with Dylan than you are about his relationship with me. Well, whether it's a mistake or not—it's ours to find out.' She stood up.

'I don't think we're finished.'

'Yeah, we are,' Tam said with a slight smile. 'I'm not doing this to get back at you or hurt you or anything like that. Dylan and

I want to be together and that's it. I don't know what the future holds but nobody does when they start a relationship.'

'So, it's just started?' Seb asked.

She shook her head. 'No, we've been together for nearly a year,' she answered before she turned and walked towards the door.

Sixteen

Christmas Eve, eight years ago

Ben Carrington hummed happily as he drove along the tree-lined driveway towards home. He'd made an executive decision and decided to close the pub early that night. The fact that it was pretty dead also helped. It's funny, he thought to himself, so many country pubs were packed out on Christmas Eve, and he'd heard that for many city nightclubs it was almost the busiest night of the year. But round here, it seemed that most of the locals were busy preparing for Christmas. For once, Ben had given himself permission to take a little time off.

The house was lit up in the golden sunlight just ahead. Everything was almost perfect. Well, as close to perfect as Ben could get. The pub was doing well and, for the most part, so were the kids. Even his dad seemed to be more like his old self now he had resettled in a retirement village not too far away. Both he and Estella would have been happy for his dad to stay at the farmhouse, it had been his home for nigh on seventy years, but he'd been determined to leave. He said that the house held too many memories—nearly all of them of his wife. He'd given the house to Ben and Estella and hoped that they would be as happy as he and Lydia had been. The stipulation was that the little cottage on the other side of the dam, down the wattle track that ran next to the boundary fence, would be for Ben's sister, Maddie, along with an acre plot for a garden. The inheritance had been unexpected and Ben believed that somehow his mother had been behind it. He loved his dad but he wasn't an easy man to get close to.

Anyway, the old man seemed happier and more at peace since the move. He'd made new friends and he was coming for Christmas lunch tomorrow. Ben hoped his sister would turn up as well, although it was probably unlikely as she seemed to spend most of her time working. She liked the buzz of the city and rarely came home, although Ben always made a point of giving her a ring every couple of weeks to check in and make sure that she was okay.

He placed his hand over the breast pocket of his shirt, checking that the small jewellery box was still there. Christmas was for the family but he wanted to carve out a few minutes with Estella this afternoon, even though he knew that she'd be gearing up with the holiday preparations.

Sometimes he missed the little things; he didn't mean to, but life and work were all-consuming and he dropped the ball. He and Estella had a strong relationship, they always had, but it got a bit lost every now and again because of the day-to-day running of family life. There had been tough years, and some had been lean, but Estella always held the family together and supported him. He knew that she'd sacrificed things that were important to her, like her art, to look after everyone. It had only been in the last couple of years that she'd got back into it. He often wondered what life would have been like if she hadn't fallen in love with him and followed him back to Kangaroo Ridge all those years ago. He blew out a breath as he neared the house—God, he couldn't imagine his life without her, not even for a minute.

Twenty years ago, on a distant Christmas Eve, they had met by accident. His parents had forced him to go to his cousin's birthday party in Melbourne. *Dragged and threatened* was probably a better way to describe it. Ben couldn't stand Stuart but it was his twenty-first and he was expected to attend. That's where he saw Estella for the first time, she stole his breath and his heart that night and still did to this day.

Ben parked the car and walked in the side door and into the kitchen. Estella was icing some biscuits on the bench.

'Hey,' he said as he walked over and hugged her from behind. She smelt of her favourite soft floral perfume and vanilla.

She turned her head and smiled back at him. 'You're early.'

'Yep, decided to close at six.' Ben dropped a kiss on the top of her head. 'Kids all here?'

'Yep, except Tam.'

'Where is she?'

Estella turned around in his arms. 'Supposedly at Gemma's,' she replied as she reached up and wiped a bit of icing on his nose.

'Hey!' he laughed as she wiggled out of his embrace.

She gave him a quick kiss on the mouth. 'I'm glad you're back.'

'So am I, and I've decided to close the pub tomorrow and Boxing Day as well.' Ben ran his hand through his dark brown hair.

'Really? We get you for two whole days?'

He nodded with a grin as he tried to catch her. 'I figured it was time to put in our own family tradition—from now on the pub is closed at Christmas and Easter and any other day I want.'

'That's good. The kids will be happy that you're here.'

He nodded. 'It's been a hard year, but things are picking up and I reckon we can afford a couple of days off.'

'Best Christmas gift.' Estella smiled.

'Talking about gifts, turn around and look out the window,' he said and waited for her to do it.

Estella frowned. 'I can't see anything out there,' she said.

Ben pulled the jewellery box out of his pocket and took out a gold heart on a shiny chain. 'There isn't anything out there,' he responded. 'I needed you to turn around so I can put this on your neck. Can you lift your hair up for a sec.'

Estella complied and Ben fastened the gift around her neck. 'This isn't for Christmas. This is to remember that we met all those years ago on a different Christmas Eve and that, no matter what, you hold my heart and always will.' He bent down and kissed her neck.

Estella held the heart in her hand. 'It's beautiful—thank you. I love it and you.' She turned around to face him and placed her hands on his shoulders.

Ben wrapped his arms around her and pulled her close. He bent down and started to kiss her.

'Oh geez, guys,' Seb exclaimed as he walked into the kitchen. These words were accompanied by Felix's and Grayson's laughter. The boys got on so well, considering they were two years apart in age, Felix being fourteen and Gray twelve—normally an insurmountable barrier.

Estella and Ben broke the kiss but kept holding each other. Ben looked down at Estella and grinned. 'We got caught.'

'I guess we did,' she answered with a laugh.

Ben waved one of his hands as if he was trying to shoo his sons away. 'You can all just turn around and walk away,' he said with a laugh.

'Sorry, Dad, we can't do that,' Seb said. 'Apparently Lix is dying of hunger and Gray isn't far behind.'

Lix looked over to the biscuits on the bench. 'Are they ready?' he asked hopefully.

'Don't even think about it, Lixie,' his mother said. 'I haven't even finished icing them yet.'

Grayson broke into laughter and he nudged his brother. 'She called you Lixie again.'

Lix screwed up his face in a frown. 'Mum, we talked about you not using the baby name. You said that you'd stop.'

'I did, didn't I?' Estella stepped away from her husband and headed over to ruffle Lix's hair. 'I'm sorry—I promise to do better.'

'Aw, Mum,' he said as she scrunched up the hair on the top of his head but he didn't pull away.

Ben sighed. 'Well, so much for stealing a moment,' he said with a wistful air.

Estella gave him a smile. 'Later,' she promised before turning back to her sons. 'Okay, so you're all hungry and won't last until dinner—right?'

The three of them nodded in unison. 'Starving.'

'All right, there's dip, cheese and celery in the fridge,' she said. 'Oh, there's some seaweed biscuits in the pantry. But don't touch the other stuff because it's for tomorrow's lunch. Deal?'

'Deal,' said Grayson. 'How long until dinner?'

Estella shook her head as she glanced back at her husband. 'I just can't fill them up,' she said with a laugh as Lix and Gray headed to the fridge, while Seb walked into the pantry.

'They're the epitome of *growing boys*.' Ben chuckled before calling out, 'Hey, make sure your sister gets some.'

Estella opened her mouth to say something but her phone on the bench started to ring.

'It's Tam,' she said before answering it. 'Hey, sweetheart, is everything all right? Do you need a lift?'

Ben watched as the laughter in his wife's eyes faded.

'Tam, Tam what's happened? Darling, I can't understand you.' She looked at her husband. 'Calm down and tell me.'

'What's happened?' Ben asked as a tight knot of fear began to build in his stomach. 'Stell, what's happened? Is she all right?'

Estella shook her head as she tried to make out her daughter's garbled words. 'Ben, I don't know . . . wait, who's that?'

'Who's what?' Ben demanded.

'All right, yes . . . I understand, thanks, Dylan. And you'll stay with her until we get there, Gemma too? Okay thanks, I'm leaving now.' Estella ended the call.

'What the hell's going on?' Ben asked.

'Mum, is Tam all right?' Lix asked.

Estella took a breath. 'She's okay, she's with Gemma, Will and Dylan. They're at the Henderson place and we have to go and pick them up.'

'Why on earth is she there?' Ben demanded.

Estella put a calming hand on his chest. 'Apparently there was a party up there. Seb already told me about it but I wasn't sure if she'd actually gone or not.'

'Geez, the freaking Hendersons . . . really? She knows better.' Ben dug his keys out of his pocket.

'Come on, darling, some of the family is lovely,' she said.

Ben gave a half-hearted nod. 'Come on, let's go and get her. You can tell me the rest in the car.'

'Mum, she's not hurt is she?' Seb stood in the doorway of the pantry.

'No, love—she's fine,' Estella said a little too quickly. She walked over and gave him a brief hug. 'Hold the fort until we get back, all right? You'll look after your brothers and Lucy while we're gone?'

'Yeah, of course, I promise—don't worry about it,' Seb replied.

Just then Lucy came running into the kitchen and could sense the tension in the room. 'Mum, what's the matter?' She was only eight years old, but she was very perceptive for her age.

'Nothing, darling,' Estella said. 'Your dad and I have to go and pick up Tam, that's all.'

'I'll come,' Lucy said.

Ben bent down and tapped her playfully on the nose. 'Not this time, pumpkin. You stay here with your brothers.' Then he loudly whispered, 'Someone has to keep them in line.'

Grayson took Lucy by the hand. 'Want to play a game?'

She grinned up at him. 'Can I choose?'

Lix muffled a laugh as Gray reluctantly nodded. 'Sure.'

'Right, we're going,' Ben said as he touched Estella on the shoulder to hurry her along. 'Love you all, and we'll see you when we get back.'

'Take care of each other, be good and I love you,' Estella said as she hurried out the back door with Ben right behind her.

'Bye,' came a chorus of voices but Estella barely heard them as she and Ben were already down the steps and running to the car.

Seventeen

Tamara didn't hang around, she got on her bike and rode away from the pub. She was glad that she'd spoken to Seb, at least now her relationship with Dylan was out in the open—and that was a good thing, wasn't it? As she rode back towards home she tried to block that last bit of her thought out. She loved Dylan and now they could be themselves without having to sneak around. She knew that he'd wanted this for a long time—to take their relationship to the next level and build upon it.

Tam slowed the bike down once she was at the edge of town. She pulled off the road near the old stone bridge and killed the engine. The afternoon sun was hot but the bridge was sheltered by a series of poplars, gums and an old willow. She got off her bike, removed her helmet and let the warm breeze blow through her dark hair. The little creek that flowed under the bridge gurgled and splashed over smoothed stones as it ran by. The sound of the water and the breeze in the nearby trees was soothing. Tam left her bike and wandered over to where the ground began to slope down towards the gully below. She sat on a rock beside the base of a gum tree, closed her eyes and took in a deep breath, hoping that she could breathe in the peace and tranquillity.

The problem was she was worried that she wasn't ready to totally commit to Dylan. Yes, she loved him and didn't want anyone else but was she ready for what he wanted—a wedding, a house and babies? That was the question she didn't have an answer for. She'd come a long way from the dark place where she'd been after her parents' accident, and was proud of how she'd pulled herself together, but maybe the picket fence and the happy family was a step too far. When she and Dylan had been sneaking around, there hadn't been any pressure or expectations—at least not on her part. And that was the thing: since no one knew they didn't ask difficult questions. For Tam that meant a bubble of security, she could love Dylan on her terms and not have to think about a future.

Had she been using not telling Seb as a ploy to keep Dylan at bay? Tam frowned at the thought. Initially, she had been worried about how her brother would react to the news. Her being in an entanglement with his best friend could make things awkward between all of them, especially if it all crashed and burnt. She understood that Seb would be wary. But if she really thought about it, maybe there was some truth that she'd used Seb as an excuse. It wasn't a pretty thought because what kind of person would that make her?

Tam didn't want to hurt Dylan—hell, she didn't want to hurt anyone, she'd already done enough damage. As she watched the sunlight glint upon the creek, she wished that everything could stay as it was: in limbo. Limbo was safe.

She was shaken out of her thoughts when her phone rang. It was Dylan.

'Hey, how's it going?'

'I've just left the pub,' Tam said.

'How did he take it?'

'Better than I thought but I don't think he's particularly happy with either of us.'

'Well, here's hoping that he'll get over it,' Dylan replied.

Tam paused. 'I wouldn't hold my breath,' she said. 'And don't be surprised if he calls you any minute now.'

'He already has,' Dylan admitted. 'I let it go to messages because I wanted to talk to you first.'

'Well, in a nutshell—he's not breaking out the champagne. He thinks we're too different to make it work,' Tam said.

'He doesn't know how we feel about each other and how good it is.'

'Or maybe he thinks that I'm taking away his best friend and somehow going to screw up everything.'

'Nah, he's just being his overprotective self. You know how he gets—always taking on everyone's problems and trying to fix them.'

'Don't you mean, control them?' Tam replied.

'Look, he can overreact and be overbearing, but it's not done out of malice. He loves you all.'

'Yeah, but it doesn't make it easier,' Tam said. 'I understand why he's worried. I've put you in the middle and now you'll have to mediate between us. I'm sorry about that.'

'Don't be, I can handle it. Are you coming over?'

'Later tonight. I've got a heap of work to do and I want to start decorating the summer house.'

'No worries, I'll see you later then.'

'Okay.'

'Hey, babe, don't worry so much. Seb will come around and everything will be okay. See you tonight,' Dylan said in a bright voice before he ended the call.

Tam looked back at the creek and hoped that he was right.

* * *

About twenty minutes after Dylan had talked to Tam, the sound of a car coming up the drive caught his attention. He wasn't expecting anyone, except Tamara but she wouldn't be there for hours yet. He looked out the kitchen window and sighed as he saw Seb's dark blue ute pull up. He knew this conversation was inevitable but he thought he'd have more time to work out what he was going to say.

Seb got out of the car and banged the door shut before heading into the house. *Oh this isn't going to be pretty*, Dylan thought as he heard the back door open.

'What the hell have you been doing, you bloody dog,' Seb yelled as soon as he laid eyes on Dylan.

Dylan held up his hands. 'Seb, calm down.'

'Calm down! You've been banging my sister behind my back,' Seb roared.

'Well, there's a hell of a lot more to it than that,' Dylan said indignantly. 'I happen to love Tam and want to spend the rest of my life with her.'

The words seemed to take Seb aback.

'Calm down and let me explain,' Dylan said, trying to sound as soothing as he could.

Seb took a breath, pulled out the nearest chair and sat down. 'Fine,' he said with a wave of his hand. 'You can start by telling me how you've been seeing Tam for a year without mentioning it.'

Dylan gave him a wary glance before pulling out the chair opposite and sitting down.

'It's true, Tam and I have been seeing each other for a year. At first she wanted to keep it a secret in case it didn't pan out. I probably did too. Don't get me wrong, I've had a thing for her since we were seventeen and I always hoped that it would build into a fully-fledged relationship.'

Seb looked him in the eye and held his gaze. 'Okay, but why did you think going out with her was even a good idea?'

Dylan shook his head. 'Geez, Seb, why do you think it's such a bad idea? We're not doing anything wrong, we just want to be together.'

'Until you're not and then I'll have to pick up the pieces,' Seb said quickly.

Dylan let out an exasperated laugh. 'Wow, thanks for the confidence. I'm really happy that my best friend has my back in this,' he said with a sarcastic tone.

'You're just too different for it to work long term. You want different things and Tam is . . . well she's still got some demons to face.'

'I know that,' Dylan snapped. 'But you're not giving us a chance to prove that we can make it work. You've already made up your mind.'

Seb didn't say anything for a while. The silence seemed to illuminate the widening gap between them.

'You still should have told me,' Seb said petulantly.

'I wanted to but Tam wanted to keep it a secret.'

'Why?'

'You'd have to ask her,' Dylan replied. 'Although it's pretty obvious from this conversation why she might be unwilling to tell you.'

Seb shifted in his chair. 'I suppose Lix knew?'

Dylan shrugged. 'If he did, he never said anything to me. But I wouldn't be surprised, they're pretty close.'

'Like we're not,' Seb said.

'No, you're actually not.' Dylan looked up. 'And you haven't been for a long time.'

Eighteen

Tam was down by the summer house, she wanted to lose herself in work and try to put the whole conversation with Seb out of her mind. Walking around the summer house, her plan was to start thinking about the placement of furniture and general decor. She took out her tablet to make notes as she went.

The space was fairly small, so she needed to be clever in her design. She was going for a romantic fairy tale look without it turning into a caricature. She'd already put in an order for a chandelier and other lighting, as well as half-a-dozen chairs that with any luck would be delivered tomorrow. She called up the dimensions of a table she already had, to see if it would fit in the space. Grabbing her trusty tape measure she measured it out and smiled with satisfaction as she realised it would fit.

'Hell yes,' she murmured under her breath.

'Talking to yourself again?'

Tam started in fright. She turned around and saw Maddie standing in the doorway.

'You scared me,' Tam said with a nervous laugh.

'Sorry, darling, I thought you'd hear me walking on the deck.'

Tam shook her head. 'No, I'm afraid I was miles away.'

Maddie came in through the old French doors and glanced around the summer house. 'It came up rather well, don't you think?'

'It's amazing what a decent coat of paint can do,' Tam agreed. 'I was just seeing if that old Georgian table I found over at Maryborough would fit here.'

'Oh, the lovely mahogany one with the cabriole legs?'

'Yes, that's the one. And it'll fit,' Tam said. 'I always knew I bought it for a reason.'

'Well, it did take you a long time to restore it but it turned out wonderfully,' Maddie said. 'It'll look fantastic here, especially with the rest of the pieces.'

'I hope so. I know that the bride is anxious about the wedding and wants to see the place as soon as possible.'

'Don't feel rushed though. We have to do this right, not quick,' Maddie said.

'Yes, ma'am,' Tam said with a laugh.

'That sounded like I'm really old, didn't it?' Maddie screwed up her face. 'Like I'm a hundred-year-old dowager.'

Tam chuckled. 'There is still quite a bit to do but it won't take that long because of the size. If I can source the last few pieces and all the deliveries arrive in the next few days, I think it should be ready in a week or so.'

'So when are you going to let her come and look?'

'Early next week? It's easy to envision your wedding if you can see the venue set up and dressed.'

'Right,' Maddie mused as she leant against the wall. She glanced out the old leadlight window into the grey-green beyond. The summer house looked splendid with its new paint and furnishings. It was a link back to a more refined time—open to the lake at the front, with beautiful windows, and gorgeous wooden posts between the panel walls and beamed cathedral ceiling.

'What are you thinking?' Tam asked.

'The week after that is when our first wedding is booked and it's pretty full on from there. It's going to be a little tricky trying to fit this one in. We'll do it but the noise and traffic from the other weddings could be an issue. I know we always stagger the times so there's hardly any crossover but this is throwing a third site into the mix. I just hope we can pull it off.'

'Don't worry, Angie knows that we're fully booked and that we're trying to do her a favour by fitting her in. I'm suggesting that we do an evening wedding on the Friday night,' Tam explained.

'And she's okay with that?'

'Yep.'

'Then there isn't a problem at all,' Maddie said with a smile. She looked at her niece. 'So, did you talk to Seb?'

'I did.'

'And?'

'Kind of like I expected. He wasn't happy, although we didn't end up in a yelling match, so I guess that's a win.' Tam shrugged her shoulders.

Maddie walked over and gave Tam a hug. 'Don't worry, he'll come around.'

'Maybe. I don't know, Maddie—it seems that the two of us keep drifting farther and farther apart. I love him, but nearly every conversation between us is contentious and strained. I'm not saying it's all his fault, it's not—but it seems to me that we've forgotten how much we actually used to like each other.' Tam let out a sigh.

Maddie nodded as she gave Tam an extra squeeze. 'I know it's been difficult. I've tried to get him to open up about it, and even get some help, but he always shuts down the conversation.'

'After the accident we all had counselling. From what I can remember, Seb was always angry and stopped going as soon as he could,' Tam said in a quiet voice. 'He said that it was a waste of time and he had a family to hold together. Like the rest of us didn't contribute to that.'

'I know, but I think it helped us—especially the younger ones—get through that awful period,' Maddie answered.

'Lix always said that he was grateful to be able to talk about his feelings with no judgement, and away from all of us, so he didn't feel like he had to react the same way as the rest of us. I suppose that was one of the things I learnt: none of us grieves the same way,' Tam said as she tried to shut down the disjointed images that flashed through her head.

'It was beneficial for all of us, I know it helped me,' Maddie said. 'All our lives changed so much in the blink of an eye.' She sighed.

Tam took her hand. 'Thank God you came—we wouldn't have made it without you . . . and Rori.'

'Yes, you would have—you're all very strong in your own individual ways. I'm just thankful that I was able to help,' she said. 'Every one of you stepped up and helped hold the family together. Your parents would be so proud of you all.'

'Do you really think so?'

'I know it,' Maddie reassured her.

'The accident affected us in different ways. It took me a long time to start to move past it,' Tam said. 'Sorry, I was such a brat to you at times.'

'You certainly didn't make life boring, darling,' Maddie said. 'But I understood why you acted up. But what happened to your parents wasn't your fault.'

'I know I wasn't to blame but back then I thought I was. Even now sometimes, in the middle of the night after a terrible day, those thoughts still prey on my mind,' Tam confessed.

'You can't think like that. It was just bad timing,' Maddie said.

'If I had just gone to Gemma's place, like I'd said—they wouldn't have been coming to get me,' Tam whispered.

Maddie shook her head. 'You don't know that, the same thing might have happened if they had come to pick you up from Gem's place. You can't think about the what-ifs. They'll consume and destroy your whole life, and that's the last thing your parents would want. They loved you and they would want you to be happy—remember that.' Aunt Maddie held onto Tam's shoulders and looked her dead in the eye.

Tam took a deep breath and blinked away the misting in her eyes. 'I know they'd want us all to be happy, healthy and together.'

'That's right and don't ever forget that. When you look back, don't go to that day. Think about all the good times you had and the wisdom and love they gave you. The accident swept the foundations out from under all of us but it made us stronger too. It made us all grow up, including me,' Maddie said with a wistful look in her eyes. 'Before all this I was just Ben's little, somewhat silly, sister. Whenever I got into a scrape he'd be there to bail me out and give me a lecture along with it.'

'Did he?' Tam asked.

'Always,' Maddie said. 'I got the help but also a dressing-down, particularly if I'd done something monumentally stupid. As you know, there was a big age gap between us, almost twelve years. Your grandma always said she never thought that she was pregnant with me; apparently I was indigestion. So, you can imagine, for your dad I was the annoying little, spoilt sister and he was the older and at times overbearing big brother.'

'Sounds like Seb,' Tam commented.

'It does,' Maddie agreed. 'I always thought that Seb was very much like your dad. Maybe all older brothers are bossy?'

Tam looked back through the open French doors. 'Maybe, but then perhaps not all brothers blame you for their parents' deaths.'

'Tam, you don't know that,' Maddie said with a gasp.

She glanced back at her aunt and nodded. 'Yeah, I reckon I do.'

Nineteen

Christmas Eve, eight years ago

Tam was still walking down the dirt track from the Henderson's place. With every step she felt a little safer but she wouldn't breathe a sigh of relief until she was home. The tears kept welling up but she pushed them down and refused to shed another, at least not in front of her friends. It was probably stupid but it was the only way she could keep control of herself. Inside, her stomach felt like a cold, hard stone and her heartbeat still hadn't slowed. Dylan remained by her side but Gemma and Will had fallen a few steps behind.

'I overheard what you said to your mum,' Dylan said as he walked in step with her. 'Did Taylor Henderson hurt you?'

Tam was silent as she tried to find the right words. 'He did but I think it would have been a whole lot worse if Blake hadn't come along and stopped him.'

Dylan blew out a breath. 'I should go back and say something, or at least do something.'

Tam reached out for his hand. 'No, you'd only end up getting hurt and the whole thing would be worse.' She saw him frown. 'It's not that I don't think you could take on Taylor but he's got all his friends there and they'd all start in on you. Blake wouldn't be able to protect you.'

'Blake is the one who really needs protection. I bet he paid for standing up to Taylor for you,' he said.

Tam felt sick, the thought hadn't even occurred to her. 'You think Taylor would hurt him?'

'Taylor doesn't like being told no,' Dylan said.

'I hope he's okay. I don't know what would have happened if he hadn't interrupted Taylor.'

Dylan scowled and set his mouth in a grim line. He looked as if he had a pretty good idea what would have happened.

'I'll call Blake later,' Dylan replied. 'He won't want to make a big thing about it. The more attention Taylor receives the meaner he gets.'

'They're so different,' Tam said quietly. 'How does he stand it?'

'Blake stays for his mum and sister. He can't help it that his brother and dad are both scum,' Dylan explained.

'But why does his mum put up with it?'

Dylan shrugged. 'I don't know, maybe she thinks she doesn't have anywhere else to go.'

Tam couldn't imagine anything worse than living like that. Although Gemma would be quick to remind her that many of their friends weren't as fortunate as she was. It was true, she did have a pretty great family life and she should be grateful for it.

Tam glanced at her phone and saw that it had been almost half an hour since she'd called her mum. They were still walking down the track but just over the hill it met the old highway, which ran all the way into Kangaroo Ridge.

'What's wrong?' Dylan asked.

'I thought mum would be here by now. She said that she was coming straight away and it doesn't take that long to get here.'

'They probably got held up or maybe had a flat. I'm sure they'll be here soon,' Dylan replied. 'If we keep walking, we'll run into them at some point.'

Tam nodded but looked at her phone again. 'I'll call again and find out what's happening.'

'Fair enough.'

'Are you okay?' Gemma asked from behind.

Tam stopped and looked back. 'I'm going to ring Mum because she should be here by now.'

'Yeah, I was thinking that,' Will said as he pointed ahead. 'We're not that far away from the main road.'

Tam's brow creased with worry as she dialled her mum's number. After half-a-dozen rings it went to voicemail.

'She's not answering,' Tam said as her stomach clenched.

'I'm sure it's fine,' Gemma said.

'Yeah,' Tam said. She turned around and started walking again. 'But it's really not like her—she's never late.'

'I'm sure she'll be here in a minute,' Will added behind her, holding on to Gemma's hand. 'This is the only road to the Hendersons'. It's not like we'd have missed her.'

They kept walking and by the time they reached the main road, Tam was certain that something bad had happened. She kept telling herself that she was being ridiculous but she couldn't shake the feeling. Her mum should have been here well before now—she could have even made the journey twice by now.

'That's weird,' Dylan said as Will and Gemma caught up with them.

'What?' Tam asked.

He nodded towards a line of cars that had banked up in the far lane, the one heading to Kangaroo Ridge. The road was always fairly busy but never backed up like this.

'Maybe they're doing some roadwork,' Gemma said as she glanced at Tam.

'Nah, it's Christmas Eve,' Will said as he looked at his watch. 'It's five thirty.'

'Maybe there's been a bingle or someone's broken down,' Dylan said. 'That would explain why your mum's late. She's probably in the waiting traffic.'

'Yeah, you're right,' Tam said. 'Well, if she can't get to us, we should go to her.'

'Seems like a plan.' Dylan took her hand and they started walking down the side of the road, heading towards town.

Every now and again, a handful of cars drove past them. Tam kept an eye on them in case one of them was her mum. She couldn't see too far ahead as the road swept around a bend, which must be where the hold-up was.

'I hope it's just a breakdown,' Gemma added. 'I'd hate it to be an accident.'

'We'll know soon enough,' Dylan replied. 'It shouldn't take us too long to get to the bend.'

Tam increased her pace and the others followed suit. She kept telling herself that everything was all right, that soon she'd be in her mother's arms, she would be safe and she could have a good cry. But that sinking feeling wouldn't go away.

'Hey, Tam, can we slow down a bit?' Gemma called out.

Tam looked back over her shoulder. 'No, I want to find Mum.'

Gemma blew out a breath and tried her best to keep up.

Tam kept going, the air was hot and smelt of dust and the occasional burst of exhaust fumes. The tall eucalypts offered a little shade but the sun was sinking in the sky and bathing Tam and her friends in its direct light. A small trickle of sweat ran down the side of her neck, she brushed it aside with her free hand and kept walking.

'We're almost there,' Dylan said beside her. 'We'll find your mum, don't worry.'

'I don't understand, if she was just stuck in traffic, why didn't she answer my call or at least ring me back?'

'I don't know, maybe she was helping?'

His words calmed her. Yes, if there had been an accident her mum wouldn't have hesitated to go and help. That was the type of person she was.

After another couple of minutes they finally rounded the bend. Several hundred metres away there was a congestion of vehicles, including a truck. There was a fire engine and Tam could see the flashing light of an ambulance.

'This doesn't look good,' Will said.

'No, it doesn't,' Dylan replied quietly.

'Maybe we should wait here,' Gemma said and then quickly added, 'we don't want to get in the way.'

'You can stay here if you want,' Tam answered. 'But I need to find my mother.'

'I'll come with you,' Dylan said but Tam had already taken off.

Will waved his hand. 'We'll catch up.'

Dylan gave him a brief nod before running after Tam. She got a few curious stares from the people in cars, but Tam didn't care; something inside her told her she should run as fast as she could. Her breath was beginning to be laboured but she kept running.

There were heavy footsteps behind her and then Dylan drew alongside her. Now she could see a couple of police cars and a barrier had been set up. They slowed their pace and finally came to a stop by the barrier.

'Hey, Dylan, you can't be here,' a young constable said as he held up his hand.

'Hi, Mark,' Dylan replied to his cousin. 'Looks nasty.'

Mark gave a nod. 'It is. Why are you even here?'

'We're waiting for Tam's mum.'

The colour drained from Mark's face as he looked over to Tam. 'Sorry, Tamara, I didn't recognise you straight away.'

Tam shrugged. 'That's okay, Mark, it's been a while.' She pointed past the barricade. 'Listen, I have to get to the other side, Mum will be waiting.'

'No, if you can just wait until I get—'

'I promise I won't get in the way,' she said as she took another few steps. There was a gap between the vehicles and Tam peered through it. A large delivery truck was smashed into a silver Hilux, the front end was crumpled and there was a tarpaulin covering what used to be the windscreen. Her eyes travelled to the side of the door, on it was a drawing of an old two-storey building with the words *Come and unwind at the Kangaroo Ridge Pub*.

'That's my dad's car,' Tam whispered before her world tilted on its axis and the realisation penetrated her brain. Everything began to swim in front of her before she lost consciousness and hit the dirt.

Twenty
Christmas Eve, eight years ago

Seb wiped down the kitchen bench. 'Thanks for your help,' he said to Felix who was putting the last of the ingredients away.

'No worries. I think the last of the biscuits turned out okay.' His younger brother grinned. 'Mum will be proud.'

'Especially since you only managed to nick two,' Seb said with a laugh.

'But they're soooo good,' Lix replied. 'I don't suppose . . .'

'No!' Seb chuckled. 'Mum will kill us if she gets home to find them all gone. You know she wants them for tomorrow.'

Lix wrinkled his nose. 'All right, I'll leave them alone. I might go skateboarding down by the old barn for a bit.'

'Go on then,' Seb said. 'Is Gray still with Lucy?'

'Yeah, he's suffering through the princess game again.' Felix rolled his eyes. 'I don't get how she can play it over and over again.'

'Me neither.' Seb glanced at the wall clock. 'I thought they'd be home by now.'

'Yeah, right? It's been over an hour. Maybe Mum stopped for some last-minute things in town.'

'But she went in with Lucy earlier.'

'Maybe Dad had to stop in at work or something,' Lix said with a shrug. 'Anyway, I'm off.'

'Have fun and don't break your neck.'

'I'll try not to.' Lix scooped up his skateboard at the back door.

Seb looked around the kitchen, everything was put away except for the trays of iced biscuits. He eyed the biscuits for a second before nabbing one for himself.

* * *

Lix had been skating for about half an hour. He was in the zone, speeding around the old concrete footpath and driveway near the barn. He was having fun but it would have been better if Tam or Gray was with him. He checked his watch and figured that Gray would still be playing with Lucy. Weird that Mum and Dad weren't back yet.

He was about to do another circuit when he heard a car pull up. He jumped off his board and ran up the hill but when he got to the top he saw that it wasn't his dad's ute but a police car. His heart started pounding. This couldn't be good. He ran towards the car as fast as he could.

'Hi,' he said warily to the two police officers who got out. 'Can I help you?'

The older policeman smiled. His eyes were brown and a little crinkly around the corners but they seemed kind.

'Hello, son,' he said. 'I'm Senior Constable White and this is my colleague Constable Jefferies.'

'I'm Felix. If you're looking for Dad, he and Mum have gone to pick up my sister, Tam.'

'Well, it's nice to meet you,' the policeman said. 'Can I ask who is home?'

'Seb, Gray, Lucy and me,' Lix said.

'Seb is your oldest brother, is that right?'

'That's right, he's seventeen.'

'And how old are you?'

'Fourteen,' Felix replied.

'Lix?' Seb was walking out the front door with a worried look on his face. 'What's going on?'

Senior Constable White gave him a soft smile. 'Hello, Seb. Can we all sit down for a minute? I need to tell you something.'

Lix sat down next to his brother on the top step and looked expectantly at the policeman. His gut was twisted in a knot. Something really, really bad had happened.

'Should I go and get Gray and Lucy?' he asked Seb.

His brother shook his head. 'No, not yet,' Seb said in almost a whisper.

Lix nodded and leant against Seb. He reached down, took a hold of his hand and waited for Senior Constable White to speak. He was terrified but he didn't know why. Seb squeezed his hand tight and waited.

* * *

Time was fractured, at least that's how it appeared to Seb. One moment the clock said that an hour had passed and yet the next time he looked the hands seemed frozen in time. Everything was topsy-turvy and he couldn't get his head around any of it. He leant his hands on the sink with his head hanging down and tried to remember how to breathe. His whole world had just collapsed around him. How could they be dead? They were here in this very room talking, laughing only a few hours ago.

He felt cold, chilled to the bone, but the summer night air was still warm around him. He had to move, he had to do something, but like the clock he was immobile. Seb scrunched his eyes shut, they stung from all the tears he'd shed. But he couldn't stay like this, he had to pull himself together. There would be things that had to be taken care of, including his brothers and sisters. It's what Mum would have wanted; he'd promised her that he would always look after the others.

Gray and Lucy had cried themselves to sleep. Maybe it was a good thing, at least the pain would stop while they slept. Tam was in hospital, according to the policeman she'd seen the crash and fainted. God, he had no idea what that would do to her. Gemma and her mum were at the hospital in Bendigo with Tam and would keep him updated. Grandad had arrived from the retirement village and was crying on the couch in the living room, and apparently Aunt Maddie was on her way.

Seb glanced towards the front of the house. He should go and check on Lix again, who was still sitting on the front steps. He'd called him in once but Lix said he was waiting—for what he didn't know.

Seb pushed himself away from the sink then walked over to the fridge and yanked open the door. All the food that Mum had prepared for tomorrow's feast was tucked away safely in bowls and cling-wrapped dishes. A lump started to form in his throat again, so he grabbed a couple of cans of drink quickly and slammed the door shut. He took a moment and pushed the fear and grief down; he couldn't break down again—his family needed him. Seb drew in another deep breath and tried to centre himself. He could do this, he would do it.

He walked through the living room and glanced at his grandfather on the way. He looked ancient and broken, tears streamed down his face and he didn't even acknowledge Seb. It was probably just as well, Seb thought as he kept walking. He didn't need his grandfather's grief, he had enough of his own. Opening the front door, he sat down next to Lix and handed him a can of drink.

'Are you okay?' he asked.

Lix glanced at him as he took the drink and shook his head. 'No,' he said simply. 'I'm not.'

'Me neither,' Seb replied as he cracked open his can and took a swig.

'How are Gray and Luce?'

'They're asleep in Lucy's room,' Seb said. 'Maybe you should come in?'

Lix shook his head. 'No, I can't breathe in there. I'm fine here.'

Seb nodded like he understood but he didn't, not really. 'Gemma's mum rang. They're staying with Tam in the hospital tonight. She said that they'll bring her home in the morning.'

'Good,' Lix replied.

He nudged Lix. 'I don't know how but I promise we'll get through this. I promise we'll all stay together and everything will be okay.'

Lix looked at his brother, his eyes swimming in tears. He didn't say anything, just nodded his head in agreement. The noise of tyres on gravel in the distance made them both look up. A light from car headlights was bouncing its way up the drive. Pretty soon a small red hatchback came to a stop right next to the steps. A young woman with dark hair, a pregnant belly and a leather biker jacket got out of the car. Both boys stood up as she slammed the door and hurried towards the house. She stopped as soon as she saw them and opened her arms.

'Aunt Maddie!' Lix cried out.

Seb and Lix raced down the steps and hurled themselves into her waiting embrace. She hugged them tight.

'I'm here and I'm not going anywhere,' she vowed.

Twenty-One

Everyone was sitting down to breakfast, when Seb walked through the back door. This was pretty odd as his day usually started a bit later because of the pub's hours.

'Hey,' he said as he looked around. 'Where's Maddie and Rori?'

'They've already eaten and gone for a walk,' Lucy said as she glanced up from her plate.

Lix looked over at the old wall clock. 'You're early,' he said. 'You want some pancakes? Gray just made a stack of them.'

'I've already eaten,' Seb said. 'I came by to see if I could borrow Gray.'

Grayson looked over from where he was standing at the stove. 'What's up?'

'I've got several deliveries coming in today and my barman has called in sick. It's a paying gig and I'll even throw in lunch,' Seb said with a persuasive smile.

'Sounds good,' Gray replied as he looked at Tam. 'That is if I haven't double booked myself. Was I meant to help you and Maddie today?'

Tam shook her head. 'Tomorrow,' she said. 'We have to start configuring the barn for our first wedding of the year.'

'Well, I guess I'm all yours then,' Gray said, turning back to Seb.

'I was hoping that you'd say that,' Seb answered. 'Can you come now?'

'Sure, if someone else can do kitchen duty.'

'I'll do it,' Lucy said. 'It's not like I've got anything else on today.'

Tam leant towards her sister. 'I'm going to Bendigo to pick up the final few pieces for the summer house, you wanna come? That's if I can borrow a car?'

Lucy broke into a grin. 'Absolutely!'

Lix reached into his pocket and pulled out his car keys. 'Here, take mine. I'm only taking photos today.'

'Won't you need it?' Tam asked even as she held out her hand.

'Nah, it'll be fine.'

'Thanks,' she responded before turning her attention to Seb. 'I might drop by later. I need to grab a bottle of wine.'

Seb didn't even look at her. 'Yeah whatever,' he said quickly. He caught Grayson's eye. 'You ready?'

'I just have to grab my phone.'

'I'll meet you in the car,' Seb said. 'See you later,' he called to the others before he headed out the back door.

Lucy stared at Tam for a moment. 'Is he angry with you?'

Tam wrinkled her nose. 'When isn't he?'

'Are you okay?' Lix asked as he cut into another pancake. 'I take it Seb is still annoyed.'

'You know how he gets when he thinks he's in the right.'

'I did tell him that it wasn't any of his business,' Lix confessed.

'I did too, but that just made it worse,' Tam replied.

Lucy held up her hands in front of her. 'Okay, everyone just hold it right there. Am I the only one who doesn't know what's going on?'

Tam raised her eyebrows at Lix.

'You might as well tell her, Tam,' he said. 'You can't leave her out.'

Tam turned and faced Lucy. 'Dylan and I are going out together.'

Lucy rolled her eyes. 'Well, about time. It took you long enough.'

Tam sat back in her chair with surprise and Lix let out a laugh.

'What do you mean?' Tam asked.

'I'm not blind, you two have been eyeing each other for as long as I can remember.'

'So much for secrets.' Lix chuckled. 'Luce knew what was going on from the get-go.'

'Lucy knew what?' Grayson had walked back into the room.

'That Tam and Dylan are seeing each other and that Seb is pissed about it,' Lucy explained.

Gray looked shocked. 'What? Really? You and Dylan?'

Lucy let out an exaggerated sigh. 'Seriously, you really have to pay a bit more attention to what's going on in this family.'

'You knew?'

'Not officially until now, but it was pretty obvious,' Lucy said. 'They've always liked each other.'

'Since when?'

Lucy rolled her eyes. 'Haven't you noticed the way she looks at Dylan every time he walks in the door?'

'That's not true, Luce,' Tam said as her cheeks tingled with heat.

'Yeah right,' Lucy scoffed back.

Gray looked puzzled as he glanced back at Tam. 'So why is Seb annoyed?'

She shrugged. 'He thinks we're not suited and that everything will crash and burn and it will be a disaster.'

'Subtle,' Lix added.

'Well, he'd be wrong then,' Gray said with a smile. 'Look, I'd better go because he's waiting in the car. But, remember, just because Seb thinks he's right, it doesn't mean he is.'

Tam grinned at her youngest brother. 'You've always had a way with words.'

He walked around the table to where she was sitting and gave her a quick kiss on the top of her head. 'Don't let him get you down. He'll get over it, it just might take a while.'

'Thanks, Gray,' Tam said as he gave a wave and disappeared out the back door.

* * *

Tam took the old back road to Bendigo, it took a little longer but in her opinion it was certainly more scenic. Lucy gave her a smile from the passenger's seat as she put on some of her favourite melodic soft rock music. Tam realised that it had been a while since it had been just the two of them together and she made a mental note to spend more time alone with her sister. She thought about how similar they were physically, and how Lucy was showing much more independence now that she had turned sixteen. She seemed to really have her head on straight, and in that way was much more stable than Tam had been at her age.
Once they left town there were a lot of long paddocks which were beginning to dry off in the summer heat. In one paddock a small flock of sheep were sheltering from the sun beneath the spreading boughs of an ancient gum tree, and in another a mob of kangaroos hopped away from the car and up a hill.

'So what's the plan?' Lucy asked.

'I want to pick up a couple more things for the summer house. I was thinking along decorative lines, but the truth is I'm not one hundred per cent sure what I'm looking for.' Tam kept her eyes on the road as she spoke.

'I'm sure we'll find something,' Lucy replied.

'After that, I thought we'd grab some lunch and have a look around the shops.'

'Sounds good.' Lucy cast a glance over at her sister. 'So, how long have you and Dylan been seeing each other?'

'Almost a year.'

Lucy chuckled and shook her head. 'Maybe you're better at hiding things than I thought. I thought it must have been a recent development.'

'No, we've just been keeping things under wraps.'

'Why?'

Tam drew in a breath. It was a reasonable question but she found it very hard to answer.

'Maybe I was afraid about what people would think.'

'You mean Seb,' Lucy countered.

'Well, yes, but it wasn't just that. Oh, truth is, I'm not sure.' She quickly added, 'Any plans with your friends for these holidays?'

'Not really,' Lucy said. 'We'd planned to hang out over Christmas but Heather had to spend it at her dad's place in Bendigo and Eric's been dragged off to a family reunion in Melbourne.'

'That sounds like fun,' Tam commented.

'Apparently not,' Lucy said. 'He barely knows his grandparents because his mum isn't on the greatest terms with them. So he thinks it's going to be super awkward. He says that his cousins, or rather his mum's cousins, are nice to him but they're all older. Everyone else ignores him because *he's just his mum's mistake.*' Lucy held up her hands and did air quotation marks.

'Wow, really? That's awful,' Tam said.

'Yeah I know—judgey much? So we're all counting down the days until they get back home.'

'Why would Elise even put herself and Eric through that if the whole family is so toxic?'

'Because her aunt and cousins begged her to go, and they're nice. It's just that everyone else is weird.'

'You know Eric could have stayed with us while his mum went.'

Lucy nodded. 'I did offer but he said he couldn't let his mum face the "wolves" all by herself. His words, not mine.'

'Sounds horrible,' Tam said with a shudder. 'I know we all have our disagreements, but nothing like that.'

'Yeah, everything is fine until Seb decides to be a jerk,' Lucy said.

Tam was torn for a moment because she kind of agreed. 'He does what he thinks is right,' she said measuredly. 'I mean, we have to cut him a bit of slack sometimes.'

Lucy screwed up her face. 'Says the woman who was told that she shouldn't be with Dylan.'

Tam gripped the steering wheel. 'Point taken.'

Twenty-Two

Dylan parked his ute on the main street and looked down at his phone. Seb still hadn't responded to his messages. He understood that his friend was angry but this was becoming straight-out childish. Dylan had asked to meet so they could talk it out and he could get to the bottom of why Seb was so dead against his relationship with Tam.

Seb had said things like they were very different people and that the whole thing was doomed before it started—which was weird and didn't take in the fact they'd already been together for so long. To Dylan, it sounded like a lot of bullshit. There was something else going on with Seb and he was determined to find out.

It wasn't just because they'd been friends since they were kids, Dylan had spent more time at the Carringtons' than his own house. No shocking revelations there, all you had to do was meet his dad and the reason why was clear. The old man was a piece of work and Dylan had decided at an early age to spend as little time at home as possible. Thank God for Seb's mum, she welcomed him at their house and never once sent him home. At first she'd asked if he wanted to stay for dinner, after a while she just kept setting a place for him.

Dylan scrunched his eyes shut as an image of Estella Carrington materialised in his mind. Her death still hurt. He never said much around Seb, in case it appeared that he was trying to take away from his grief, but Dylan had lost the closest mother figure he'd had. He couldn't remember his own mum as she'd taken off when he was still a baby. Sometimes he blamed her for not taking him with her but he also understood why she'd run away.

He redialled Seb's number and waited, but once again the call went through to the message bank.

Dylan sighed. 'How long are you going to keep this up?' he asked after the beep.

He shoved his phone into the pocket of his pants. All he wanted was for everyone to get along and be okay with the fact that he was with Tamara and was happy.

He understood Seb was hurt because Tam and his best friend had gone behind his back. But there was more going on, too. He couldn't quite put his finger on it but he knew something wasn't right. The same way he knew that there was a deeper problem with Tam, who had been so insistent that they keep their connection a secret. He'd spent so much time with the Carringtons over the years, he could tell when they were lying even if they didn't realise it themselves.

He'd been euphoric that their relationship was finally public. But he didn't get the same vibe from Tam. She didn't seem happy about it at all. When he'd asked her about it last night, she said she was happy that the truth was finally out there but she was still worried about Seb's reaction. He wanted to believe that was all it was. In his own happiness, he'd chosen to ignore the sense he had that something was wrong, to push it under the rug, but something was there, and he guessed it was a whole lot more than just Seb being annoyed.

Dylan got out of his ute and headed towards a house just off the main street. He knocked on the door and waited. After a moment he could hear the tap of brisk footsteps. The door swung open to reveal a middle-aged woman in a dark green dress with her auburn hair pulled up in a bun.

'Hey, Ms Winter,' Dylan said with a smile.

'Hello, Dylan.' She stood back to let him into the house. 'Like I said on the phone, I was hoping that you could help me sort out my little office and shelving problem. I didn't realise you were on holiday. It can wait a while if it's a problem.'

'No worries,' Dylan said as he stepped inside. 'I need something constructive to do at the moment.'

'So I was thinking about remodelling a couple of rooms into an office library,' she said as she walked down the hallway. 'I knew when I bought this place, I always wanted to combine the rooms.'

'Sounds good.'

'I think it will be,' she answered. 'I get too distracted when I write in the bedroom or here at the kitchen table,' she said as she gestured into the open doorway.

'I understand,' Dylan replied with a nod. 'You need a designated place to make you feel like you're actually going to sit down and work.'

Ms Winter glanced over her shoulder. 'Exactly. So, the idea is to open up both of these small rooms. They're both rather small so combining them into one would be a lot more useful.'

'Let's take a look.' Dylan followed her into a room on the left.

'It's through here,' Ms Winter said. 'Oh by the way, I heard a little rumour about you.'

'Really?' Dylan raised his eyebrows. 'Can't imagine that it would be very interesting.'

She smiled. 'A little bird told me that you're going out with Tam Carrington.'

Dylan stood there, dumbfounded. As far as he knew Tam had only told Seb and the rest of the family. 'How could . . .' he started to say.

'This town is very good at finding out secrets and spilling the tea. Mind you, I think it's lovely. You two will make a great match—that is, if it's true?' she added with a wink.

'Um, yes,' Dylan said. 'We're seeing each other.' He felt compelled to say something because she was looking at him expectantly, the way his English teacher used to when she was waiting for an answer.

'That's wonderful! Now, here's the first of the rooms—do you think it's doable?'

'Let's have a look,' he said, happy to change the subject.

* * *

Seb was in the cellar when he heard his phone ping. With a sigh, he put down the box of wine and dragged the phone out of his pocket. A voicemail from Dylan. He almost deleted it but then thought better of it.

He was annoyed that his sister and best friend had been sneaking around for a year without saying anything to him. He didn't think they were right for each other, but he also recognised that he was hurt that they hadn't told him. He played the message.

'So how long are you going to keep this up?'

Seb sat down on the nearest stack of boxes. Maybe Dylan was right, giving them both the cold-shoulder treatment was pretty juvenile. The problem was that Seb couldn't work out how he really felt or what he wanted to say.

He understood why Tam hadn't wanted to tell him. If he put himself in her place, he probably wouldn't have wanted to either. Their relationship wasn't good and it hadn't been for a long time. He closed his eyes and fragmented images flashed within his mind's eye. They were out of sequence but all of them were snatches in time where he and Tam were at odds with each other.

On the big things, the important things that had to do with the welfare of the family, she always had his back. But on the general day to day, they snapped and snarled at each other like dogs about to fight.

He'd promised his mum that he'd take care of his younger siblings but when it came to Tam, it was complicated. An uncomfortable thought surfaced, it was the same one that Felix had scratched at recently. The one that said he still blamed her for the death of their parents.

He ran both his hands through his hair. That was ridiculous, it wasn't Tam's fault. It was the idiot truck driver's fault who didn't know the road and took the bend too quickly. He lost control and slammed into the oncoming car, which happened to be Estella and Ben's.

Tam had been in trouble and his parents naturally went to help her. It was inept driving and a big dose of bad timing that had stolen his parents away from him, nothing else.

He hated thinking about that day. For his own peace of mind he'd mentally locked it away and rarely let it out. The past was done and no amount of thinking or wishing would ever change it. These were the cards he'd been dealt and he just had to get on and make the best of it. This had basically been his motto ever since that fateful day. And he had to admit, he'd been shouldered with the task of holding the family together but he hadn't done it by himself. He always had Tam and Aunt Maddie to lean on and he knew that there was no way he'd have done it without them.

He appreciated his sister, she'd given up just as much as he had, including going to university, because she felt she was needed at home. Felix was wrong about him blaming Tam and wanting to punish her. That was plain ludicrous.

Seb stood up and brushed the imaginary dust from his jeans. He'd go and get something to eat and maybe ring Dylan then. He knew he had to get past this thing. Tam and Dylan were going out together and he had to accept it. He started to head towards the stairs when a little inner voice asked, *But why was she even at that party? If she hadn't gone, your parents would never have been on that road.*

Twenty-Three
Eight years ago

Seb was only going through the motions, at least that's how he felt. He was sitting in the front row of the packed church with his brothers and sisters jammed up against each other. He was hollow, present only in body—it was like everything that was actually him was missing. He sat up straighter and Lucy wiggled beside him. He fixed his eyes ahead, purposely blurring his sight so he didn't have to focus on the two flower-strewn caskets before the altar.

He gripped on to the order of service until his knuckles were white. Time was out of whack, it had been ever since they had found out about the accident. It sped up, slowed down and sometimes just froze. That's what it was like now, Seb thought—it was as if he was frozen in this agonising moment and there was nothing he could do about it.

Lix sat on the other side of him, and without turning his head he reached over and placed his hand over Seb's. The warmth from his hand seemed to penetrate Seb's clutched fingers and he slowly released his grip on the screwed-up bit of paper.

Seb glanced over his left shoulder and saw that all the pews were full and a handful of people were standing in the doorway. He recognised nearly everyone; it appeared that the entire town had turned up to say goodbye. It was humbling to know that his parents had touched so many lives.

'Are you all right?' Lix whispered beside him.

Seb turned back and nodded to his brother.

It wasn't true, he wasn't all right but then none of them were. The minister spoke but Seb couldn't take in the words. He had wanted to say some words himself but he had realised that he could barely put together a cohesive thought let alone attempt to speak in front of a church full of people. His father's best friend Mick had spoken instead, as well as Aunt Maddie.

He looked down the pew past Lix and saw that Tam was sitting with Dylan. She was very pale and her eyes were brimming with unshed tears. He caught Dylan's attention and gave him a pointed look towards Tam. Dylan nodded before slipping his arm around her for support. His friend had been helping at the house ever since the news broke of the accident, for which he was eternally grateful. Dylan had taken calls, fended off well-intentioned neighbours and looked after the younger kids while Seb and Maddie organised the funeral. Grandad was there too but the accident had shaken him to his core. Seb understood but he resented him as well. Someone had to take responsibility, and when his grandfather refused to pull himself together, Seb realised that he was going to have to be that person.

That sounded harsh and perhaps it was. But his grandfather was so consumed with his own pain that it didn't seem to even cross his mind that they were all grieving too. Two nights ago, Lucy had been crying and she'd gone to their grandfather for a cuddle but he'd turned away from her. Thank God that Gray had been there and scooped her up. But the action had shown Seb how self-absorbed his grandfather could be.

He cast a glance now at the other end of the pew where his grandfather sat. The old man looked frail and shattered. Seb dug down deep and tried to find his compassion but he couldn't. He turned his head and looked straight ahead again.

The organ began to swell and the congregation got to their feet. Lucy clung on to him and all he could think was—*Oh God, I can't do this. I can't do this.*

* * *

Tam was sitting on the hard wooden pew between Dylan and Lix. The world about her appeared distorted, especially the sound, almost as if she was underwater. She blinked her eyes shut as she tried to concentrate on what the minister was saying. She caught a few words but couldn't focus on the whole.

Ever since the accident she felt as if she was submerged and she couldn't surface. It had been this way since she'd returned home from the hospital, moving through the days and the hours as if in slow motion. She wanted to scream, to call out for help, but no one could help her.

Images of that terrible Christmas Eve kept appearing unbidden in her mind. If she'd only left the party sooner . . . If she hadn't gone to the stupid party none of this would have happened. Her parents were on that road because of her. The guilt twisted in her stomach and ate her from within. If her family blamed her, she wouldn't try to defend herself because she knew that they would have been right.

But none of them had blamed her, or at least not openly. Aunt Maddie had been a godsend, she'd given all the support she could while letting Seb and Tam make the final decisions on everything. Tam winced, she'd allowed Seb to take the bigger lead because she really couldn't do it right now. She wanted to—to step up and be strong like her parents would have wanted her to be—but no matter how hard she tried over the past few days, she just couldn't do it.

Tears began to well in her eyes, which puzzled her because it didn't seem possible she could have any left. The air inside the church was hot, but Tam shivered. Almost instantly, Dylan put his arm around her. She leant into his strength and his warmth, and felt the first bit of comfort she'd had since her world had been ripped apart.

The music began to swell and there was a shuffle as people stood up. As Tam stood up she was thankful that Dylan caught her hand in his and gave it a squeeze. She concentrated on his touch as it was something tangible that anchored her to the spot and prevented her from drifting away.

Tam took a breath as she thought—*How am I ever going to get through this?*

* * *

Lix sat between his older brother and sister. He looked up at the intricate stained-glass window and watched as the sun shone through the different colours. He was like the window, everything about his life was now fragmented and fractured.

When he was a little kid, he used to have a pony puppet. It had strings attached and you could manipulate it by its crossbar handles. That's how he felt right now, that he was suspended in the air with no control over his own body.

He'd tried to keep busy and make sure that his brothers and sisters were okay. But that was a joke because none of them were. He did his best to try to help anyway, even if that was just reading Lucy a story and holding her hand until she fell asleep.

It was hard, Lucy was only eight years old. She understood what had happened and that their parents weren't coming back but she still wanted her mum—but, then again, so did he.

Aunt Maddie had been amazing and tried to keep everyone calm, fed and together. He wanted to ask her about the baby, like when it was due, but it never seemed like the right time.

There was an underlying tension in the house, at first hard to detect because of the grief, but Lix could feel it. Part of it was because of Grandad, it was an awful thing to say but it was the truth. This was the hardest thing that any of them had ever had to do but everyone in the family was trying to be considerate, trying to help and trying to get through it—except for Grandad and that grated on Seb.

The other night when Grandad had ignored Lucy was pretty much the last straw. Lix was almost positive that Seb and Maddie would suggest that he go back to the retirement village as soon as this awful day was over.

The congregation was singing now, but Lix couldn't find his voice. Instead he looked up at the pretty blue-shaded piece of glass in the window. It was his mum's favourite colour; she'd planted flowers in that colour by the front steps of the house last spring. A ray of light bounced through the blue glass and reflected on the floor in front of him. Lix stared at it and wondered if it was his mum saying goodbye.

He closed his eyes and hot tears spilt down his face. He'd give anything to hear her call him that baby name again.

Lixie.

He thought he heard her voice but he knew it was just in his mind.

Twenty-Four

'So, now we're officially public, what do you want to do?' Dylan asked as he lay back against the bedhead.

Tam looked perplexed. 'What do you mean?'

'Well, for a start, I reckon we could actually be seen together,' Dylan said. 'Now everyone knows, we don't need to sneak around anymore.'

'I guess,' Tam replied. 'But what do you mean everyone knows?'

'The whole town by now,' Dylan said with a shrug. 'I checked out a job for Ms Winter and she knew about us. So I figured if she knew, everyone else would too.'

'How is that even possible?' Tam rolled on her side and looked up at Dylan.

'You know how fast gossip runs through this place,' Dylan reminded her. 'I don't know why you're so surprised—it's been a week.'

'I don't like that people are talking about us,' Tam said. 'It's got nothing to do with them.'

'Ah, don't let it get to you.' He bent down and dropped a kiss on the top of her head. 'They'll get bored and move on to someone else.'

'I suppose,' Tam grumbled.

'Anyway, you didn't answer my question,' Dylan reminded her.

'Which was what?'

'Honestly, do you even listen to what I say?' Dylan replied and added an over-dramatic sigh. 'You wanna go out somewhere, you know, on a date . . . together?'

Tam grabbed the sheet and sat up. 'I suppose we could. Although, work is about to crank up so I'll have to look at the schedule.'

A frown flickered across Dylan's brows. 'I was only thinking dinner and a movie in Bendigo.'

Tam paused before nodding. 'Yeah, let's do it,' she replied. 'But I still better check the schedule.'

Dylan relaxed a little. 'Okay. You check what night you're free and then I'll make a booking.'

Tam gave him a smile. 'I'll let you know tomorrow, once I'm back in the office.'

Dylan kissed her.

'Have you heard from Seb at all?' Tam asked.

'He rang earlier today. He didn't say much but I'm catching up with him tomorrow after work.'

'Let me know how it goes.'

Dylan hauled her up to his side and gave her a hug. 'You worry too much, all this will blow over. He's just being his over-cautious self—you know how he is.'

'Maybe,' Tam replied.

'Look, he loves both of us and when he realises that we make each other happy, he'll back off. You know Seb, he doesn't function unless he feels like he's in control of every situation.'

Tam paused. 'I suppose you're right,' she said.

'Of course I am.'

'It really annoyed me how he was talking though, like he knew better.'

Dylan laughed. 'Well, he can certainly be annoying and bull-headed but never doubt that he loves you and wants you to be safe.'

'I do doubt that though. We've really drifted apart lately. Nothing I do ever seems to please him. And yes, I know I did some dumb things in the past but I feel as if he still holds that against me. The thing that gets under my skin probably more than anything is how he acts like he's years older than me when we're the same age,' Tam said with another sigh.

'I never said he was perfect,' Dylan said with a laugh and then added, 'but you're right, he does act that way with you and I'm not sure why. Have you tried talking to him about it?'

'Of course but he chooses not to listen or takes exception to what I'm saying and we end up having another argument. Both of us saying things we shouldn't and most probably don't mean.'

'Maybe you could ask Maddie to be a mediator?'

'Perhaps,' Tam said in a quiet voice. 'It's always so much hard work and I never seem to get anywhere.'

'All you can do is keep trying,' Dylan replied before changing the subject. 'So, what sort of movie are you up for?'

'I don't mind.'

'You might regret saying that.'

Tam laughed. 'Probably.' She pulled away from him and sat on the edge of the bed.

'What are you doing?'

'I'd better go home. I have an early start and a bride is coming to inspect the summer house.'

'Oh, I thought you were staying the night,' Dylan said quietly.

'Yeah . . . but I think I'd better head back.'

Dylan reached out for her. 'Tam, is anything wrong?'

She shook her head. 'No, why would it be?' She gave him a slight smile before standing up then scooping up her clothes and heading to the bathroom.

The mood had changed, Dylan swore he could feel it in the atmosphere. It was the same sort of vibe he'd felt in the past whenever he'd suggested that they make their relationship public. It was unsettling, like she didn't want to be with him. He had given her ample opportunities in the past to end things but she didn't and always said that she loved him. But maybe she didn't love him enough, or at least not in the way he loved her. She'd always used the excuse of not telling Seb but that didn't fly now. Was she ashamed of him or their relationship? Or was she terrified of commitment?

He got out of bed and dragged on his jeans.

'You sure you want to go?' he called out.

'No, but I should,' Tam replied through the bathroom door.

'And nothing is wrong?' He asked again, knowing all too well that something was.

Tam opened the door and gave him a quick kiss on the cheek. 'Why do you keep harping on about it? I'll give you a ring tomorrow so we can organise a movie.' She put her arms around him and gave him a hug. 'I'd better go. See you later.'

'Yeah, of course,' Dylan said as he watched her go yet again. But this time an ache in his belly told him something wasn't right, and maybe it never had been.

* * *

Tam took off on her bike and headed towards home. Every time Dylan talked about future plans she felt a rising wave of panic. She didn't understand it. She loved Dylan, she really did, so why could something as innocent as dinner and a movie send her into a tailspin?

She wanted to be happy, to be normal. Dylan wanted to build a life with her, he talked about it all the time. She wanted to give that to him but something deep inside kept stopping her. Every time she thought about it, it was like she was underwater, unable to breathe. She wanted to swim to the surface but she couldn't. It was the same feeling she'd had after her parents' accident. Why did she feel it now with Dylan?

The red motorbike sped down the old dirt road, kicking up dust in its wake. The night sky was studded with so many shiny stars but Tam didn't notice them. Instead she kept her eyes straight ahead and tried not to think about Dylan alone in an otherwise empty bed. She needed to figure out what the hell was going on with her. Like Maddie always told her—she deserved to be happy . . . didn't she?

Twenty-Five

'Welcome to the summer house,' Tam said to the young blonde woman who stood by her side. 'Do you think this could work?'

Angie nodded. 'It's gorgeous,' she said softly. 'I can really get married here?'

Tam grinned. 'Of course! But like I said over the phone you'd have to be willing to hold the wedding on a Friday evening, rather than on a weekend.'

'You're that booked up?'

Tam blew out a breath. 'You have no idea. We're booked out for months but because you're planning such a small ceremony, we could hold it here—if you like it.'

Angie looked at Tam with tears in her eyes. 'I love it.'

Tam gave her a one-armed hug. 'I'm so glad,' she said. 'So I thought we could have the ceremony here on the deck with lots of candlelight and then you can use the summer house for a small reception.'

Angie looked out across the lake. 'It sounds beautiful, I can almost see it now.'

Tam opened the French doors into the tiny summer house. 'See, just big enough for you.'

Angie tried to take it all in. There was an old Georgian table surrounded by six carved wooden chairs, fairy lights, a chandelier and silk draperies.

'Now imagine all the lights on with candlelight and a festoon of flowers,' Tam said. 'Did you have any catering in mind?'

Angie shook her head. 'Not since everything was cancelled,' she answered. 'Until you rang, I didn't think any of this was even possible.'

'We can put a small buffet together, using local produce. How about your cake?' Tam asked and then kind of wished she hadn't as Angie's eyes filled up.

'All we have is the dress, the suit and the rings.'

'And that's all you need, we can take care of everything else,' Tam said gently. 'It may not be how you first envisioned your wedding but it will be beautiful, I promise. We can source a cake and if we ask my brother really nicely, I'm sure he'd be happy to take some photos.'

'Really?'

'I'm sure we can bribe him with something,' Tam said.

Angie began to brighten. 'I don't know how to thank you. I was losing hope, our wedding has been cancelled twice.'

'Well, third time's the charm,' Tam said. 'Why don't we go back to the office and we can go over some of the costs? Then you can take them home and discuss it with your fiancé.'

'Yes and my mum, she's going to pay for part of it. She's been so supportive,' Angie said. 'Rick adores her, she's like his second mum.'

Tam nodded. She was glad that Angie and her mum had a close bond. It wasn't always the case. At some of the weddings they hosted, the family dynamics were an absolute disaster. Weddings could bring out the worst in people. Tam never understood it. A wedding was meant to be a celebration about a couple and the love they shared, not a day where family members jostled for some weird pecking order in which they tried to make the day about them.

'Let's go back to the house.' Tam gestured towards the little path that encircled the lake.

'You know,' Angie said, 'I always wanted a flower girl. I suppose it's stupid, but it's one of those things you picture when you're dreaming of your wedding as a kid.'

'You don't have any children in your family?'

'Unfortunately not. Besides, even if I did find someone there wouldn't be time to get a dress.'

'Your colour scheme is pale pink and apple green, isn't?'

'That's right, why?'

'Oh, no reason, I was thinking about flowers,' Tam replied. 'Shall we go?'

'Sure.' Angie followed her along the path that led back to the house.

* * *

An hour later Maddie walked into the office. 'How's it going, darling?' she asked Tam as she sat down at her desk.

'Good. Angie's left with the breakdown of the cost for her wedding, if she decides to go with us,' Tam replied.

'You think she won't?'

'Nah, it's just a formality. She wants to talk it over with her fiancé and her mum. But her eyes lit up when she saw the summer house.'

'Excellent.' Maddie fired up her computer. 'Was there anything else?'

'If we do the wedding it will include some catering, photos and a cake.'

Maddie looked up from her desk. 'We can do simple catering for a handful of guests and talk Lix into taking the photos but as for a cake, I have no idea.'

'Yeah, I was thinking about that,' Tam replied. 'James and Laura at Whistledown Farm make fabulous cakes for their little cafe. If we have to cater, I'd go there anyway to pick up some of Laura's relish.'

'That stuff is addictive,' Maddie said with a laugh. 'It would certainly be worth seeing if they would be willing to make a cake anyway—you know, for future reference.'

'As soon as I hear back from Angie, I'll get in touch with James,' Tam said.

'Didn't he go to school with you guys?'

'Yep, he and Dylan are pretty close.'

'I love the way this town works.' Maddie sat back in her chair.

'How do you mean?'

'Well, we're all interconnected and try to support each other's businesses.'

'Yeah, most people are willing to help out,' Tam said. 'Look what happened after the accident.'

'Exactly, I don't know what would have happened if the community hadn't stepped up. So many people came to help us when we needed it the most.'

'If it hadn't been for Uncle Mick helping out at the pub, we probably would have had to sell it.'

'You know Seb still talks things through with Mick sometimes.'

'He was a good friend of Dad's so he trusts his advice—we all do,' Tam said.

'And his wife, Caro, has always been so supportive. I don't know what I would have done without her when I arrived back,' Maddie said.

They were silent as they both relived thoughts of that difficult time. Maddie was the first to recover.

'How's the whole thing with Dylan going?'

Tam gave her a smile. 'All right.'

'Is that all?'

'We're going out for a movie and meal sometime this week,' Tam said with a shrug.

'That's lovely. What day?'

'I'm not sure.' Tam grabbed her planner and checked her schedule. 'Maybe Wednesday.'

'And have you and Seb managed to mend some bridges?'

Tam closed her planner and then glanced back to her aunt. 'Not yet. I get the feeling we're both trying to avoid each other.'

'You can't do that forever.'

'I know,' Tam responded. 'Apparently he and Dylan are seeing each other after work. So maybe I'll see how that goes before I try again.'

'That sounds like a plan,' Maddie said with an encouraging smile.

'At the moment it's the only one I've got.'

Twenty-Six
Late February, eight years ago

It had been one of the hardest decisions that Tam had to make but it had to be done. And yet it felt like she was betraying her parents and doing the right thing all at the same time. How was that possible? Tam and her brothers had been circling around this topic for weeks. Aunt Maddie had basically put her life on hold to come and stay with them. Words could never express how grateful Tam was for that.

The farmhouse was big enough for most of them to have their own rooms, Lix and Gray were the only ones who shared. Aunt Maddie had been staying in the tiny box room ever since she arrived. It had a flimsy old single bed, which wasn't good enough for a pregnant woman.

The Carrington siblings had come up with the solution that they should pack up their parents' room so that Maddie could have it for her and the baby. At first it didn't seem right and they shied away from it but then Maddie said that she was thinking about doing up the tiny cottage at the front of the property. That didn't sit well with them either—she was a part of the family, and the family lived in the house. So they talked it out again and again, and finally came to the decision that this was what their parents would have wanted. Which was why they were all gathered in the bedroom that night.

'So take what you want,' Seb said. 'Tam, you'll help Luce, won't you?'

Tam, who was sitting on the bed with her little sister by her side, nodded as she stroked Lucy's hair. 'Sure.'

'It feels weird.' Gray was standing by the door of the walk-in wardrobe. His eyes glistened with tears. He dashed them away and pretended that no one noticed.

'I know,' Lix replied. 'But if Maddie is going to stay with us, she should at least be comfortable, especially with the baby coming.'

Seb gave Lix a smile. 'You're right,' he said as he opened his father's nightstand. 'We should do this quickly because, honestly, I don't know how long I can be in here.'

They started to move about the room silently.

Lucy tugged on Tam's sleeve. 'Can we take that,' she said as she pointed to the small jewellery box on the old dresser. 'It's got Mummy's pretty things inside.'

'Of course we can, sweetie.' Tam picked up the box and handed it to her.

'Um, guys, maybe you should come here.' Gray stuck his head out from the inside of the walk-in.

'What's up?' Tam asked as she made her way towards him.

Gray waited until they crowded in. 'The Christmas presents are still here. They're all wrapped up and have our names on them—I guess Mum didn't get the chance to put them under the tree,' his voice was cracking as he spoke.

Seb put his arm around him. 'It's okay,' he said as he gave his younger brother a hard hug. 'It's going to be okay.'

Lix looked at the brightly wrapped packages. 'Should we even open them?'

Tam put her arm around him. 'Of course we should, they would have wanted us to have them.' She let go of her brother and reached out and took a present. 'This is yours—it's got your name on it,' she said as she handed it to Lix.

He took the box and then looked at Seb.

'Go on, Tam's right—you should open it,' Seb said with an encouraging smile.

Lix carefully undid the wrapping. Tears fell down his cheeks as he stared down at the box. 'It's the camera I wanted—I didn't think I'd get it because it's so expensive.'

Lucy wrapped her arms around her brother. 'Don't cry, Lixie,' she said.

'Here, Tam, this is yours.' Gray handed her a tiny present.

'Thanks.' She took a moment to centre herself before she opened it. As she unwrapped it she saw it was a small red jewellery box. Opening it up, she discovered a small gold compass on a long chain. Sitting in the lid was a card in her mother's handwriting. Hot tears pricked her eyes as she read the words.

To our darling daughter, so you never lose your way.

* * *

The warm morning sun shone through the first-storey window, casting a long beam of light down the hallway. The summer air was hot but Maddie shivered as a chill ran up her spine.

'Get it together, get it together,' Maddie whispered as she squeezed her eyes shut in an attempt to stop the tears from falling. She was standing outside her brother and sister-in-law's bedroom trying to find the courage to walk in.

Taking a deep breath, she braced herself and opened the door. She and the kids had had several discussions about this room.

At first after the accident, no one wanted to touch it, including Maddie. She couldn't be in that room without an overwhelming wave of grief washing over her. She felt the loss of her big brother deeply but she did her best every day to mask it so she could be there for the kids. The atmosphere of the room was bittersweet, the sadness was tempered with memories and the love Estella and Ben had not only for the children but each other.

In those first dark days she'd crept in here in the middle of the night and cried for the injustice that they'd been taken away; for the fact she didn't get to tell Ben one last time how much she loved him and confess how scared she was now that she was responsible for their children, and her own child on the way. She hadn't even had a chance to share her joy about her pregnancy, and she wondered if he would have approved that she was going ahead with this unplanned pregnancy by herself; but she was sure he would have been happy for her either way. He would have loved being an uncle.

Seb and Tam were trying their best but they were still only seventeen and grieving the loss of their parents.

Her father, the kids' grandad, hadn't helped at all. Although, she didn't know why she'd expected he would. She and Ben had both had a problematic relationship with him and it was their mother who had held everything and everyone together. Her father had always been self-absorbed, and the accident seemed to highlight these traits rather than show him as a loving grandfather. He made a couple of helpful gestures, like handing her a wad of bills for the children, as if that was all the emotional care they needed. A few days after the funeral he returned to his retirement village, and Maddie had been glad to see him go. That was awful, wasn't it? But she couldn't help how she felt.

Maddie stood in the open doorway, rubbing her hand over her ever-growing baby bump. If anyone had told her last year that this was what her life would be now, she would have laughed in their face. Life had thrown her some pretty wacky curve balls, first the surprise baby and now her nieces and nephews.

Maddie had been surprised when Seb had told her that they had all decided she should have their parents' room because she and the baby would need more space. It was true that the box room off the kitchen she'd been staying in was tiny, there was barely enough room for a single bed and a bedside cabinet, let alone anything else. Even so, she'd refused at first but Seb was insistent, saying that it was the right thing to do. She knew the kids wanted her under the same roof and she understood why: they were scared and lost and hoping to cling on to anyone who seemed present.

All the kids had come up to the room last night, they had taken mementos and anything else they wanted. Now it was her turn for one last moment to remember Ben before she packed up the room. They had decided to put most of the furniture into one of the sheds for storage, as Maddie had her own furniture and didn't want to feel like a visitor in her own room.

Which was why she was standing in the doorway with a heap of empty boxes at her feet. Maddie stopped for a moment while she steeled her resolve, then she picked up a couple of the boxes and stepped inside.

Twenty-Seven

It had been a good evening. The dinner was lovely—it was at one of their favourite local restaurants in Kangaroo Ridge, after which they drove to Bendigo for the movie, which had been one of those big blockbusters with loads of effects and mind-boggling explosions. Going to the movies was still a treat and Dylan had picked her up from the house, since he preferred to go in his car rather than her motorbike. Tonight she didn't care, at least her hair wouldn't get messed up by the helmet.

Going out openly with Dylan felt a bit weird, especially because most of their relationship had consisted of secret rendezvous in other towns and general sneaking about. They went out but it was always somewhere other than Kangaroo Ridge. But all that was done with—it was a new start and Tam had to learn to embrace it.

'So did you like the movie?' Dylan asked as he drove down the dark road towards home.

'I wasn't sure at first but it drew me in,' Tam said as she watched the headlights illuminate the gum trees as they passed.

'The opening was a bit slow but then it took off,' Dylan agreed as he reached over for her hand and then brought it to his lips. 'I liked tonight, there was something freeing about it.'

Tam gave him a smile. 'It was lovely.'

'We didn't have to worry if we ran into anyone, it was good. Hey, tomorrow, do you want to get coffee at the bakery,' he asked.

'Okay, but why?'

'Because then I'll really feel like we've turned a corner and everything is out in the open.'

Tam stifled a sigh. 'I don't know if it's necessary as you think the entire town already knows about us.'

'I'd still like to do it,' Dylan said as he glanced over at her. 'So are you coming to my place tonight?'

'Nope, I have an early start and my bike is at my place.'

'Damn, I really didn't think that one through, did I?' Dylan chuckled.

'If you're good I might be persuaded to come over tomorrow night,' she replied.

'How?'

'You buy the coffee tomorrow,' she said with a laugh.

'Done.' He grinned at her.

'I was going to ask you before but I wanted to enjoy our date: did you see Seb?' Tam turned her attention back to the road.

'No, he couldn't make it in the end but he gave me a quick call and we're going to catch up in a couple of days.' He gave her a nudge. 'Don't worry, if he wasn't open to talking about it, he wouldn't have rung at all.'

'I suppose that makes sense,' she said. 'We've been avoiding each other.'

'Probably a good thing, the two of you can be a little ... volatile.'

Tam laughed again. 'Well that's one way of putting it.'

'But seriously, give him some time to get used to the idea and then sit down and have a talk with him. Meanwhile, I'll try and smooth things over when I see him in a couple of days.'

'Do you really think you can?' Tam asked.

Dylan shrugged as he turned down her road. 'I don't know, but if it comes down to it he'll be angrier with me than you. You're his sister . . . his twin.'

'Perhaps, but you've been his best friend since you were kids.'

Dylan was silent for a moment as he pulled into her drive. 'Which means that he can't stay annoyed at us for long. Besides, you know that he's all bluster. Just chill, it'll be fine.'

'You sound so confident.' Tam wanted to believe him but she wasn't convinced.

'Babe, it'll be fine,' he said as he stopped in front of the house. 'It's about us, our decisions and our plans for the future. Once Seb finally gets that in his head, he'll stop being an idiot.'

'I hope so.' Tam unclipped her seatbelt.

'You're allowed to be happy and have a future, Tam,' he said. 'Let's make it together.' He leant over and kissed her.

Her mouth softened under his, he tasted of coffee and sugared popcorn. Her arms wound around him and she kissed him back. He was like her touchstone, whenever he kissed her, held her and cherished her all her doubts and worries subsided. His calming presence had pulled her back from the enveloping darkness more than once.

They savoured the kiss, postponing the moment until they finally pulled away.

He gave her a wink. 'Now, get out of here before I change my mind and drag you back to my place,' he said with a glint of laughter in his eyes.

'I'll see you tomorrow,' Tam replied as she started to get out of the car.

'Looking forward to it,' he said. 'I'll meet you at the bakery.'

'Are you tempting me?'

'Always,' he said with a laugh. 'See you tomorrow.'

* * *

Tam lingered on the top step and watched as Dylan drove away. He was right, they did deserve to have a future together. As his tail-lights disappeared down the drive, she wondered why she sometimes got those dark and twisty thoughts telling her otherwise.

Walking into the house, she found Lix in the kitchen, watching the newly filled coffee plunger.

'Smells good,' she said as she sat down at the kitchen bench.

'Yeah, it's almost done.' He looked up and smiled. 'Want one?'

'Please.'

Lix grabbed another mug from the cupboard. 'So how was the movie?'

'Good, you and Gray would love it.'

'Maybe I'll see if he wants to go,' Lix replied as he poured the coffee. 'After you left, one of your brides and her boyfriend dropped off some signed paperwork.'

'Ooh, which one?'

'Angie Stevens,' Lix said. 'I put it on your desk.'

'Thanks. You could have given it to Maddie.'

'She wasn't here either. She and Rori went to a barbecue, they're still there as far as I know.'

'Oh, I forgot about that,' Tam said with a shake of her head. 'I swear if I don't write things down, I forget them.'

'I took Angie and her fiancé down to the summer house. She said that she'd seen it but he hadn't,' Lix explained.

'And?'

'They both seemed happy and excited about holding their wedding here. Apparently, that's why they showed up after closing because she was determined to get everything set in concrete—those are her words by the way.'

'She's a bit jittery about the whole thing because she's already had to cancel her plans more than once,' Tam said before biting her lip. 'I kind of, sort of offered your photography services.'

'And you're only telling me now,' Lix said with a chuckle.

'Sorry. It's only a very small wedding, I promise.'

'It's okay. So when is it?'

'The actual date hasn't been agreed on yet. Although it's probably going to be on a Friday night.'

'I'm sure I can fit it in.'

'Thanks, Lixie, I owe you one,' Tam said as he handed her a coffee.

'I might even hold you to that,' he replied with a smile.

Twenty-Eight

Tam's phone had been ringing almost continually this morning with hopeful brides trying to secure a venue. It seemed like everyone was keen to get married this year. They tried hard to fit new bookings in but they were fully booked for the next six months, with the first reception happening this Saturday at 2 p.m.

Maddie sat back in her chair and blew out a long sigh. 'Are we all set for Saturday?' she asked.

'As far as I know,' Tam replied. 'Let's hope it goes off without a hitch.' She was scrolling through the Carrington Farm website. 'Did you see that Lix has rejigged the website and added some more seasonal photos?'

'We're so lucky to have him,' her aunt said. 'He's so talented.' Then she changed the subject. 'I just had an interesting conversation. A couple of local writers are toying with the idea of doing some in-person classes and maybe even a writing retreat.'

'That could be beneficial,' Tam said, 'especially in the quiet season.'

'That's what I was thinking,' Maddie replied. 'Only problem is that Kangaroo Ridge doesn't have a lot of accommodation. There's only the motel and a couple of bed and breakfasts.'

'Maybe we should refurbish the hotel—it used to have guests there back in the day, so why not again?' Tam mused.

'I'll have a chat with Seb later and maybe even crunch some numbers,' Maddie said.

'I meant to ask, how was the barbecue last night? Did Rori have fun?'

'She had a great time playing with Katie. Those two are inseparable,' Maddie said.

'Was it just you guys and Katie's family?'

'No, there were a few other kids and parents from Rori's class, as well as a handful of other friends.' Maddie started to toy with some of the documents on her desk.

'Oh yeah, like who?' Tam asked.

'You know, the usual crowd. Jenny and Bill were there, so was Josie and her hubby and Luke Miller,' Maddie said with a shrug.

'Oh, Luke Miller was there, huh?' Tam raised her eyebrows and slowly nodded. Luke Miller had moved into Kangaroo Ridge about three years ago when he took over the veterinary clinic. He was single, dashing and somewhere in his late thirties and his gaze had been lingering on Maddie for quite some time.

'Oh shut up,' Maddie said with a laugh. 'We've barely said two words to each other.'

'You don't need to, staring is enough communication,' Tam teased.

'It's not like that,' Maddie responded.

'Sure, of course not.' Tam pretended to rearrange her desk. 'Just keep telling yourself that,' she said before bursting into laughter.

'Stop it.' Maddie laughed. 'There's nothing going on.'

'Isn't it about time that you had a little fun?' Tam replied with a pointed look.

Maddie gave her a bright smile. 'I'm happy as I am. And I have enough on my plate with the business and Rori. I don't need another distraction, even if it is a cute one.'

'So you think he's cute?'

'Tam!' Maddie laughed again. 'Seriously though, I haven't got time for anything else in my life at the moment.'

Tam looked at her. Maddie had the dark hair and light eyes that ran through the entire family. She possessed a pretty face with delicate features but what made her beautiful was her selfless heart. In all these years after the accident she'd never put herself first.

'When was the last time you went out and enjoyed yourself?' Tam asked.

Maddie frowned as she tried to recall her social calendar. 'Well, Shelley and I took Rori and Katie to the waterpark just before Christmas. The kids had a great time.'

'When was the last time *you* had fun?'

'Oh—I don't know. Maybe when I took off for a day of shopping in Melbourne.'

'That was back in June. But I'm not talking about shopping, when was the last time you went on a date?'

Maddie shrugged. 'It's been a while,' she answered as she suddenly took a great interest in her computer.

'Oh my god, you haven't had a date since you came back to Kangaroo Ridge,' Tam said as the situation dawned on her. 'Am I right?'

Maddie hunched in her seat before she straightened up and looked across the room at Tam. 'I was way too busy to think about things like that,' she said simply. 'If you remember, we had a family to keep together.'

'You put your life on hold—' Tam started to say but Maddie didn't let her finish.

'We all did,' Maddie said quickly. 'And I don't regret it for a second.'

Tam nodded. 'Okay, neither do I, but I seem to remember you telling me that this is the time to live my life. Perhaps you should start taking your own advice.'

* * *

As Tam drove down the main street of the town, she saw that it was quite busy. Well, at least busy by Kangaroo Ridge standards. As it was still school holidays, there were a lot of tourists in town, which was always a good thing. The whole region was filled with interesting little towns with their own special flair and Kangaroo Ridge was no exception. It was sheep country around here but the town had at some point branched out and become a magnet for artists. Some came to find inspiration in the countryside and enjoy the slower pace, while some discovered a close-knit community that welcomed blow-ins with open arms. There were some interesting shops that showcased the talent of the town's inhabitants and Gekko Gallery was one of these little gems, and it had plenty of parking at the back.

Tam was on her way to grab lunch at the bakery. Dylan had cancelled their lunch booking due to an unexpected call out, but the idea of a ham and cheese croissant and caramel latte could not be ignored. Walking briskly down the footpath, she told herself to keep walking and not glance into the gallery's window. She had a weakness for interesting earrings and Yvette always stocked ridiculously desirable things.

She noticed a movement from the corner of her eye and she saw Yvette, the temptress, waving at her.

Tam waved back and, with a sigh of resignation, headed towards the store, knowing how this would end before she'd even opened the bright green door. The shop was fairly small, there was a little counter by the far wall with a vase of white flowers sitting on one corner. The rest of the store was filled up with several large display cases and a few shelves. A small table in the middle was covered in a stack of interesting books and a few knick-knacks.

'I'm glad I caught you, Tam,' Yvette said brightly. 'I just got another consignment in and I thought you'd like to have a look.'

'How are you going, Yvette?'

'Business has picked up quite a bit—so that's great.' She brushed her blonde bangs out of her eyes. 'How about you?'

'We're about to kick off with our first wedding this weekend. So, what fabulous things are you going to entice me with today?'

Yvette grinned. 'I've got these new earrings and I thought of you as soon as I saw them.' She reached under the desk and drew out a small box. 'I figured that I should show them to you before I put them out in the store.'

'You know my earring collection has expanded exponentially since you opened,' Tam mused.

'And I appreciate your support,' Yvette answered with a smile as she unboxed a pair of beautiful, dangly earrings. 'I thought they were your style as well as being in that shade of blue that you like.'

Tam stared at them. 'They're gorgeous.'

'I know,' Yvette agreed. 'Turquoise, blue topaz, a couple of pearls and some Mediterranean blue glass all suspended on some lovely sterling shepherd hooks. They've got your name all over them.'

Tam laughed. 'You know I'm buying them. It's already a done deal.'

'Really? You haven't even heard the price—although it's mate's rates as usual.'

'Thanks, Yvette. Wrap them up,' Tam instructed. 'It looks like lunch is going to be more expensive than I thought.'

Tam pulled out her wallet as Yvette started to wrap up the earrings.

'So, I heard a rumour that you're going out with Dylan Petersen—is that true?' Yvette asked.

Tam was a little taken aback by the question. 'Um, well, yes it is. How did you . . .'

Yvette handed her the prettily bagged earrings and took Tam's card. 'The girls next door in the bakery,' she explained. 'You know how this place is?'

'Right.' Tam held on to the bag, not really sure how to deal with this information. Why the hell was everyone so interested in her private life?

Twenty-Nine
Six years ago

Tam cracked open her eyes and then instantly regretted it as the sunshine blaring into the bedroom was unbearable. Throwing the covers over her head, she lay in the semi-dark cocoon and wondered what time it was.

She'd been out last night, clubbing, drinking and getting up close and personal to a guy who she only vaguely remembered. She tried to recall exactly what had happened but it was a messed-up blur. She squeezed her eyes shut but she couldn't even remember coming home last night.

Maybe I'm not even at home.

The thought scared her enough to make her stick her head out from under the doona and look around the room. A sigh of relief escaped her lips when she realised that she was in her own room. She sat up and then wished she hadn't as her stomach lurched and her head began to pound. She took her time trying to centre herself enough to stand up. Her throat was dry and she was in desperate need of a glass of water.

She managed to get out of bed and shrug on her dressing-gown before heading downstairs to the kitchen.

'Ooooh.' Lix looked up from the couch as she walked by. 'One of those nights, huh?'

'Yeah, I don't think I want to talk about it,' she murmured as she went by.

'Better brace yourself, Seb was looking for you earlier,' Lix called over his shoulder.

The idea of seeing Seb right now made her screw up her nose. 'Is he still around?'

Lix shrugged. 'He could have gone back to the pub. I haven't seen him in about half an hour but that doesn't mean he's not kicking around somewhere here.'

Tam grabbed a glass from the cabinet and the water jug from out of the fridge.

'How was he?' she asked as she poured herself a drink.

Lix glanced over to her. 'Annoyed.'

She took a large gulp. 'Great,' she whispered. That was all she needed—an annoyed and judgey brother. Opening one of the kitchen drawers she helped herself to a couple of paracetamols.

Lix looked towards the front door and then called out to her. 'I reckon you've got about ten seconds if you want to hide. He's coming now.'

Tam looked around and realised that unless she hid in the pantry there was really nowhere to go.

'It's okay,' she said before she sculled the rest of the glass and filled it up again.

Lix took a deep breath as if he was readying himself for an onslaught, which she thought was probably accurate.

'I'm here if you need me,' he said as the front door swung open.

'I love you, you know that?' Tam replied.

'I know,' Lix said as Seb walked into the room.

'Lix, have you seen Tam yet?'

Lix gestured with his head towards the kitchen. 'Don't yell, all right,' he said, like an order rather than a request.

Seb looked at him. 'I'll try.'

'Good, because it upsets Gray and Lucy. Not to mention you'll wake the baby up.'

Seb gave him a nod before he headed to the kitchen.

'Morning,' Tam said as he walked in.

The side of his mouth quirked up into almost a sneer. 'Hardly. It's almost lunchtime.' He glanced up at the wall clock.

'Is there something you wanted?' Tam chose to ignore the sarcasm in his voice.

'I thought we'd discussed this, Tam. You said that you weren't going to pull this sort of stuff anymore.'

'Funny, I don't remember us having a discussion . . . maybe a lecture,' Tam said.

'Oh that's rich. Come on, Tam, when are you going to take some responsibility for your actions and this family?'

His words were soft but they cut through her. 'Responsibility? Are you kidding me? I work all week, I help you out when you need it and Maddie and I run this whole household. I step up and do my share, probably more of it—I think I'm allowed to go out once in a while.'

'You know I can't help out at night because I'm working at the pub,' Seb replied.

'Yes, I know and, unlike you, I don't hold it against you,' Tam bit back. This was how all their arguments started, sniping at each other and pointing the finger.

'No one is saying that you can't go out,' Seb said, trying to maintain his calm. 'But when you come back you can barely stand. It's not good, Tam. It's not healthy.'

'You worry about yourself and let's leave it at that,' Tam said as she picked up her glass. 'I'm going to have a shower.'

'You're getting out of control and it needs to stop,' Seb said.

'Controlled by whom?' Tam countered. 'That's the thing, you always need to control everything and everyone in this family. But it's not going to work with me.'

'I'm just trying to hold us together,' Seb said with a shake of his head. 'Don't you get that?'

'We're people not possessions,' Tam replied.

'I don't . . . well, at least I don't mean to.' Seb reached out and put his hand on her shoulder. 'I'm worried about you. You're getting reckless and I don't want you to get hurt.'

'I'm just blowing off steam,' Tam said. 'It's just a bit of fun with the girls.'

'You mean Gemma?'

'Don't start, Seb,' Tam said quickly as she pointed her finger. 'You're always trashing Gemma.'

'That's because every time you get into a situation, she's always by your side,' Seb snapped back.

'Maybe she's just looking out for me.'

'Or maybe she's dragging you into trouble, just like she's always done.'

'You always like to have someone to blame,' she replied. 'Gemma has always been there for me—ever since we were little. Don't blame her for my actions.'

'Fine, then act like you're meant to,' Seb responded.

'*Meant to*, in whose opinion?' Tam asked. 'I do everything I can for our family—I don't understand how you can stand there and not see it. Do you think I want to work at the supermarket? It's hardly my dream job. I took it because it's close to home, so I can look after our brothers and sister. I gave up what I wanted to do for them and I don't resent it because I love them. But do not stand there and tell me that I don't pull my weight and put everyone's needs before my own. I do and I have for the past two years. So what if I take one night a week to play?'

'Playing? Is that what you call it? You staggered home drunk last night.'

'So what if I did? Do I call you out if you've had one too many drinks?'

'No, because I don't,' Seb answered with a raised voice.

Lix appeared in the kitchen with a frown on his face. 'I said not to raise your voice, Seb—you'll wake the baby.'

Seb turned around and glared at his brother. 'I'm having a private conversation here,' he said.

Lix crossed his arms. 'It's not very private if it can be heard through the house, is it? If you want to shout then take it outside, otherwise shut up because you'll make Lucy cry and wake Rori. And if you do that, then you'll have to deal with Maddie.'

Seb opened his mouth to say something and then thought better of it. He gathered himself before he continued.

'You're right, I'm sorry. I shouldn't have snapped at you,' he replied before turning back to Tam. 'Do you want to finish this outside?'

Tam stared at him like he'd grown another head.

'Are you serious? Why would I put myself through that?' Tam replied with a shake of her head.

'We haven't finished this conversation,' Seb urged.

'Oh, we've finished it,' she said. 'I'm not going into the garden so you can keep yelling at me. It might make you feel better, but I don't want my day ruined any more than it already has been.'

'Tam, please, we need to talk about your behaviour. Don't you see, you're on a slippery slope?' Seb asked.

Tam grabbed her glass of water and walked past him. 'I'm done,' she said.

And as she walked back upstairs she heard Lix's voice.

'Real smooth, Seb—real smooth.'

Thirty

'Mmmm, it's good,' Dylan said as he bit into a slice of pizza. 'What do you think?'

Tam nodded. 'Agreed. Pass the salad, would you?'

'Seriously?' Dylan replied as he handed her the container. 'Why do you have to go and ruin a perfectly good pizza with salad?' he joked.

Tam ignored him while she helped herself to half the salad and then dumped the other half onto his plate.

'Hey,' he said with a laugh.

'No seconds until you eat that,' she said with a smile.

'Wow, bossy or what?' Dylan replied before picking up his fork and attacking the green salad.

'Just looking out for you,' she said.

Dylan's eyes softened as he gave her a look that made her feel fuzzy inside.

And in a blink the look was gone and Dylan was back to his normal self. It was insane. One minute they could be talking about the weather or pizzas and the next he had her hot, bothered and more than thirsty with only a look.

Tam tried to refocus and glanced down at her plate. 'So, did you have a busy day?'

'It wasn't too bad. I started measuring up and working out what materials I need for Ms Winter's place,' he said before picking up his slice of pizza again.

'Is it going to be difficult?'

'I'd like to say no but I don't want to jinx myself. You never really know what you're going to find when you start tinkering with old buildings. Like last year when I had to restump old Mr Tully's floor and we discovered that half the stumps were missing.'

'An unexpected surprise,' Tam said with a smile.

'Yeah, I hate those,' Dylan replied. 'Anyway, hopefully it will be smooth sailing. What about you?'

'I bought these from Yvette today,' she said, flicking one of her earrings.

'Pretty,' Dylan said before pausing.

Tam looked at him expectantly. 'Anything wrong?'

He shook his head and smiled back at her. 'I've been thinking.'

'Oh dear, this sounds ominous,' Tam said in an attempt to lighten the mood.

'Nah, it's nothing bad—or at least I don't think so,' Dylan said. 'It's something that's been on my mind. I've been thinking about it for ages.'

'Thinking about what?' Tam asked.

'That maybe now that Seb and pretty much everyone else knows about us . . . maybe we could do something more permanent.'

Tam stilled. She should have known that this was coming. She wanted things to stay as they were because every time he mentioned permanence she felt terrified. Once again it was as if she was submerged and couldn't break the surface so she could breathe. It made no sense, she loved Dylan yet the idea of living together and starting a new life scared her.

'I know that you were hesitant before, but now there's nothing holding us back.' Dylan reached over and took her hand. 'I love you, Tam—let's take the next step.'

Her heart seemed to increase its beats and she took a breath in order to calm down.

'What did you have in mind?' she asked as she put down her cutlery and looked back at him.

'Maybe you could move in here? Or we could get another place, if you don't like this one. I don't care where we are, as long as we're together.'

'I love you,' Tam said but before she could continue she saw the look of disappointment in his eyes. She didn't get to finish because he broke in.

'But you don't want to,' he replied flatly.

'It's not that, truly it isn't.' But Tam didn't exactly know if that was the truth or not. 'It's just that I don't think I'm ready—at least not yet.'

'Or maybe ever?' Dylan added. 'Every time I bring this up, you don't want to, but next thing you say that you love me. It does my head in. I don't mind waiting but are you going to keep putting it off for another five years . . . or maybe ten or twenty?'

'I, I . . .' Tam stammered. She wanted to be with him, to be happy and give him everything he wanted but something stopped her and she couldn't explain it. She didn't know why she felt this way.

'I what, Tam?' Dylan asked.

'I don't know,' she said as she looked back down at her plate. 'I think I'd better go.'

'You can't keep running away; we've got to deal with this one way or another. I feel like I'm in limbo and I can't break free,' Dylan said.

'Is that what you want, to break free?' Tam asked quietly.

'No, I want us to be together,' Dylan said. 'I'd live with you, marry you, have babies with you with no hesitation. When I say that I love you—I mean it. I'm not the one putting on the brakes.'

'I know, I know . . . it's just that I'm not sure if it's the right time,' Tam said quickly. 'I mean work is about to go into overdrive and—'

'Geez, Tam, I'm not asking you to marry me tomorrow. I'm only asking about taking the next step together.'

'We are,' Tam replied.

'Don't wind me up. You know exactly what I'm talking about.' He sat against the back of his chair and crossed his arms.

'I think we both have a lot of work at the moment and perhaps this isn't the right time. I'm not saying no, I'm just saying not yet,' Tam said.

'I'm beginning to think that's just another excuse,' Dylan said as his gaze bore into her. 'I know what I want, but it seems you still have to figure out what you want. I can wait, Tam—but not forever.'

'I understand, Dylan, I really do,' she said but she looked away.

'I hope so, because what we have is great but I've already waited and I need something solid that we can build on.' Dylan reached across the table and gently tilted her head back to him with the tip of his finger. 'I really do love you but the more I think about it, the more I realise that you're not as committed to this relationship as I am. I'm not blaming you, but I think we've got to work out why. Then we'll know if we have a real future together or not.'

Tam covered his hand with hers. 'I do love you.'

'I know you do, babe,' Dylan said with a sad smile. 'But I wonder if it's enough.'

* * *

Even though she was dreaming, Tam couldn't break free. The dream was the same one that had haunted her for years. Sometimes its frequency diminished, but it never fully went away.

It was hot and Tam was walking down a dirt road. She could almost feel the sun on her back, the scent of gum trees and the warmth of Dylan's hand holding hers. All of a sudden she was propelled down the road, as if she was in a movie on fast forward. She didn't want to go, she didn't want to see, because she knew what was beyond the bend. Disjointed images flashed before her—lying to her mum about the party, Taylor Henderson, the pile of unopened presents in her parents' bedroom. This was how the nightmare always went and Tam couldn't do anything about it but endure.

But this time there was a shift. The old images were punctuated with more recent memories. Maddie's face telling her, *You deserve to be happy*. All the times she'd faced off against Seb. Dylan telling her he wanted them to be together. She wanted that too but there was something in the darkness that pulled her back down, away from the warmth of his love.

Tam tossed in the bed, she swam against the force, trying to make her way to Dylan but she couldn't. All at once she was in a long dim tunnel and the only light was at the end. She knew what was there, she could feel it in her bones. It was the one thing that she never wanted to see again. A memory that was burnt into her brain so that she could never forget it. Again, the dream hit fast forward and she rushed through the tunnel until she was standing in front of her parents' mangled car. Words echoed in her head—*You did this. This is your fault.*

Tam gasped as she opened her eyes. For a second she was confused because she wasn't in her own room, it was still dark but there was a shaft of moonlight falling through the window.

She turned her head and saw Dylan sleeping beside her. Her first impulse was to roll over and hug him until the terror of her dream faded but instead she slowly sat up. The nightmare still had a tenuous hold on her. Her heart pounded as she ran her hand through her hair and tried to catch her breath.

The old guilt settled over her like a cloak of stone, she couldn't move on to the future as she was still weighed down by the past—and it might never let her go.

Tam carefully pushed the covers back and sat on the side of the bed. Maybe she was fooling herself to think that she could ever be free of this burden. Maybe she didn't deserve to be.

She got off the bed, grabbed her clothes and with one final glance at Dylan, she walked out the door.

Thirty-One

Dylan opened his eyes as Tam left the room. He rolled onto his back and looked up at the ceiling. He'd been hoping this wouldn't happen but somehow he knew it would. He didn't doubt that Tam loved him but he knew there was something that kept her from moving forward towards the future.

He sighed when he heard her motorbike firing up. She was running away, just like she always did when they'd had a conversation like that. The night air blew in from the half-open window and yet it didn't bring any clarity with it. They were trapped by the events of her parents' death and he didn't know how Tam could ever reconcile with it.

Tam had received professional help in the past, as had most of the family. As far as he knew she kept going to her therapist long after the others had stopped. For the most part, Dylan had thought it had helped her. Although every now and again there was a wild and almost destructive streak that would flare up in her. As the years passed the parties and the drinking diminished and as the business with Maddie had grown, she'd toned things down even further.

Dylan had thought that the past had been put to rest. Tam's business had been going well and so were they, at least he thought so. He knew for sure now that her reticence in going public about their relationship wasn't just because she was worried about what Seb would say. But he still didn't know exactly what the problem was.

It was true that she did love him. Dylan felt it, but was it strong enough for them to get through this together? If it was only a question of waiting for her to be ready, then he'd wait. But what would happen if she was never ready? And how could he keep trying to accommodate everything she wanted as well as his own needs when they weren't even on the same page?

Seb used to tease him that he didn't dream big and just wanted a simple life. That was true. Since he was a kid, he had promised himself he would have a stable and loving home life one day. He wanted everything that had been denied to him and he wanted to be the best father he could be so his future children would never know the kind of pain and fear that he had experienced.

He always assumed that he'd grow up, fall in love and that the person he fell in love with would have the same ideals of what a future would look like. But he was beginning to think that Tam didn't want those things and it killed him.

Dylan hoped that they could find some common ground but maybe he'd have to make a different decision soon. Was he willing to love Tam on her terms and give up on his vow?

Dylan looked around the dark empty room. He ran both hands through his hair and blew out a breath.

Why did love have to be so hard?

* * *

Tam let herself in the back door, only to find Lix standing there. He looked half asleep and a chunk of his hair was sticking up.

When she walked into the kitchen, he took a step back and let out a gasp.

Tam wrinkled her nose. 'Sorry,' she said, 'I didn't mean to surprise you.'

Lix sucked in a breath. 'Geez, you scared the hell out of me.' He placed his hand over his heart. 'I didn't think you were coming back tonight.'

'Neither did I.'

'Did you two have a fight or something?' Lix asked as he filled up the kettle.

'More of the *or something*,' Tam replied. 'I don't know what's wrong with me. Dylan wants me to move in with him and start looking to the future.'

'You mean the whole thing—house, kids et cetera?'

Tam nodded as she walked over to one of the stools at the kitchen island and sat down. 'Yes, that's what he wants. And I want that too but . . .'

'But?'

'Every time we talk about it, I get an awful panicky feeling and I bolt out of there. I'm surprised that he's still talking to me. Although, after tonight, I don't like my chances,' Tam confessed.

'You love him though, right?'

'Like crazy. And I know how good we are together. But I can't give him what he wants, even though I want to.' Tam sank down and leant her arms on the bench.

Lix didn't say anything, instead he busied himself by making hot chocolates. After a couple of minutes, he walked over to Tam and handed her a mug.

'Tam, maybe you should go and get some professional help. I mean, it helped us all after Mum and Dad's accident.' He sat down next to her. 'Perhaps you need someone to talk to, so you can find out what's going on.'

'Maybe,' she said, not wanting to admit that he might have a point. To cover, she decided to change the topic. 'So, are you going to bed late or did you just wake up?'

'I was up late working but I fell asleep on the couch.' He gestured in its vague direction.

'I thought you'd finished updating the website.'

Lix gave her a little nod. 'This was some stuff I was doing for me. I was taking some night pictures outside.'

Tam glanced down and saw Lix's old camera on the bench. It was his prize possession and he only ever brought it out when he was feeling down or nostalgic, or both. He had other cameras, better ones in fact, but this was the last gift he'd received from their parents and he treasured it. She looked thoughtful as she turned back to him.

'Has something happened?' she asked.

He shook his head and placed his hand over hers. 'Nah, it's all good. I wanted to get some shots of the moon and the trees silhouetted against the sky. I was thinking about Mum and how she always liked warm, moonlit nights and the next thing I knew I was outside taking some shots.' He gave a slight smile. 'I'm hoping that they'll turn out all right.'

Tam leant over and gave him a nudge with her shoulder. 'Since when are your pictures just all right? They'll be fabulous. Actually, you should have an exhibition or something, you're that good.'

He let out a laugh. 'You're just biased.'

'That doesn't mean you're not talented. Your photographs are brilliant. You always manage to tell a story and touch people's emotions. That's priceless.'

Lix's cheeks flushed a little. 'Stop, you're making me blush.'

'Well it's true,' Tam replied. 'Don't sell yourself short—promise?'

'Okay, I promise.' He looked over to the wall clock. 'It's almost half past three. I think I'll turn in . . . unless you need to talk?'

'Nah, I'm okay—nothing's going to get resolved tonight anyway.' She watched him stand up and grab what was left of his hot chocolate.

He bent down and dropped a kiss on her head. 'I'll see you in the morning.'

'It is morning,' Tam teased.

'You know what I mean,' Lix said with a yawn.

'Go on, get out of here.'

'Night, sis.' He headed upstairs.

Tam sat in the now silent kitchen and nursed her drink between her hands. She reluctantly stood up and made her way to her bedroom. She was tired and thoughts about her and Dylan kept spinning in her head. Sleep sounded like a good idea but she was terrified that the nightmare would return and drag her back down within its depths.

Thirty-Two

Work was ramping up as Tam prepared for the first Carrington Farm wedding of the year. In truth, this was a pretty easy one as the couple had outsourced the catering, the cake and the photographer and were having the ceremony at a local church. So really all Tam had to do was make sure that the barn was ready for the reception and decorated as they wanted. It was a nice way to ease back into the wedding schedule. Of course, she would be on hand in case any last-minute changes or emergencies cropped up.

It had been two days since she'd done the midnight flit from Dylan's place. She'd talked to him a couple of times since then and had seen him yesterday. He acted like nothing had happened but Tam could see a trace of hurt in his eyes. She wished it wasn't there and she wished that she wasn't to blame for it.

She was up a ladder repositioning a string of tiny lights that was intertwined with a green vine wound around some of the heavy wooden ceiling beams when Maddie walked into the barn carrying a box of decorations.

'How's it going?' her aunt asked as she dumped the box on the nearest table.

Tam glanced down. 'Not bad—what does this look like from down there?'

Maddie put her hands on her hips and looked up. 'Pull it a little to the left . . . Yeah, that's good.'

'Thanks,' Tam said. 'I've only got a couple more of these to do.'

'Great, I'm finishing off the table decor,' Maddie said. 'After that, we'll be ready for this afternoon.'

'I'm excited.' Tam started down the ladder. 'The place feels a bit quiet when we haven't got any functions on. It's silly really, before Christmas I couldn't wait for the last wedding but about a week after it was done, I was getting impatient for it to all start up again.'

'I understand completely,' Maddie said.

'I'm glad it's not just me then.' Tam moved the ladder and grabbed the next string of fairy lights.

Maddie came over to hold the ladder as Tam began to climb.

'So have you sorted things out with Seb yet?'

Tam focused on stringing up the fairy lights. 'We've had a talk, but haven't really resolved anything. I figure we're both busy and, to tell you the truth, I'm not up for another lecture.'

'Okay,' Maddie replied.

Tam drew in a breath and stopped what she was doing. 'I can hear the disappointment in your voice.'

Maddie looked up at her and smiled. 'Too obvious then?'

Tam chuckled as she picked up the fairy lights and continued weaving them through the vine. 'Really, Mads, you need to work on your acting and delivery.'

'Point taken,' Maddie said. 'But you will talk to him again sometime?'

'As he is my brother, I suppose I will.'

Maddie frowned. 'Come on, darling, I'm serious.'

'Don't worry about it, I'll deal with it soon.'

'Well, that's all I can ask,' Maddie responded. 'I don't want to get pushy.'

Tam looked down at her aunt and raised an eyebrow. 'I think the time for that has passed,' she quipped.

'Cheeky,' Maddie said with a laugh. 'And how are things going with Dylan?'

'Good,' Tam said a little too quickly.

'That's great.'

'You're full of questions today.' Tam tried deflecting and added a laugh to drive it home.

'Only because I love you and want you to be happy,' Maddie replied before she broke into a grin. 'And because I have no personal life, so I get to live through you.'

'Well, whose fault is that?' Tam replied. 'I told you it's high time that you started going out. Come on, you said that we all deserve to move on and have a life—that includes you too.'

'Oh I hate it when you do that,' Maddie said.

'What?'

'Throw my own words back at me.' She chuckled. 'I'll think about it—okay?'

'I guess it will have to do for now,' Tam replied as she came back down the ladder. 'Come on, let's get this finished.'

* * *

The afternoon sun added a golden glow to the dance floor as the bride and groom danced in each other's arms. Tam stood apart from the guests and watched the couple as they waltzed by on the outside dance floor. From what she could gather, the whole reception had gone off without a hitch. A mild breeze, carrying the scent of eucalyptus and faraway rain, gently tugged at the bride's train and made her look even more ethereal, if that was possible.

Tam was holding down the fort, so Maddie could pick up Rori from her friend's house. Lix had been around but as everything was running smoothly, he'd taken off as well—although he was only a phone call away if needed.

Tam looked back to the couple, Kelly and Greg. Their guests were gathered around the edge of the dance floor but neither bride nor groom gave them a second glance, as if the entire world had fallen away and they were the only two beings left. They were in their own little sphere, gazing into each other's eyes. She'd seen that look hundreds of times before and was always moved by it but today it struck a deeper chord inside her and she found it hard to turn away.

This is what Dylan wanted. And, as she watched the couple dancing, Tam realised that there was a chance that she could never give this moment to him. She'd told him that she just needed time but that wasn't true. Time wouldn't change her fears and uncertainties. He deserved a loving wife, children and a happy home but Tam couldn't give him those things—not yet, maybe never. Whenever there was a spark of happiness in her life she questioned it. It was as if a darkness closed over her and wouldn't let her break free.

Tam closed her eyes. She couldn't go on like this—hoping that everything would be fine—because she knew deep down it wouldn't. It wasn't fair to keep leading Dylan on, allowing him to think that they could have a fairy tale when there was a good chance they wouldn't. And Lix was right, she needed to talk to someone and put her life back together.

She was broken, and had been since she was seventeen. She pretended otherwise, for the sake of her family and those who loved her, but it wasn't the truth. She'd been temporarily patched together with sticky tape and bandages, but if you looked closely you could see them unravelling. She loved her family and didn't want them to worry but there was a void within her that never healed.

The wedding progressed around her and love seemed to almost permeate the air but Tam was detached from the happy scene. The full weight of her realisation settled heavily upon her and she knew instinctively what she had to do.

Thirty-Three

Seb sighed as he got out of the car. He'd put this off for too long and was now feeling nervous about catching up with Dylan—*stupid, huh?* He yanked open the back door of the car and retrieved the burgers he'd brought and a few beers. Yeah, it was a peace offering, no doubt about it.

He walked up to Dylan's cottage. For a second he wondered if he should knock on the front door but then thought better of it and went around the back like usual. He was being ridiculous, Dylan was like his brother.

'Hey,' Dylan said as Seb walked into the kitchen. 'I thought I heard your car.'

'Hi.' Seb handed him the food. 'I thought you'd want a snack.'

Dylan looked down at the burger, one side of his mouth quirked up into a smile. 'Well, I'm always open to bribery,' he said.

'It's an apology,' Seb replied. 'I've been a jerk.'

Dylan grinned back at his friend. 'So what's new?'

'Yeah, yeah, you don't have to rub it in.' Seb smiled. 'Forgiven?'

'For my part, yes,' Dylan said as he put the food on the table. 'You want to sit down?'

Seb gave a nod and pulled out a chair. 'What do you mean *for my part?*'

'Listen we've been friends ever since we were kids. Whatever happens between us, we always sort it out. Generally because we sit down and talk it out, even if we have to take a week or so to cool down first,' Dylan replied.

'So . . .?'

'So, why don't you do the same with Tam? It seems to me that both of you talk and butt heads but don't listen to what the other one has to say.' Dylan tried to make his words as gentle as possible.

'I do talk to her,' Seb said in a defensive tone.

'See?' Dylan replied with a shrug.

Seb sighed and relaxed in the chair. 'I do try and talk with her. It's just that one minute we're okay and the next minute we're yelling at each other.'

'Well, I'm now officially smack bang in the middle of you both so how about I try and mediate?' Dylan suggested. 'I get that there's always two sides to a story but sometimes, Seb, you've got to sit down and listen to what's being said.'

'I know I can be difficult,' Seb said. 'I don't mean to be.'

'When we were kids you and Tam were really close,' Dylan said.

'Things changed.'

'Why?'

Seb sat back in his chair and gave him a puzzled look. 'You know why. After the accident, I had to step up and look after everyone.'

Dylan nodded but was silent for a moment. 'I'm not taking that away from you, you did an amazing job,' he said. 'But so did Tam and Maddie.'

'I've always acknowledged that. It's just that in the past, Tam's behaviour was . . . well, you remember.'

Dylan nodded. 'Tam definitely had some issues she had to work through and I suppose there were times when she felt so overwhelmed she reacted and did some dumb stuff. But we've all done that.'

'Not to that extent,' Seb said. 'All I know is that back then things were hard, for all of us, and as soon as she turned eighteen she started disappearing for days. I can't count the times she came back drunk or stayed out all night.'

'But she's a very different person now. She's not a belligerent eighteen-year-old girl anymore.'

'I guess I still have that version of her in my head,' Seb said, 'and so maybe I don't trust her as much as I should. I know that she still hangs out with Gemma and her friends every now and again.'

'It's hardly the same as it was years ago. The outings now generally consist of a dinner and a couple of bottles of wine.' Dylan reached for the beer and handed one to Seb. 'Maybe you should ask why she behaved like that in the first place?'

'What do you mean?'

'Why was she on such a destructive path?' Dylan asked.

Seb looked uncomfortable and concentrated on opening the beer can and having a swig. 'I haven't really thought about it.'

'Yeah you have,' Dylan said. 'It's just that you don't want to deal with it.'

'Oh come on, that's a bit unfair.'

'I reckon that's the problem: neither of you want to get to the bottom of it.'

'Bottom of what?'

'Why Tam has a destructive streak,' Dylan answered. 'You both blame her for your parents' deaths.'

'Oh that's bullshit,' Seb said quickly. 'I don't blame her at all.'

'That's what you keep telling yourself, but your relationship nosedived after the accident and it's never recovered.'

'Are you saying that I don't love my sister?' Seb looked amazed at the very thought.

'I'm not saying that at all,' Dylan explained. 'But on some level you blame her and you haven't been able to move past it. You're stuck just as much as she is.'

'All I've ever wanted is for our family to be safe and cared for—*all of my family*, which includes Tamara,' Seb said with a slightly raised voice.

Dylan waved his hands in a downward motion as if he was trying to de-escalate the situation. 'All I'm saying is there's something more, buried deep inside you, that still blames her. The more I think about it, the more I believe that Tam doesn't feel like she deserves to be happy. Every time she starts to live her life, she does something to sabotage it.'

Seb got up from the table and for a moment Dylan was worried that he'd walk out the door. Maybe he'd gone too far this time? He held his breath until Seb walked over to the window and looked out into the garden.

'Maybe you should have been a shrink rather than a builder,' Seb said quietly as he leant his forehead against the cool glass of the window pane.

Dylan smiled. 'I'm a better builder,' he replied. 'I'm only saying these things because I love both of you. I could be way off base, but I don't think I am.'

'No, I think there is something there, even if I don't want to admit it.' Seb turned back to his friend. 'Lix accused me of a similar thing recently. I brushed it off because I couldn't get my head around it.'

'It's hard to admit that you could have made a mistake or acted in a certain way,' Dylan said.

'I expect others to hold themselves accountable for their mistakes and shortcomings, it's only right that I do the same,' Seb said. 'The accident wasn't Tam's fault, I know that.'

'But?'

'There's a tiny voice in my head that always says it wouldn't have happened if she hadn't gone to that stupid party,' Seb confessed.

'That doesn't mean it may never have happened.' Dylan went over and placed his hand on Seb's shoulder. 'Thinking about what could have or should have happened won't bring you any peace. We have to use what we're dealt—it's all we can do.'

'I suppose you're right,' Seb said with a slight smile.

'A whole lot of things could have been different,' Dylan replied. 'Sure, maybe Tam shouldn't have gone to the Henderson party with us. But if Taylor hadn't been a shit, then Tam and Gemma would have waited for her brother to come and pick them up. If that had happened, your parents wouldn't have been on the road at all.'

'What did you say?'

Dylan stilled. He saw the confusion and surprise on Seb's face.

'Surely you knew about that?' he replied.

'Say it again,' Seb said quietly. 'I know that Taylor Henderson is a nasty piece of work but what does that have to do with Tam?'

'She didn't tell you?' Dylan asked with disbelief.

'Tell me what?'

'That Taylor tried to . . . well, he tried to kiss her and force himself on her.' Dylan picked his words as best he could but felt like he still failed miserably.

Seb's face grew dark. 'She never said a word,' he said slowly. 'You knew?'

'I was there, that's why we left the party straight away. Will came with us too. We tried to get someone else to pick us up but there was no one, so even though she was upset and afraid—Tam called your mum.'

'Why didn't you tell me?' Seb asked, staring at his friend.

'Because I thought that you knew,' Dylan replied. 'I'm sorry, bro, if I'd suspected you didn't know I would've said something.'

Seb stood there silently for a moment. And then another one, as if he was absorbing everything Dylan had just said.

'I can't believe she didn't say anything,' Seb murmured. 'Why didn't she tell me?'

Thirty-Four
Six years ago

Tam hurried into the dining room and stopped short. Maddie, Seb and Felix were already sitting at the table.

'Sorry I'm late, one of the girls didn't turn up for her shift and I had to cover for half an hour,' Tam explained as she sat down next to Felix. 'What's wrong?'

Maddie gave her a smile. 'Everything is fine, it's just that we need to have a family meeting and sort a few things out.'

Seb blew out a breath. 'That doesn't sound ominous at all.'

Tam and Lix exchanged glances.

'I've also invited Uncle Mick to stop by in about half an hour,' Maddie said.

'Now I'm worried,' Lix murmured. Uncle Mick had been running the hotel, until Seb was old enough to take over the reins. 'Wait, if it's a family meeting where are the others?'

'I talked to Gray and he agreed to watch Rori and Luce for a while so long as we fill him in later,' Maddie said. 'Okay, I don't want to be dramatic but we're kind of at a crossroad.'

'What do you mean?' Tam asked.

'We need to think about the future. The way things are at the moment, well, there won't be enough to sustain us all. We had the payout from the accident which helped pay things off, and I put what was leftover in an education fund for you all because I know that's what your parents would have wanted. Seb is bringing in some money from the pub but it's not a huge amount. Neither are the wages that Tam and I contribute—we're okay but we don't have a lot to fall back on if we have to.'

'So what are you suggesting?' Tam asked.

Maddie shrugged. 'We have a lot of land and none of us really know what to do with it.'

'You want to sell the farm?' Lix's eyes widened at the thought. 'Where would we live?'

Maddie shook her head. 'No, I didn't mean all of it. Maybe just a bit so we have a buffer.'

'Well for a start,' Tam said as she glanced at Maddie, 'you can take my share of the education fund because I'm not going to uni.'

'But I thought you were only going to take a year off.' Maddie's brows furrowed. 'We all know that you don't want to keep working in the supermarket.'

'I'd rather work at the pub with Seb, but we need to bring in extra money, so for now it's the supermarket. It's not what I want to do, but going to uni isn't my thing either.'

'You can add my uni money to that,' Seb said. 'I have a pub to run.'

'I'm not sure if I—' Lix started to say but stopped when Maddie held up her hand.

'Sweetheart, you're sixteen and still in school. You're not sure what you want to do yet. There's time to decide.' She looked at the others. 'Look, I'm not saying that it's an emergency and that we have to act right this minute. I've still got some savings left and we're all going to be fine. I just thought we could have a conversation about our future.'

Seb was quiet as he tried to read through Maddie's words. 'We need to work out what we have, what to keep and what we want.'

Lix nodded. 'Okay, I don't want to sell the house. I love it, it's been in the family for generations and we all have to live somewhere. But it hasn't been a working farm in decades and I don't want to be a farmer.'

'Neither do I,' Tam replied. 'We'd have to ask Gray and Lucy, but I doubt they'd want to either.'

'We need to keep the pub. The family has owned it forever too,' Seb said. 'I can run the pub, I'm learning everything I have to from Uncle Mick—you won't have to worry about that, we won't lose it, I promise.'

Maddie reached over and squeezed his hand. 'We're all very proud of you and how you've really thrown yourself into learning about the hotel,' she said before glancing at Tam and Lix. 'For the past couple of years we've been trying to survive day to day. But it's time to think about what we really want to do.'

'You don't like your job either then?' Lix asked Maddie.

She gave him a smile. 'I feel the same way Tam does. I'm grateful for the job and the people are lovely, I just can't see myself being an accountant's assistant forever.'

'So what do you want to do?' Seb asked her.

'I'm not sure, but wouldn't it be great if we could find something that we could do together?'

'Like a family business!' Tam said.

'We kind of already have one,' Seb added.

'That's true, darling,' Maddie replied. 'But I don't think it's enough for all of us.'

'We should list what we have and then work out what we could do with it,' Tam said.

'So, we have about one hundred and fifty acres, right?' Lix said.

'Yep, about that—give or take,' Seb said.

'We have the pub, the house, the barn and the greenhouse, three dams, one of which is the size of a small lake,' Lix reeled off.

'And there's the old summer house and the rose garden,' Tam said before she took a sip of her apple juice. 'Oh, and Maddie's little cottage.'

Maddie nodded. 'Yep, that's about it—so any ideas?'

They all sat silently for a while, thinking, until Tam looked up. 'Maybe I have an idea,' she said with a smile. 'Wanna come for a walk?'

Seb frowned but nodded. 'Sure, what are you thinking?'

'It's just a vague idea and I think we need to check out the barn first,' Tam said as she stood up.

Tam led them outside, down the gentle hill towards the big dam.

'Why are we out here again?' Seb called out.

Tam glanced over her shoulder and smiled. 'You'll see.' She increased her pace down the hill until she stood outside the barn. It was old—no one was sure when it had been built but it predated the farmhouse that had been erected over one hundred years ago. Tam opened the first of the double doors, she pushed it and the bottom of it scraped against the gravel.

'You want us to use the barn,' Maddie said with a surprised look. 'I'm not sure I understand.'

Lix walked over and opened the second door before peering inside. It was pretty dark and cluttered with old tools, a broken-down tractor and a heap of cobwebs.

'It's in rough condition,' Seb said as he ventured in. 'Although there doesn't seem to be any water damage and it bucketed down last night. So, what's your plan?'

Tam gestured towards the dam, which was dotted with reeds, bushes and one ancient willow that hung over the water. 'We've got this beautiful site, all it needs is a spruce-up, some replanting and maybe even a jetty or something like that.'

'Go on,' Maddie said.

'We also have the barn. Like Seb said, it's a bit rough but watertight. So why not fix it up and rent it out for events or parties?'

'Or weddings,' Lix said with a spark of excitement in his eyes.

'Exactly,' Tam said with a grin. 'The barn is huge, it would hold a heap of people. But we've also got the old orangery, it's small but we could renovate it as well.'

'I don't know what hoops we'd have to jump through but I'll find out,' Maddie said.

'Not bad, Tam,' Seb said. 'It's a good idea.'

'I know there's so much we have to think about but it's something to go on.'

'It would be expensive,' Seb agreed. 'But it might pay for itself in the end.'

'There'd be a lot of hard work and it will be expensive but we could sell off some of the land to finance it,' Tam replied.

'It's certainly a great idea but we need to sit down and think it through,' Maddie said evenly. 'First of all, I'm going to see what competition there is around the area and if there's a need for such an event site.'

'There will be, I'm sure of it,' Tam replied as she looked back to the old barn. 'Just think how beautiful it will be when it's all fixed and decorated. It'll be wonderful.'

Thirty-Five

Seb got out of his car and walked towards the farmhouse. Rori let out a whoop of delight and ran over to him. He picked her up and swung her around.

'Hey, munchkin, how are you doing?' he asked with a smile as he put her back down.

'Good,' Rori said. 'I just got back from Ally's birthday.'

'Did you have a good time?'

'Yep. I won this when we played pass the parcel.' She held out her arm so he could admire her brightly coloured bead bracelet.

'Very pretty,' Seb said. 'Do you know where your mum is?'

'Finishing the cleaning up after the wedding,' Rori said. 'It was too late to do it last night, so they're doing it now.'

'Is Tam down there too?' Seb gazed over his shoulder towards the old barn.

'Nah, she left not long before you came.'

'Thanks,' Seb replied. 'I've got to talk to your mum for a minute.'

'That's all right, Lucy promised she'd make us a milkshake.'

'What flavour?'

Rori gave him a look like he had two heads. 'Strawberry, of course.'

Seb chuckled. 'Of course.'

'Say goodbye before you go?' Rori asked as she turned to run back into the house.

'Promise,' Seb called back. He watched her scamper up the steps before he turned around and headed towards the barn.

As he neared the open doors, he could hear soft music coming from inside.

'Maddie?' he called out. 'Maddie, are you in there?'

'Just a tick, Seb—I'm down the back,' Maddie called out.

He walked into the barn to see Maddie perched all the way up a ladder. He hurried over and held it steady.

'You okay up there?'

'Yeah, it's this damn bulb that blew last night. Thank goodness it was right at the end of the night, so it didn't matter that much,' she answered as she fiddled with the globe. 'There, that should do it,' she added with a smile.

'Good, now get down—you're making me nervous.'

'That's only because you're not great with heights,' she said as she started to climb down.

Seb waited until she had two feet back on the ground.

'There's something I want to ask you about,' he said as he picked up the ladder and leant it against the nearest wall.

'Sounds serious.' Maddie pulled out a chair from one of the tables and sat down.

'It might be.' Seb sat down next to her. 'Has Tam ever said anything to you about the party she went to on the day of Mum and Dad's accident?'

Maddie stared at him and frowned. 'Not that I remember.'

'I think if she'd said something you would have remembered,' Seb replied.

'Darling, what's this all about? Why are you bringing this up when it was years ago?'

'I was talking to Dylan earlier.'

'It's about time you sorted yourselves out,' Maddie said with a little nod.

'Yeah, but the thing is we were having a slightly heated conversation about Tam and me when he brought up what happened at the party at the Hendersons. I didn't know what he was talking about.'

Maddie's brows drew together. 'What happened?'

'Taylor Henderson assaulted her. That's why she rang Mum to come and get her.'

'Wait. What?' Maddie replied. 'She never said a word about this to me.'

'She didn't say anything to me either,' Seb said.

'So the only person who knew was Dylan?'

'I guess Gemma and Will knew. They left the party with her too.'

'Okay, that would make sense,' Maddie said. 'Did he say anything else?'

'Just that Gemma's brother was going to pick them up later but the thing with Taylor happened and Tam wanted to get the hell out of there. Apparently no one else could pick them up.'

'Which is why she called home.'

'Yes,' Seb said with a nod. 'But I don't understand why she didn't tell us.'

Maddie was quiet for a moment. 'Do you know what happened?'

'Dylan said that Taylor kissed her and tried to force something more but she got away.'

'She was probably upset and terrified and then she stumbled across the aftermath of the accident. I can't even imagine what was going through her head.'

'So what do we do? Should we ask her about it?' Seb asked.

'I'm not sure,' Maddie replied. 'I mean I'd say wait until she tells us but obviously that's never going to happen.'

'Would this play into how she reacted to the accident?'

'Of course. Come on, Seb—you know that she already felt like it was her fault.' Maddie sighed. 'She went to therapy for a long time but I think there's still a small part of her that blames herself.'

Seb sat back in his chair and paused for a moment. 'Dylan said something along the same vein.'

'Well, he was always clever—thank heavens he was with her that day,' Maddie replied.

'Yeah, you're right. What should I do, ask Dylan for all the details?'

'Maybe you should talk to Gemma,' Maddie said.

Seb made a face. 'I doubt she'd talk to me; you know that we don't get on,' he said.

'Not surprising, seeing you like to blame anything that Tam does on Gemma,' Maddie said with a crooked smile.

'Oh, I—'

'Yeah, you do,' Maddie cut in. 'Just own it, Seb.'

'I suppose, but I don't think she'll tell me anything.'

'She's still our best bet to find out what really happened that day,' Maddie replied. 'I don't like the idea of talking about Tam behind her back—it feels like snooping, but if we're going to get to the bottom of this, we really don't have a choice.'

Seb was quiet for a moment. 'All right, I'll go and see her tomorrow.'

'You're not going to ring her?' Maddie asked.

'Like she'd even answer the call,' he replied. 'Nope, I'll drive down to Melbourne one day this week and catch her at work. She owns a shop, so she's gonna be there. If I'm there, she might feel compelled to talk to me.'

'Good luck with that,' Maddie said. 'I'm not sure it'll work but I hope it does.'

Seb blew out a breath, the last thing he wanted to do was talk to prickly Gemma but it had to be done. 'I guess we'll find out tomorrow.'

* * *

Tam sat in Maddie's car, nursing a large coffee. She had just finished getting some groceries and had decided to indulge in a good cup of caffeine before dropping the supplies back to the house. The car was parked outside the bakery and she allowed her thoughts to wander as the aroma of the fresh brew wrapped tantalisingly around her. She'd come to a decision, one she'd been putting off for a long time. Saturday's wedding had made her confront the issue. And it had been a revelation. She would walk away from Dylan for good. It wasn't what she wanted—in fact it was the last thing she wanted to do—but for his sake, she'd leave.

He deserved everything he wanted—a wife, children, a happy family life—and it had finally dawned on Tam that it couldn't be with her. For her to pretend that everything was fine and that they could have a happy future together would be a big, beautiful lie.

She breathed in the steam from her coffee, savouring the moment and clinging on to the fact that for the next hour or so Dylan was still hers. She checked the time and decided to drive out to his place around five, when he should be home from work.

Tam took another sip of her coffee and looked down the street. A familiar figure crossed the road nearby and she froze. For a moment she found it hard to breathe. Taylor Henderson was walking towards her car. Her eyes shot to the dashboard and she flicked the switch to lock the doors. Tam put her head down and waited for him to pass by.

There had been some trouble about six years back and Taylor had taken off before it could escalate. No one had seen him in town since. Tam knew Blake had nothing to do with his wretched brother these days but she wondered if he knew Taylor was back. Maybe she should get Dylan to give him a heads-up.

She picked up her phone and called Dylan.

'Hey, babe,' he said after a couple of rings.

'I'm in town and I just saw Taylor Henderson,' Tam said quietly. She knew it was ridiculous but she felt frightened that Taylor might hear her.

'He hasn't been around for years,' Dylan said.

'I know and, believe me, the town didn't miss him. I wonder if Blake knows? I'd hate it if Taylor went over there and caused a scene with him or his mum and sister.'

'I'll give him a call,' Dylan replied. 'Are you coming over soon?'

'Yeah, I thought I'd drop by after work.'

'Fantastic,' Dylan said.

She could hear the happiness in his voice but she knew he wasn't going to be happy when he heard about her decision.

'I'll see you soon,' Tam said quietly. 'I have something to tell you.'

Thirty-Six
January, eight years ago

Dylan rested his head on the chipped green paint of his back door and tried to catch his breath. His stomach hurt, blood seeped from his nose and his left eye was beginning to swell.

He was an idiot. He should never have gone after Taylor Henderson. Taylor was older and had a stockier build, Dylan knew he hadn't stood much of a chance but he still felt compelled to confront him.

The only upside of this disaster was that he'd at least landed a couple of good punches, one of which potentially had broken Taylor's nose, or at least he hoped it had.

He drew in another breath and noticed that his ribs on one side hurt as well. Great, just great. He managed to open the door and walk into the tiny kitchen.

'Is that you?' came his father's voice from the lounge.

'Yeah, Dad,' Dylan called back as he slowly made it to the doorway.

His father was propped up on the old threadbare couch with his ever-present glass of bourbon in his hand. Dylan clocked the table to see that the bottle was still almost full. He let out a sigh, maybe it would be okay. Jack Petersen had once been a handsome man but years of neglect and alcohol abuse had left him bloated with a coarse and ruddy complexion. He worked at a factory a town over, somehow he managed to drag his arse there each morning, which was a miracle in itself as each evening he'd drink himself into oblivion.

'What the hell happened to you?'

'I got in a fight.'

A slow smile spread across his father's face. 'Oh yeah? With who?'

'Taylor Henderson.'

His father let out a laugh. 'Well I'll be, this is a first. You didn't embarrass yourself, did you? What did you do to have him come after you?'

Dylan tried to stand a little taller. 'I went looking for Taylor.'

His dad stared at him. 'Did you win?'

'Probably not but I managed to stagger away and I might have broken his nose.'

His dad gave him a nod and for the first time in his life he thought he saw a speck of respect in his eyes. *Typical*, Dylan thought, *I can get great marks and line up an apprenticeship but the only time he's proud of me is when I hit someone.*

That's how screwed up their relationship was, if you'd even call it that.

'Why'd you hit him?'

'He did something he shouldn't have and no one called him out on it,' Dylan said without going into the details. 'He needed to know that you can't act like that and get away with it.'

'Broken nose, huh?' his dad added.

'It was a lucky punch.' Dylan shrugged.

'Maybe you've picked up some of my moves.' He grinned as he did a punch and dodge motion from where he was sitting.

'Yeah, maybe.' Dylan found it hard to forget that the old man had used those same moves on him.

'You want a beer, son? There's a couple in the fridge.'

Dylan frowned at the word. *Son*. He couldn't remember the last time his father had called him that. Was this some sort of twisted bonding moment? Dylan gave his father an insincere smile, which he didn't even notice.

'I might grab that beer later,' he said. 'I think I'd better wash some of the blood off first.'

'Good idea. Grab a bag of frozen peas for your eye.'

Dylan started to walk down the short hall towards his bedroom. But he stopped when his father called out to him.

'Was that Carrington boy there? Did he fight?'

Dylan closed his eyes and willed himself to keep calm. He looked back at his father and gave a laugh.

'Nah, this had nothing to do with Seb.'

'I guess they're all still grieving up at the house?' his father asked.

The comment took Dylan by surprise. The accident had happened less than a month ago, of course everyone was still grieving, including him. The Carringtons' farm had always been his safe place. A place where he wasn't judged, hit or ignored. His heart ached that Estella Carrington would never give him a smile or a hug ever again.

'Yes, they are,' he replied flatly as he tried to push all the pain he was feeling back down inside. He'd learnt long ago to never show his dad any weakness because some day he'd be sure to use it against him.

'Rumour has it that young Maddie Carrington came back pregnant with no husband in sight, is that true?'

Again Dylan shrugged to give the impression that it didn't mean anything to him. 'She's pregnant and I haven't seen a partner. All I know is that she's moved back for good to take care of the family.'

'Bet there's a story there,' his father said as he took a gulp of his drink.

'I'm sure you're right,' Dylan said, thinking it was easier to placate him. His stomach hurt, mainly from where Taylor's punch had landed but the old prickliness was there too. His father could go from a fun and tipsy drunk to a monster, it was the difference of only a couple of shots or glasses. Dylan always knew when he was about to snap, he could see the change in his eyes. He could tell it was coming now and he needed to get to the safety of his room.

'So if it wasn't about protecting your precious Carringtons, what was it about?' his father continued with a sneer.

'A girl,' he answered with a fake grin. It wasn't a lie, he'd purposely sought Taylor out because of what he'd tried to do to Tam at the Christmas party. He didn't know if she'd told her family about what had happened yet but they were all grieving their loss. Taylor had to be held accountable and, as far as Dylan could see, he was the only one who could do something about it.

His father put down his drink and clapped his hands together with glee.

'A girl.' He said again and laughed. 'That's brilliant. Maybe you're not such a useless sissy after all.'

Dylan smiled and nodded. 'Maybe not, eh?' He gave a forced laugh, playing along. 'I'm going to grab those peas from the freezer.'

'Do that.' His father reached down and topped up his glass.

Dylan quickly backtracked to the kitchen. He yanked open the fridge and took the peas out of the freezer section. Then he also helped himself to a can of soft drink and a packet of chips from the cupboard. He needed to grab something to eat because he couldn't come back into the kitchen until his dad had passed out. He snagged an apple from the counter on the way.

'I'll go and clean up then,' he said as he walked through the lounge.

His dad looked up but didn't say anything else, just waved his hand like he was a king dismissing his servant.

Dylan hurried down the hall and locked himself in his bedroom, hoping against hope that this would end up being a quiet night.

Thirty-Seven
December, thirteen months ago

Tam was sitting in the pub looking at the glass of sparkling wine in front of her. She barely drank anymore, well, not like she used to anyway. Occasionally she'd let her hair down and she'd get a bit tipsy with the girls but not the mind-numbing drunk she once did. Some would say she'd grown up, others would say it was because she had a business that she loved and had to look after. There was some truth in both tales, but Tam was just doing her best to keep the darkness inside her at bay without having to self-medicate with booze.

With each year it got a little easier. Not that she ever forgot what happened nor stopped missing her parents but time eased the rawness from the wound. The lead-up to Christmas, however, was always the worst and this year was no different. She fiddled with the little gold compass that hung around her neck as she eyed the sparkling glass in front of her.

The dreams had already started. For the past three nights they had haunted her, dragging her back to the one day she never wanted to revisit. They always left her feeling prickly, uneasy and guilty.

Her home had felt suffocating. After the nightmares, everything about Carrington Farm today reminded her of what she had lost. She had felt twitchy and in need of escape.

Which is why she'd taken off and found a pub two towns from home.

Her phone rang and shook her out of her thoughts.

'Hi Gemma,' she said.

'Where the hell are you?' Gemma asked quickly. 'I've sent you a dozen messages and you haven't answered one of them.'

Tam frowned. 'Sorry, I must have missed them.'

'So where are you?' Gemma asked again.

Tam looked around and saw the name of the pub written behind the bar. 'The White Stag.'

'Where the hell is that?'

'Lawson's Bend.'

'Oh for God's sake, what are you doing all the way over there?'

'I don't know, I decided to go for a drive and I ended up here,' Tam replied.

'Are you by yourself?'

'Well, you're not here, so who else would I be with?' Tam replied with a slight laugh.

'I thought that maybe Lix might be with you now uni has finished.'

'No, he's still in Melbourne. There's some exhibitions he wants to go to. He'll be up next week.'

'Did you ride?' Gemma asked.

'No, I borrowed Maddie's car. It's been raining on and off all day.'

'That's good,' Gemma replied.

'You don't have to babysit me, you know,' Tam said. 'Anyway, are you coming back for Christmas?'

'Of course,' Gemma said. 'I've only got a week off but it's better than nothing.' Then she went in for the kill. 'Tam, just get up and go back home. You don't want to be sitting there all by yourself. You'll end up regretting it in the morning.'

'Gem, I'm fine—'

'No, you're not,' Gemma cut her off. 'I know what's going on. It's almost Christmas and I bet your dreams have started again, just like last year—am I right?'

'Well, I . . .'

'And all of a sudden you're beginning to feel empty and blaming yourself for something that was never, let me say that again, never, your fault. So you took off and now you're staring at a drink debating whether or not to get hammered. Tell me I'm wrong.'

Tam sat back in the chair and looked out the window. 'You're not wrong.'

'Okay, you've got two choices,' Gemma told her. 'You can get up and go home or you can order a steak to have with that one glass and then go home.'

'You were always bossy,' Tam said.

'I know, and I'll keep doing it until you come to your senses,' Gemma said. 'So what's it going to be?'

'I'll order the steak.'

'Good, and then straight home.'

'Yes, Mum,' Tam answered with a slight smile. 'I'll talk to you soon.'

'Okay, bye,' Gemma said before she hung up.

Tam put down the phone, took a deep breath and then sculled the glass in front of her.

* * *

Dylan frowned as his phone rang and Gemma's name flashed up on the screen.

'Gem, how's it going?'

'Hi, Dylan. I'm good, how about you?'

'I can't complain,' he answered. 'What's up?'

'I think that you might have to go and retrieve Tam,' Gemma said. 'I've just talked to her and I don't think she's in a good place. It's almost Christmas—you know how she gets.'

'Where is she?'

'The White Stag. It's a pub in Lawson's Bend. Could you go and get her?'

'I'm on my way,' Dylan said as he picked up his keys and headed for the door.

* * *

It took forty minutes to get to Lawson's Bend and another five to find the pub. He noticed Maddie's car parked outside the hotel and pulled up next to it. Dylan turned to Joey Mackles who was sitting beside him. Joey was a friend and they had done their apprenticeship together.

'I really appreciate you driving out here with me,' Dylan said. He pulled out his wallet and handed Joey a couple of notes.

Joey looked puzzled. 'What's this?'

'I dragged you out here—I should at least shout you dinner,' Dylan said with a smile.

'Driving your car back home is not exactly a hard job,' Joey replied before he closed his hand around the money. 'But if you're offering . . . thanks.'

Dylan grabbed his wallet and phone as he got out of the car and waved Joey off.

He stood on the footpath and watched as Joey drove his car away. Then he turned and walked towards the pub. He pushed open the bar door and walked in, a quick glance showed him that

Tam wasn't there, so he kept going into the lounge. He found her sitting by a window up in the back corner. There were a couple of empty glasses in front of her but she seemed okay.

'Hey, Tam,' he said as he walked up to the table.

She seemed confused as she looked up. 'Dylan? What are you doing here?' Then she shook her head. 'Gemma rang you, didn't she?'

Dylan pulled out a chair and sat down next to her. 'She did. You okay?'

She gave him a nod. 'Yes, no . . . maybe.'

'Nice and decisive then—I like it,' he said with a smile.

She wrinkled her nose and gave him a look. 'I should be mad at Gemma,' she said. 'But I'm glad you're here.'

'Really?' Dylan leant on the table.

Tam nodded before she gave him a small smile. 'You can buy me dinner.'

'Cheeky,' he replied. 'But seriously, Tam, are you okay?'

'I wasn't but I think I will be.'

'Good, I'm glad.'

'So after dinner, I suppose I'll follow you back to Kangaroo Ridge,' she said.

'We can go back together. I had Joey drop me off,' Dylan explained. He picked up the menu. 'So what do you want?'

'Gemma told me I should have a steak,' Tam said with a shrug.

'Sounds good to me,' Dylan responded. 'I'll put in an order.'

Tam reached out and took his hand before he could get up from the table. 'Thanks for coming, I really mean it.'

The look in his eyes softened as he squeezed her hand back. 'You don't have to do this alone, Tam. I'm not going anywhere.'

Thirty-Eight
One year ago

Summer was waning and Dylan could feel the change in the air. There was a hint of crispness in the early mornings that up until now had been missing, and the breeze seemed to blow a little cooler than it had. The season was turning and the thunderstorm that had settled over Kangaroo Ridge three nights ago had watered the parched earth and settled the dust. Soon the leaves on the planted European trees that were dotted about the town would change from green to red and brown. As the rains came the surrounding bush would begin to green and the brown dirt would be replaced with the first tufts of grass.

Dylan drove down the bumpy road towards Carrington Farm. It was late and the moon was high overhead. He wound down the window and leant his arm on the window ledge as he continued down the gum-lined track. The wind blew away the tiredness that had been sneaking up on him. The same couldn't be said for Seb. Dylan turned his head and saw that his friend looked pretty out of it; his head leaning against the passenger's door with his eyes closed and the scent of alcohol emanating from him. It was unusual, as he was always cool, calm and collected; but something had rattled him today. Dylan had his suspicions but he was keeping the reason close to his chest.

Seb had called him earlier and said that he wanted to blow off some steam, apparently a session at the local gym hadn't been enough. Dylan suggested that they go to Bendigo, maybe to a club to grab a drink. He offered to drive as he could see that Seb was agitated. In Bendigo, they grabbed some pizza before heading to a club where Seb began to throw back drinks in quick succession.

Dylan sat opposite, studying him. 'So do you want to talk about it?'

Seb shook his head. 'It's nothing.'

'Yeah, really looks like it.' Dylan raised his eyebrows.

'It was a frustrating day,' Seb said as he put his half-empty glass back on the table. He glanced up at Dylan, who was waiting for him to expand. He let out a sigh before continuing, 'The orders that I was waiting on were delayed . . . again. Then one of the guys managed to drop a case of prosecco and shattered nearly all the bottles. Then the kitchenhand quit and to top everything off I had another run-in with Gemma.'

'How did that go?' Dylan asked, a smile tugging at the corner of his mouth.

'It wasn't pretty.'

'The two of you should make a pact to not interact. It would be easier for all of us,' Dylan added with a laugh.

Seb made a face. 'Oh shut up.'

That just made Dylan laugh harder.

'I always tell myself to ignore her,' Seb continued, 'but we just seem to rub each other the wrong way. She's so prickly and difficult.' Seb gulped down the remainder of his drink.

This time Dylan bit back a smile. He'd known Gemma for years, since high school, and he'd never had a problem with her. She could hold her own and was outspoken, especially if she was defending her best friend, Tam. And generally, that's why she and Seb clashed. Dylan was going to point that out to him but Seb got up to get another drink and the moment was lost.

After a couple of hours, Dylan helped Seb back to the car, poured him into the passenger's seat and drove back to Kangaroo Ridge.

Seb opened his eyes and straightened up in his seat about twenty minutes into the trip.

'Where are we?'

'About halfway,' Dylan replied without taking his eyes off the road. 'You're a bit out of it. Do you want to stay at my place?'

Seb shook his head and it seemed to take him a little time to get his thoughts together. 'Nah, I need to go home.'

'Right, but you're half cut and the pub will still be open by the time we get back. It's not a great look for the owner to turn up drunk.'

'I'm not drunk,' Seb mumbled.

'Of course not,' Dylan scoffed.

Silence filled the car and Dylan thought that Seb had fallen asleep.

'Maybe we should go to the farm?' Seb whispered as he leant back and closed his eyes.

'Good idea,' Dylan said as he gave Seb a quick glance.

About twenty minutes or so later, Dylan pulled into Carrington Farm's drive and drove up to the house. He was relieved to see the lights of the house come into view, at least the family was still up. A brief frown marred his face, maybe that wasn't such a good thing—at least not for Seb. By the time he'd stopped the car and managed to manhandle his friend out, the lights on the front verandah had been switched on and the front door creaked open.

Felix walked down the steps to meet them.

'Seb had a few drinks,' Dylan said. 'And he wanted to crash here, rather than at the pub.'

'A few?' Lix echoed. 'What the hell happened? He's never like this.'

'Not one hundred per cent sure,' Dylan replied. 'But something about a bad day and a run-in with Gemma seems to have been a part of it.'

'Ah,' Lix said as if the whole thing was crystal clear.

Felix grabbed hold of the other side of his brother and together he and Dylan managed to half walk, half stagger Seb up the steps and into the house.

'Where do we put him?' Dylan asked.

'I reckon the couch is the best bet.' Lix had already begun to veer in that direction.

'Good call,' Dylan replied as they manoeuvred Seb over to the couch and dumped him down. He straightened up and blew out a breath. 'You'll be all right with him?'

'Of course,' Lix said. 'You can take off.'

'Anyone else here?'

'Maddie is out with some friends, so Tam and I are officially babysitting Rori. Both she and Lucy have gone to bed but Tam's down by the summer house; you should swing by and say hello on your way.'

'I should get going.' Dylan slapped a hand on Lix's shoulder. 'I'll catch you later.'

'Yeah, no worries,' Lix said. 'Have a good night.'

Dylan bounded down the steps and headed towards the car. He was about to open the door but his hand paused on the handle. He looked across the dark waters of the dam to where a trail of solar lights marked the narrow path to the summer house.

The bright moon bathed the dam in its sensuous light, the night air was warm and scented with a hint of honeysuckle. He tilted his head back and looked up at the twinkling night sky. Maybe he should go and see Tam; it wasn't as if he was in any hurry to get home. He walked down towards the dam and began to follow the path around its edge. The chorus of frogs stopped their song as he walked past but resumed their boisterous croaking as soon as he had moved further along.

He knew he should turn around and walk back to the car. He'd wanted her, dreamt about her and been secretly infatuated with her for years. But if he and Tam ever got together, what would that do to the dynamics of the family? And if it all went pear-shaped and they broke up, what then? Seb would hate him and there was a good chance that he'd lose the closest thing he had to a family. That thought should have been enough to stop him in his tracks, but the lure of seeing Tam propelled him down the path.

The summer house was on the opposite shore from the main house so it took him a while to get there. He called out as he approached, to give Tam a heads-up.

'Hey, Tam, it's just me—Dylan. You there?'

Other than the frogs in the distance, Dylan was met with silence. He wondered if she'd already headed back to the house. If she had gone back using the other path, it was quite likely that they would miss each other.

'Tam, are you there?' he called out.

There was a splash in the water which drew his attention.

'Dylan? What are you doing here?' Tam asked. She was standing naked in the shoulder-deep water.

Thirty-Nine
One year ago

Dylan stood transfixed by the vision of Tam in the water. Her dark hair was wet and slicked back, emphasising the creamy expanse of her shoulders in the moonlight.

'Dylan? What are you doing here?' she asked again.

Her words shook him out of his trance and he tried to gather himself.

'Um . . .' He gestured towards the house. 'I brought Seb back.'

Tam frowned. 'Why isn't he at his place?'

'We went out and he's a bit drunk. I figured he'd be better here than at the pub.'

'Wait . . .' She held up a hand. 'Did you say that he was drunk?'

'A bit,' he said with a nod.

'Well, that's new,' Tam said. 'Is he all right?'

'Yeah, I think so. He said that he had a bad day and then he and Gemma crossed swords.' Dylan walked down the slight incline so he was a little closer to the edge of the water and crouched down.

Tam let out a laugh as she swam closer. 'Hah, I guess she's finally driven him to drink.'

'I guess.'

Tam was silent for a moment as she seemed to study Dylan's face. 'So have you been ghosting me, Petersen?'

Dylan's eyes widened in surprise. 'What do you mean?'

'Before Christmas, when I was in a bad place and you came to the rescue. You drove over to Lawson's Bend to pick me up, remember?'

Dylan nodded. 'Of course.'

'And after that you said that I could count on you, but you bailed on me,' Tam said with a lift of her eyebrows.

'I've never done that,' Dylan replied. 'If you ever need help, you know that I'll be there for you.'

'But ever since that night, you've gone out of your way to avoid me—why?'

'I haven't,' Dylan responded.

'Yeah, you have,' Tam said. 'Just admit it—you're scared.'

'Of what?' he scoffed as he shook his head.

'Of me, of you . . . of us,' Tam said softly as she came a little closer.

He froze at her words before saying with a laugh, 'Ah, stop winding me up, Tam. Why would I be scared of you?'

'Because you're terrified about what will happen if we actually get together. You put up a wall and pretend to treat me like a sister, but I know that's not what you want. I see right through you, Dylan.'

'Tam,' he whispered, not really knowing if it was a warning to stop or a plea not to.

'You want me, I know that you do,' Tam said as she bobbed in the water. 'So don't you think it's about time you did something about it?'

He stared at her, drinking her in. She was there, naked in the water, right in front of him, and he could feel the urgency growing in his body. She was right, he wanted her so bad it almost hurt, but he was scared that he could lose everything he held dear.

Should he risk it? He'd been asking himself that question for years now.

'You know that it could be difficult,' he replied.

'Anything that's worth a damn is always difficult.'

'The family might not understand,' he said as he felt any remaining resistance he had beginning to crumble.

'You mean Seb,' Tam said. 'Sometimes you have to do what's right for you and not worry about what others might think.' She turned around and swam a couple of strokes back out into the lake. The moonlight caught her lithe figure as she cut through the water and Dylan saw a tattoo of a crescent moon and three small stars nestled above five red roses on the back of her shoulder.

'That's new,' he called out after her.

She turned her head and gave him a smile. 'You're changing the subject but yes, it's new. I've got a thing for the moon, and the roses represent the five of us. Mum and Dad's initials are hidden in the petals.'

'It's pretty,' he managed to get out. It was a lame response, but she had him rattled and it was the best he could do.

'Come in for a swim,' Tam said after another moment. 'I really want you to.'

Dylan looked into her eyes. 'Do you mean it?'

'Yes, I mean it,' Tam said softly. 'Will you come?'

In the moonlight, Dylan could see the vulnerable look in her eyes and he realised that, for all of her bravado, she was just as uncertain of this next step as he was. She knew what the dangers and possible consequences could be but she was willing to take the risk.

He was quiet for a moment. He was at a crossroad and he knew it. He couldn't play it safe any longer, if he turned away now, she'd never give him a second chance. He also knew that if

Seb found out, there'd be hell to pay. But . . . maybe he was all right with that.

He pulled off his shirt and quickly discarded the rest of his clothes. His excitement was obvious, even in this half-light, and he stood for a moment in front of her, so that she could see all of him, and then he walked into the water.

Tam watched him undress, and stand there before her. His need was obvious. As he stepped down into the water, she knew that something had changed indelibly. There was no going back. Forces were in motion that neither of them could stop now, and the fires of need could not be quenched without their desire's fulfilment.

Dylan kept going until it was deep enough to dive in and then he swam out to where she was waiting for him. As he surfaced he wiped his hair back off his face and gazed into her pale eyes. A heartbeat went by and then another before they moved together, slowly at first until they were almost touching.

Dylan reached out and pulled her close. His kiss was filled with the longing he'd been holding back. Tam's arms wrapped around his back and drew him in tighter. She kissed him back and met his ferocity; lips to lips, tongue to tongue and body to body, until their heat almost threatened to overwhelm them. She would not have been surprised if the water had started to boil around them, and she could feel the insistence of his need as he pressed his hard body against hers.

All of Dylan's doubts had vanished, and his whole being was enraptured by every part of her. His hands roamed over her water-slick body and explored her curves and taut lines. His heart raced—all he could think of was having her, holding her and staying like this forever. To hell with any consequences, he couldn't breathe without her.

He broke the kiss and rested his head on hers, so he could catch his breath.

'Don't stop,' Tam whispered. 'I need you, Dylan.'

'You know how I feel about you, don't you?' Dylan asked as he looked into her eyes.

She nodded without breaking eye contact. 'I think I've always known but I didn't want to hurt you. I've been in a dark place for years but I think that's behind me now. I care about you, Dylan. You've always been so constant and dependable, even when the rest of my life was a shambles. I want you in my life, I need you.'

They were the words that he'd always hoped to hear. He dropped a kiss on her forehead. 'I think I've always been in love with you,' he confessed.

Tam wrapped her arms around his shoulders. 'Then show me, make me feel it.'

He lifted her up in the water, she wrapped her legs around his hips and slowly he lowered her back down and slipped inside her. She sucked in a breath as he marvelled at the juxtaposition of the cool water and the heat of Tam's body. Together they began to move in unison and finally release the yearning of buried desire.

Tam's senses were attuned to the night and to Dylan. When she felt him enter her for the first time, she felt a sense that maybe this was what destiny had intended for them all along. The overwhelming feeling of rightness was intoxicating. As he began to move in her, she felt as if a stronger power had overtaken her body, and she answered his movement with her own—thrust with thrust—until he touched a deep place in her soul that no one had ever reached before. She cried out—an almost primal sound of desire and overwhelming pleasure. She knew that this moment would stay with her forever, regardless of what the future might bring. This was a joyous counterpoint to the bleak memories that had plagued her for so long.

Their tempo increased until Dylan held her tight. When he reached the moment of release, he called out her name; and the moon shone down from the cloudless night sky.

Forty

The afternoon sun shone golden through the gum trees that lined the road to Dylan's cottage. Normally Tam would have revelled in the beauty but today she kept her eyes strictly on the road. She'd dropped off the groceries at home and swapped the car for her bike. Turning off the road, she bumped down the familiar dirt track. Dylan would be home from work by now and it was time for her to step up and do what was right.

As she crested the hill, the little cottage came into view. A wave of sadness swept over her and she almost stopped and turned the bike around. She didn't want to do this, she didn't want to lose Dylan, but he deserved better.

Parking her bike near the front door, she paused to take her helmet off. She ran her hands through her dark hair and readjusted the gold chain around her neck. Her fingers lingered over the little compass that dangled between her breasts. Taking courage from it, she headed towards the cottage, only to find that Dylan had already yanked open the front door before she had a chance to reach it.

'Hey,' he said with a soft smile. 'I've missed you.' He leant in and gave her a kiss on the lips.

She pulled back and gave him a nod. 'Me too,' she said before she walked past him and into the cottage. 'Did you ring Blake?'

Dylan frowned but followed her. 'Yeah, he thanked me for the heads-up. The poor guy has worked so hard to make sure his mum and sister finally escaped the toxic half of the family.'

Tam nodded but she didn't turn around. 'His little sister, Diana, has really flourished since their dad went to jail and Taylor took off. I'd hate to think he was back now to muck everything up again.'

'No one is going to let that happen. Don't worry about it, Tam. Blake's got a lot of support in town and nobody holds his father's sins against him. Like they always say, you can't choose your family. A lot of us would be in trouble if we did. I mean, hell, just look at mine.'

'It must be hard though for Mrs Henderson, Taylor is still her son,' Tam said.

'That's true, but I think they've grown stronger without him,' Dylan replied. 'Blake told me that once his father was gone, it was like the dark cloud hanging over them had finally blown away. I'm sure even Taylor's return can't overturn all the things they've achieved.'

'Let's hope that he doesn't hang around,' Tam said. 'Kangaroo Ridge is better off without him.'

Dylan walked over to her and hugged her from behind. 'Just put him out of your mind, babe. He's not worth a second thought.'

She stood there, wrapped in Dylan's strong arms. There was safety in his embrace and she was cocooned by his warmth and the faint scent of his aftershave. Everything was about to change but she was determined to hold on to this feeling for another second or two. She relaxed in his arms and savoured it.

'So, you said you had something to tell me?' Dylan rested his chin on the top of her head.

Tam closed her eyes, not wanting this moment to end. But knowing that it would.

She broke from his arms.

'I've been thinking about us lately,' she said, unable to look him in the eyes. 'About our future.'

Dylan's smile began to fade as if he sensed the change in the air. 'Okay?' He took a step back and looked at Tam. After a moment of silence he asked, 'What do you want to say?'

Tam walked over to the couch and leant against it, in a way she hoped it would give her some sort of tangible support for what she was about to do. 'I'm beginning to think that we want two different things. You want the perfect family life with a wife, house and kids. But I don't think I'm the one to give you those things.' She ran her fingers across the well-worn fabric of the couch nervously.

'You just came to this decision, did you?'

Tam shook her head. 'No, I've been thinking about it for quite a while. I love you, Dylan, but I can't give you what you want. At first I thought that I wasn't ready, but it's more than that.'

'We can work this out, Tam,' Dylan replied. 'If you want to wait then . . .'

She shook her head. 'No, that's not fair—to either of us. What if I'm never ready? What then?'

'Then we'd still have each other,' Dylan said.

'That's too much for you to give up. Sometimes love isn't enough, no matter how much we want it,' Tam said. 'It's better that we end it now, rather than let it go on until you end up resenting me.'

'That's never going to happen.'

'Perhaps it would, especially if I end up being the one who stands in your way of getting everything you ever wanted,' Tam replied. 'I couldn't live with that.'

'So you're just going to decide for the both of us?' Dylan shook his head. 'Don't I get a say in this?'

Tam glanced back at him. 'You'll talk me out of it and we'll end up having the same conversation next year or maybe the one after that.'

'You're going to walk away and give up on everything we've got?' Dylan folded his arms and leant against the doorway.

'It's the only way that you can have what you want,' Tam said as tears began to prick at her eyes.

'You really believe that, don't you?'

'Yes, this is the only way forward and it's not together,' Tam said. 'I've tried to want the same things as you do but . . .'

'So you're going to give up? It's that easy for you?' he responded with an incredulous tone.

'Nothing about this is easy,' Tam said with a shake of her head and then started to walk past him. She had to get away.

His hand caught her arm. 'Why are you doing this, Tam?'

'I've just told you,' she said.

Dylan let go of her arm. 'You're doing this because you're scared. You're too frightened to have a life with me because you think that you don't deserve it and that's bullshit. The one thing your parents would have wanted is for you to be happy.'

'I'm sorry, I've got to go.' Tam took another step away from him. 'I can't do this.'

'Aren't you even going to try?' Dylan asked quietly as she ran out the front door.

Forty-One

Dylan stood by the door as the sound of Tam's motorbike faded in the distance. Part of him had known that this would eventually happen, the signs were there but he had tried hard to avoid seeing them. He understood that she was scared and that, even though she would never say it, the past still had her tethered. Sometimes he wondered if she'd ever break free of it.

He sighed as he shut the door. He didn't know how to help her and it ate him up inside. It was crazy, they both loved each other but here they were breaking up. He'd stand by her decision if it was what she really wanted, but he wasn't convinced that was the case. He didn't want to be *that guy* who dismissed his girlfriend's feelings and wishes because he knew better. This was about what she believed about herself and Dylan was pretty sure that most of it was warped and blown out of proportion.

He headed to the kitchen and grabbed a bottle of water from the fridge. *What the hell am I going to do?* he thought as he cracked open the lid and took a swig. Maybe he should talk to someone in the family. Was that being a little possessive? Yeah, maybe, but he had to do something. The first person that popped into his mind was Seb but perhaps he wasn't the right choice. He needed someone who could look at things more objectively, or someone who at least knew what Tam might be thinking.

'Lix,' he said under his breath. 'If he doesn't know what's going on, then no one will.'

Dylan pulled out his phone and scrolled through until he found Felix's number.

'Dylan?' came Lix's voice after a couple of rings.

'Hey, Lix. Yeah it's me,' he said quickly. 'Are you in the middle of anything?'

'I'm out at the old Darcell property,' Lix said.

Dylan was taken aback. 'Why the hell are you out there?'

'I'm taking pictures for a series I'm working on,' Lix replied. 'What's up?'

'I need to talk to you about Tam,' Dylan said. 'She just told me she wanted to break up.'

Lix let out a long sigh. 'Okay, I'm not sure how you think I can help but I'll try.'

'It's not so much that I want you to intercede; I just need to get my head around what's going on with her,' Dylan said. 'Can I come out so we can talk in person?'

'Only if you're not scared of ghosts,' Lix said with a laugh.

'Yeah, right. I'll see you in about ten minutes.'

'Okay, I'm in the back garden. See you soon.'

Still carrying the water bottle, Dylan snatched up his keys and walked out of the house.

The Darcell place wasn't far from Carrington Farm, but you had to drive up past the old dam and along an overgrown dirt track. The house had once belonged to a wealthy sheep farmer but had fallen into disrepair after the Second World War. There had been some sort of tragedy back then involving a child. The story had evolved into gossip and then legend with each generation whispering that the Darcell family was cursed and their home, Peppercorn House, was haunted. Every now and again the property was listed for sale but nothing ever came from it. It was understandable; ghost stories aside, the property was a little isolated and out of town. And it needed a lot of work. Most potential buyers ran away as fast as they could.

Before too long, Dylan was pulling into the driveway of the old house and peering through the windscreen at the two-storey home. He could tell that once, long ago, it would have been impressive as it had a balcony with iron lacework and large stone steps leading up to a pretty portico. He got out of the car and shielded his eyes from the sun as he looked up at a copper rooster weathervane on the roof. The whole place had a desolate feel about it. Dylan resisted the shiver that was waiting to skim down his spine and walked towards the back garden.

He pushed his way through a rusted iron gate and found Felix taking a photograph of an old forgotten sundial.

'Hi,' he called out as he got closer.

Lix looked up from his camera and smiled. 'Hey, Dylan, I won't be a sec,' he said as he turned back to his camera and took a couple of shots.

Dylan waited until Lix looked as if he was finished. 'Creepy place,' he said, half to himself.

'Nah, it's just old and a bit neglected, that's all.' Lix sat down on a nearby slate-covered garden edge.

'Are you even allowed to be here?' Dylan asked.

Lix grinned back. 'I've got permission from old Mrs Knightly, she's the one who owns it. It was her childhood home.'

'So she was a Darcell?'

'Yep, she's in a nursing home in Bendigo. I go and visit her every now and again and she tells me stories about the house. I think the family is going to try and rent it out,' Lix said.

'It needs work.' Dylan looked at the crumbling building. 'Does it even have a flushing toilet and running water?'

'Oh come on, it's not that bad,' Lix said with a laugh. 'If I had the money, I'd buy it. It's got a great vibe to it.'

'Yeah, if you like something out of a horror movie,' Dylan quipped.

Lix chuckled before he changed the subject. 'So what happened with Tam?'

Dylan sat down next to him and shrugged. 'I'm not exactly sure. One minute, we're okay and the next she's cooling it off. Every time I suggest taking the next step, she freaks and changes the subject but this time it went a whole lot further.'

'So what do you want me to do about it?' Lix glanced at Dylan.

'I'm not sure if there's anything you can do. I just want some clarity about what she thinks about us,' Dylan replied. 'I mean, I think that she's scared of living . . . or maybe even being happy. I figured that maybe you were the person to talk to because you guys are so close.' He looked at the ground and toed a rock with his boot.

'I don't tell secrets.' Lix gave him a slight smile. 'But I can give you my impression of what I think is going on in her head.'

'Thanks, Lix. I'd appreciate it. She says that she loves me but she's breaking up with me for my own good. She's not ready to commit. That's fair enough and I'm willing to wait but she doesn't want to lead me on and then never marry me,' Dylan said quickly. 'Sorry, did that even make sense?'

'Yeah, I understand,' Lix replied. 'So you want to know if she really feels that way or if there's something else coming into play, is that right?'

Dylan nodded. 'Yeah, I've had some thoughts but I'm not sure.'

'Go on.'

'I think she's still troubled by your parents' accident. Sorry, I know it's a tender subject.' Dylan glanced at Lix.

'It's okay,' he replied. 'You think that she blames herself for the accident, don't you?'

'Yes, I do.'

'So do I,' Lix said. 'I think she always has. She tells herself that she can't have a life because she doesn't deserve to be happy.'

Dylan stared at him for a minute. 'I had the same kind of thought.'

'Whenever she gets any happiness, she'll push it away or sabotage it because she believes that she needs to atone for her mistake,' Lix continued. 'This is the story she tells herself, even though it's not true.'

'So what do I do?' Dylan asked.

'I think it's something that Tam has to confront by herself. We can help but ultimately it's up to her.'

'I love her and I don't want to lose her.' Dylan ran his hand through his hair.

'Then you'd better figure out a way to fight for her.' Lix gave Dylan a smile. 'She's worth it.'

Forty-Two

Later that night Tam sat outside under the boughs of the spreading peppercorn tree, staring into the night. The air was warm and scented from the nearby jasmine that climbed over the front fence. The sound of frogs croaking happily in the dam wafted through the night air along with the occasional hoot of an owl.

Tam was shattered after the break-up with Dylan but sitting here, listening to the night, eased the pain enough for her to breathe. She watched the moon's reflection in the water and tried to find a little peace from the turmoil within her.

What she'd done was for the best, she reminded herself, at least for Dylan's sake. But the more she sat quietly with her thoughts, and the realisation of what her life would be without him, the more she doubted her decision.

Dylan had always stood by her, even long before they were together. She closed her eyes and remembered walking down that dusty road from the Hendersons' place. He'd been with her then, supporting her. He'd stayed with her on the worst day of her life and had never turned away; not even when she'd tried to push him.

She wanted him and loved him, so why was she so scared to have a full-blown relationship with him? It didn't make any sense. Her hand reached for her pendant and she rolled it between her fingers.

A gentle breeze blew across the water, making it ripple. With a sigh she sat back against the garden seat. Perhaps she should follow Lix's advice and find someone she could talk to. For the past couple of years, she'd wanted to pretend that everything was okay. She'd kept telling herself that she hadn't been all right in the past and that her parents' deaths had profoundly affected her but, with therapy and the help of a loving family, she'd made real progress. And that was true, or at least partially so. The problem was that there was still a tiny voice inside of her that would reach out through the darkness and snare her. It happened when she didn't expect it, often when she was at her happiest. The voice condemned her, blamed her for the accident and whispered that she would never deserve happiness because of what she did.

Tam tried her best to ignore it but more often than not it sowed a seed and she would end up sabotaging herself, or her happiness. With Dylan it had been a little different. When they had just been sneaking around, the voice was held at bay but any time Dylan suggested going to the next level, it would hiss its vicious words in her ear. Then the nightmares of the past would plague her sleep until she started to pull away from Dylan. It was only when he would drop the idea that the voice would fade and the bad dreams dissipate.

Tam pulled her knees up and leant her arms on them. If she allowed this guilt and fear to control her life—she would end up not having one and she deserved more than that. Aunt Maddie had told her that and so had Lix and Dylan. Maybe it was time that she started to listen, before it was too late.

* * *

The next afternoon, Seb pulled into a car space in a high-rise parking lot in the middle of the city. He made his way to the lift on the far side of the building. It had taken him about an hour and forty-five minutes to get to Melbourne from Kangaroo Ridge as the drive down the Calder Highway had been pretty clear and he was able to make decent time. That had been the easy bit, it was meeting Gemma that would be . . . challenging.

Seb headed down Bourke Street, deciding to stop and grab a coffee to fortify himself before his encounter. The heady aroma of the coffee was mixed with the smell of exhaust fumes in the warm air. He'd always liked Melbourne, you could lose yourself for hours, and he liked being anonymous, not like in Kangaroo Ridge. Once, long ago, he'd toyed with the idea of moving down here, just for a couple of years. But things changed.

He kept going, over Elizabeth Street and through the Bourke Street Mall. There was a rumble as a tram ambled its way past him and Seb caught the faint scent of perfume as he walked past the front doors of Myer. Turning left at Swanston Street he walked about a block before he came to a small lane. He paused and looked at the dress shop that had a double window; one that faced the main street and the other that looked out into the busy lane. It was decked out with several mannequins modelling different styles as well as some handbags and other accessories. The sign above the window said Sweet & Savage Boutique. Seb frowned. Well, the savage part described Gemma, he wasn't so sure about the sweet bit.

He started walking towards the busy shop. There was no point putting this off, even though he'd like to. He pushed open the door and stepped inside. The air smelt of white flowers and there was soft barely audible music playing in the background. It appeared to be quite busy and it was a bit difficult for him to navigate his way deeper into the shop. He glanced around but couldn't spot Gemma, so he walked up to the counter.

'Hi, can I help you?' a girl with red shoulder-length hair and a quick smile asked.

'Maybe. I'm looking for Gemma—Gemma Allen,' Seb said. 'I'm Seb Carrington, a friend of hers.'

'Oh, okay. I won't be a minute—Gem's out the back,' the girl said before she turned and disappeared through a thick curtain.

Seb waited by the counter. He gave an apologetic smile to the women behind him waiting to be served then looked straight ahead. The girl reappeared after a couple of minutes.

'Gemma will be down in a moment,' she said with a smile.

'Thanks.' Seb stepped to one side to get out of the way.

Before long, a slim blonde walked out from behind the curtain. A frown danced across his brows for a second. She looked different somehow, maybe it was because she'd grown her hair out a bit and it was pulled back in an updo.

She looked around the shop and then her pale blue eyes pinpointed him and she strode over.

'God, what's happened? Is Tam all right?' she asked in a low voice so she wouldn't be overheard.

'She's okay,' Seb answered quickly.

Gemma narrowed her eyes. 'Then why are you here?'

'Can we talk somewhere?'

'Is this an emergency?' Gemma asked. 'Or can it wait until I close the shop?'

'It can wait.'

'Okay, good,' Gemma said. 'We close at five thirty, come back then.'

Seb nodded and started to turn away until he felt her hand touch his arm. He looked back at her expectantly.

'You're sure she's all right?' she asked.

'Yeah, I promise,' Seb replied.

'Okay.' Gemma let go of his arm and took a step back. 'I'll see you later.'

'You can count on it,' Seb said before he wound his way back through the shop and out the front door.

*   *   *

Seb made his way back towards Gemma's shop around five o'clock. He'd already killed a couple of hours having a look around and doing a little shopping and he figured he could have a coffee at a cafe he'd seen near her shop until she finished work.

He sat by the window nursing his coffee and glanced across the street to the Sweet & Savage Boutique. At least she'd been willing to talk to him, he supposed that was something. He took another sip of the coffee. It was probably mostly his fault that he didn't get along with Gemma. Like Maddie had said, he had to own that.

Over the years he had tended to blame Gemma for leading Tam astray. It was easier to be mad at an outsider rather than his twin sister. But maybe that had been unfair.

Maybe it was because of his attitude that Gemma had become cold and sometimes downright argumentative whenever they were in the same room.

He just hoped that she could put all of that aside and tell him what had really happened at the Henderson party. Seb took another sip of his coffee. Maybe he should apologise to her as well—it wouldn't hurt.

Forty-Three

Gemma sat opposite Seb in a small Italian restaurant. They had been seated now for a couple of minutes and the silence between them was becoming more than awkward.

She sat back and crossed her arms. 'So, what's all this about, Seb?'

'I need to ask your opinion about a couple of things,' he replied as he looked across the table at her.

'Really?' She raised one of her eyebrows.

Seb stifled a sigh, this was going to be more difficult than he thought. 'I guess first of all I want to apologise.'

'For what?' Gemma replied quickly. 'There's a long list, so I'm wondering which things I should cross off.'

She wasn't going to make it easy, but maybe that's what he deserved.

'I want to say sorry for always jumping to conclusions and blaming you for when Tam went off the rails.'

Gemma snorted and picked up the menu. She took a minute or two to read through the options before putting it back down and staring at Seb. 'Fine, I accept your apology even though it sounds half-hearted,' she said. 'So what do you want?'

'I wanted to ask you about the day of the Hendersons' party. I want to help Tam, but I don't know what to do.'

'You said that she was all right,' Gemma replied with concern in her voice.

'She's physically okay,' Seb said. 'But I think she needs some help. If you ask me, she's still not over our parents' accident.'

'You're only coming to this conclusion now?' Gemma gave a shake of her head. 'She's been trying to get you to see what's going on for a long time. She reaches out for help and you just follow the same narrative you've been telling yourself for years—she's wild, unpredictable and will never settle down or grow up.'

Seb's eyes widened at the accusation. 'That's a bit much, isn't it?'

'See, defensive without taking a look to see if there's any truth to what I just said,' Gemma replied. She went to say something else but the waiter came to the table and they spent the next couple of minutes ordering.

Seb waited until the waiter had gone before resuming the conversation.

'Let's say that everything you said is true, I've been a jerk and haven't seen what's really going on,' he began. 'After all, I didn't know that Tam and Dylan were even seeing each other until recently. So tell me the truth.'

'She self-sabotages,' Gemma said as she looked Seb in the eyes, almost challenging him to say otherwise. 'Because a tiny piece of her still blames herself for your parents' death.'

Seb nodded. 'I tend to agree with you.'

Gemma took a moment then continued. 'And because of that, she believes that she doesn't deserve to be happy. As soon as things begin to go well, she bails. The exception is Dylan. She really loves him but even that's not enough. Somehow, she'll wreck that relationship too.'

'So what can I do to help?'

Gemma narrowed her eyes. 'Do you really want me to answer that?'

'Of course, I wouldn't have asked otherwise.'

'You're not going to like the answer,' Gemma said quietly.

'Okay, but say it anyway.'

Gemma bit her bottom lip before she spoke. 'You can stop blaming her for your parents' death.'

Seb stilled for a moment before he shook his head. 'That's crazy, I don't.'

Gemma stared at him—she seemed to be able to look inside him. 'You do. You may never admit it to yourself, but you do blame her, Seb—you always have.'

'I've never said anything like that,' he stated quickly, trying to defend himself.

'You don't have to say it. It's how you treat her, how you talk to her and how you dismiss the real problems and instead say she's unpredictable or wild.'

Seb was silent as he absorbed her words.

Gemma continued, her voice a little softer. 'I can't imagine how difficult it was for all of you to lose your parents. And I know how much you stepped up to help the family. And even though you might not have voiced it, it's a whole lot easier to blame someone for the accident than accept that it just happened.'

'Lix said a similar thing to me, and I refused to believe it,' Seb said. 'I justified my reactions and decision when it came to Tam. I couldn't wrap my head around it.'

'Yeah, I understand, Seb—I do.' Gemma reached across the table and gave his hand a quick squeeze and then snatched it away when she realised what she'd done. 'But think about how close you guys used to be when we were kids and how much distance there is between you now. We all have guilt about that day but if we don't come to terms with it, it'll eat us alive.'

'I'm sorry,' Seb said.

'For what?' Gemma replied but this time her voice wasn't tainted with anger or frustration.

'Being an idiot. I should have known there was more going on.'

'We're all idiots sometimes,' Gemma answered with a slight smile.

He nodded. 'What did you mean about us all feeling guilty?'

Gemma drew in a deep breath and then blew it out. 'I made Tam go to that party,' she explained. 'I had a crush on Will Griffith and I made Tam come with me. I even blackmailed Jace to drive us. So you can actually blame me for that, Seb. I made her go.'

'Gem, I didn't mean—'

Gem held up her hand. 'No. If it weren't for me, Tam would never had been at that stupid party.'

'It's all right, I don't blame you,' Seb said gently. 'But can you tell me what happened?'

Gem took a sip of water. 'That day was awful. I should have listened to Jace, he told me it was a bad idea to go. And I knew that Tam didn't want to be there but I guilted her into it. At first, it wasn't so bad. Will and Dylan arrived and we all hung around together but later in the afternoon, the guys went off to get food or drinks or something. Tam was getting anxious about going home and didn't want to wait for Jace who was picking us up around six o'clock. So she went to find Will and Dylan and ask them how they were getting home, thinking that maybe we could hitch a ride with them.' Gemma started to fiddle with her serviette.

Seb was about to urge her to carry on but the waiter arrived with their food and delayed the rest of the conversation.

Gemma picked up her fork and toyed with her pasta. 'Then of course, you know what happened next,' she said.

Seb shook his head. 'That's just it, Gem, I don't.'

She frowned at him. 'But surely Tam told you about Taylor Henderson?'

'No, I've only just found out about it. She never said a word to Maddie either.'

'But how is that even possible? I understand with the trauma of the accident she may have not said anything straight away but I always thought that she would have told you or Maddie.'

Seb shook his head. 'I haven't had a chance to talk to Lix yet but I don't think she told him either.'

'So she's been carrying that all by herself as well?'

'Geez, Gem, I wish I knew but I don't,' Seb said. 'Did you ever talk about it with her?'

'I was pretty stupid back then and I didn't really understand what had happened until a bit later. When I did try to talk to her she said that she just wanted to forget it. All I know is that he kissed her and then he assaulted her and if Blake hadn't stopped him it could have been even worse.'

'Bloody hell, I'm going to beat the crap out of Taylor Henderson,' Seb said quietly.

'Dylan already beat you to that,' Gemma said with a smile. 'Although, if I remember rightly, he got pretty messed up.'

'What?'

'You probably don't remember because you had a lot going on but Dylan confronted Taylor sometime that summer.'

'I didn't know any of this,' Seb said. 'You're saying Dylan took on Taylor?'

'Yep, even though the odds were against him. That's how Taylor got a broken nose. So there was a bit of payback although not nearly enough in my opinion.' Gemma paused for a moment before she continued. 'Anyway, now you know why we had to leave the party. Tam was really upset and we tried to get a ride back to town but no one could come and get us.'

'So that's when Tam called Mum,' Seb said. 'I was there when she rang. Mum didn't say what had happened but I got the feeling it was something bad. They both took off to get her but never made it. After the accident I forgot to find out what the phone call had been about, or that Tam had been upset.'

'So, now you understand why Tam blames herself. She's carried that with her over the years and you've reinforced it. Not intentionally, but it happened.'

Seb sat back in his chair and rubbed his hand across his mouth. 'I never meant to . . . I know that it wasn't her fault.'

'Then maybe you should tell her.'

'Yeah . . . I will.'

'And, Seb?'

'What?'

'Give me a call and let me know how it goes, all right?'

'I will,' Seb said quietly.

Forty-Four

Seb got back to Kangaroo Ridge around nine o'clock that night. He'd taken the solitude of the drive to think about what Gemma had said. He'd made some mistakes and he was ready to admit it. Above all, even though it may have been subconscious, he had at least partly blamed Tam for their parents' death and hadn't given her the support she'd deserved.

That was wrong and he wondered if he'd managed to screw up anyone else in the family while he'd blustered along. He knew now that things had to change and the first thing was to sit down with Tam and actually listen to what she had to say. He owed her that, and an apology. He just hoped that it wasn't too late.

Instead of going home to the pub, he kept driving out to Carrington Farm. With luck, Tam might be at home. He'd thought about ringing her but he figured they needed to have a face-to-face conversation.

'Hey,' he called out as he walked through the back door. 'It's just me.'

Gray stuck his head around the corner. 'Hi, what's up?'

Seb gave him a smile. 'Oh nothing, I wanted to catch up with Tam. Is she here?'

Gray gestured up the stairs. 'She's in her room, or at least she was earlier.'

'Thanks,' Seb said as he started up the stairs.

When he knocked on Tam's door, there was a rustle from inside before the door opened.

'Seb, what are you doing here?' Tam asked.

Seb smiled at her. 'I wondered if we could talk for a bit.' He noted that she looked as if she'd been crying.

Tam frowned. 'Is anything wrong?'

Seb shook his head. 'No, not really—I just need to talk to you.'

'Okay, shall we go down to the kitchen?'

'I was thinking somewhere a little less public.'

'The garden then,' Tam said.

Outside, Tam led the way over to the garden seat under the peppercorn tree. After taking a seat she looked at him expectantly.

'It's bad, isn't it?' she asked.

Seb sat down next to her. 'Are you all right? You've been crying.'

Tam glanced down at the ground. 'I kind of broke up with Dylan,' she said quietly. 'You were right, we weren't suited to each other.'

Seb was quiet as he recalled Gemma's prediction that this would happen—one way or another Tam would get scared and call off her relationship with Dylan.

'No, I was wrong,' Seb said. 'I had no idea what I was talking about.'

'Where's this coming from? You were so set against—'

Seb didn't let her finish. 'I was an idiot. If the two of you are in love and happy, then I have no business trying to interfere. Your relationship had nothing to do with me, which I think you've pointed out to me more than once.' He took her hand. 'You're my sister and I love you, Tam. If Dylan makes you happy then you should be with him.'

Tam gave him a wary glance before asking, 'Okay, who are you and where is my brother?'

He let go of her hand and gave her a nudge with his shoulder. 'I'm sorry, Tam—I was an overbearing jerk. I don't know why you put up with me.'

Tam stared out into the night. 'That thought had crossed my mind,' she answered with a twitch of a smile at the corner of her mouth.

'I've been having a few conversations lately that have driven home just how unfair I've been to you.'

Tam looked confused. 'With whom?'

'Dylan, Lix and Gemma,' he said.

'Gemma! You two hate each other. When did you talk to her?' Tam gasped.

'Earlier today,' Seb said. 'We had a chat over dinner.'

'Wait! What?' Tam's eyes widened in surprise.

'I've just got back from Melbourne,' Seb explained. 'I went to ask her something and she put me straight on a couple of issues.'

'I must be dreaming,' Tam said. 'You've been at each other's throats for years.'

'Yeah, I apologised for that too,' Seb admitted.

Tam looked at Seb in disbelief. 'What the hell is going on?'

'Okay, I don't want to throw him under the bus but . . .'

'You're going to anyway,' Tam cut in with a smile.

Seb nodded. 'Dylan told me what really happened at the Henderson party all those years ago. He assumed that I knew. Tam, why didn't you tell me?'

Tam's shoulders slumped. 'I try not to think about it,' she said. 'Besides, it was a long time ago. What happened could have been a whole lot worse than it was and Taylor left town.'

'I wish that you'd had enough confidence in me to say something,' Seb replied. 'Although I get why you didn't. But Taylor Henderson should never have touched you.'

'I know. But at the time, it didn't seem that important—not after Mum and Dad's accident.' Tam shrugged, as if she didn't know what else to say.

'That prick is lucky I didn't know at the time—he would've got a lot more than the broken nose that Dylan gave him.'

'What?' Tam looked shocked. 'Dylan broke Taylor's nose?'

'You didn't know? Apparently he confronted him and punched him fair in the face. Although it sounds like he got fairly beat up in the process.'

'Did he tell you that?'

'Gemma told me.'

Tam went quiet. She had always known that Dylan had her back, and was always there for her, but she never realised how far that went.

'I need to tell you something,' Seb said as he glanced at his sister. He paused for a second before he continued. 'I don't blame you for the accident.'

* * *

Seb's sentence seemed to hang in the air between them for a long time. Tam bit her bottom lip to stop it from quivering.

'I always thought that you did,' she whispered.

'I'm sorry, Tam,' Seb said. 'I really am. I think that maybe I did, at the beginning anyway. It wasn't right and it certainly wasn't fair but I suppose it was easier to bear the pain when I could blame someone. I was so wrapped up in my own grief and I threw myself into caring for our family and taking on as much responsibility as possible. I always blamed the truck driver but I guess there was a tiny fragment inside me that asked all the wrong questions about why our parents were driving on the other side of town to begin with.'

Tam took in a couple of deep breaths before she could trust her voice to answer. 'They're the same questions that I've always asked myself. The truth is, if it wasn't for me, Mum and Dad would never have been on that road.'

'You're not to blame,' he said as he put his arm around her and gave her a squeeze. 'It was an awful, stupid accident—that's all. Do you really think that Mum and Dad would want you beating yourself up over this? They loved us and only ever wanted us to be happy.'

A lump formed in her throat and she tried to push it down. 'I know,' she said softly as she leant into him. 'I know that. It's just sometimes I have these dreams and I begin to think that I don't deserve to be happy because it's my fault that they're not here.'

'It's not, Tam, and it never was. You have to move past it and begin to really live your life—because that's what they would have wanted for you. If you want to honour Mum and Dad then live and be happy.' Seb's voice cracked a little. 'I'll help you through this, I promise.'

She nodded as she wiped away a tear. 'Lix suggested that I go and get some professional help. I think he's right.'

'It's a good idea,' Seb said. 'I'm sorry I've been such a shit brother.'

The comment made her smile through the tears and she nudged him back. 'You haven't been . . . well, maybe a difficult brother.'

'Forgive me?'

She looked over at him. 'Always.'

Forty-Five

Over the next couple of days Tam busied herself organising an upcoming wedding at Carrington Farm. The fact that she was assisting in the beginning of another couple's life together, when her own had all but fallen apart didn't escape her. She hadn't spoken to Dylan, even though he'd left several messages on her phone. She was too much of a coward to answer them. She still didn't know how she really felt, and if she could ever give him what he wanted.

She'd taken Lix's advice and had booked in to talk to someone in a couple of weeks. Maybe it was too late to help her relationship with Dylan but at least she was taking a positive step forward. The conversation with Seb had also helped her decide it was time to reach out for help. The shadows of the past had kept her captive for too long.

But today she was doing her best to push those thoughts aside as she had to make sure that everything was in place for her favourite bride's wedding tomorrow night. It was wrong to have a favourite but that's how she felt about Angie. This wedding was so different from the first one Angie had imagined before her plans had been ruined. So Tam and Maddie had pulled all the stops out for this event. Even though it was only for a handful of people, they wanted it to be perfect. It was all hands on deck. Carrington Farm was responsible for every aspect of this wedding, from the food to the venue to the photography. The only things

Tam had outsourced were a surprise for the couple and the cake that she was picking up from the bakery this afternoon.

Just then Lix stuck his head around the door of the office. 'Is everything sorted?'

Tam glanced up from her desk. 'I think so. Who knew that such a tiny wedding would take so much work,' she said with a smile.

Lix chuckled. 'It'll be worth it,' he replied. 'Let's just be thankful that the storm isn't meant to turn up until Sunday. I don't think Angie would cope if this wedding got cancelled as well.'

'Storm?'

'There's meant to be a big one rolling in on Sunday. Just as well we don't have anything planned.'

'Well, we did have another wedding booked for then but the groom toppled down a flight of stairs on his buck's night. Apparently he's still in hospital.'

Lix grimaced. 'Ooooh, how much trouble is he in?'

'A lot, I'd say. The poor bride is beside herself but we've managed to postpone and re-book. Although, I think they may have lost some money on the catering.'

'Listen, I'm going into town—do you need anything?'

'You could drop in to the bakery to see if the cake's ready,' Tam said.

'Not a problem,' Lix replied. 'Oh, by the way, did you hear about Taylor?'

'I knew he was back in town—I saw him. Is he causing trouble again?'

'Not anymore. It seems that Blake saw him off the property, and threatened him with all hell if he ever came back.'

'Really? Blake?'

'Yep. The tables have turned. The last anyone saw of Taylor, he was heading out of town with a look of thunder on his face.'

Tam felt a little shaken. Any mention of Taylor Henderson brought back dark memories. His was a name she would rather forget. 'Let's hope he stays away forever—but somehow I get the feeling that he's not done yet.'

'Well, he's gone for now,' Lix said. He started to walk away then paused and turned back. 'Are you okay?'

She gave him a brief smile. 'Of course I am.'

He looked at her. 'You're a terrible liar,' he said with a shake of his head. 'Just so you know, I spoke to Dylan the other day.'

Tam shuffled a few papers on her desk and pretended to be disinterested. 'Oh?'

'Also a bad actor,' Lix added with a smile.

'What did he have to say?'

'He's worried about you, he wants to be with you and he loves you,' Lix said simply. 'You know, sis, it seems to me that you've got a whole lot of happiness in your reach—all you have to do is be brave enough to take it.'

'That was very poetic of you,' she said as she tried not to let the words wind around her heart.

'It was, wasn't it?' He grinned as he walked away. He called back over his shoulder. 'You should think about it. Catch you later.'

* * *

Dylan checked his phone for the tenth time, but she still hadn't responded. He needed to talk to her but she was avoiding him. *Fine, that's just fine*, he thought as he drove back to the cottage.

Lord, she could be exasperating sometimes.

It was just after five—he may have finished for the day but he knew that there was a good chance that Tam would work later as there were weddings booked over the weekend.

He contemplated pulling over and ringing her again but he'd probably go straight to voicemail. He wanted to just head on over to her place but he knew she might need a few more days to mull things over. If he hadn't heard from her by Sunday, he'd go over and try to get her to see sense.

He'd spent some time thinking long and hard about what was going on in her head. She said that she was breaking up with him for his sake, so he could have the future he wanted with a happy family. And it was true that's what he'd always thought his life would be. He didn't need to be rich or drive a flashy car, he just wanted for his business to stay afloat and have a good life. At least that's how he imagined the future—him, Tam and a couple of kids running around the cottage. Maybe even a dog, if Red would allow it. But as each day went by, another one with no contact from her, he began to rethink how much he was attached to that perfect picture. The more he thought about, the more he began to realise that all he wanted—no, all he needed—was Tamara. The future could take care of itself. All he had to do was work out how the hell to get her back.

* * *

It was Golden Hour, that magical time of day when the sun begins to set and bathes the countryside in its warm, rich gilded light. Rori, dressed in a pale pink dress which was topped with a circlet of rosebuds, preceded the bride as she walked to the end of the deck outside the old summer house. She couldn't contain her happiness about being a flower girl, and grinned back at Angie as she scattered petals from the small wicker basket she was carrying.

The incandescent sky was reflected in the water of the lake as a light breeze wound through the weeping willow and the reeds, until it spiralled around Angie and playfully tugged at her veil. The setting sun illuminated the bride as she walked towards her groom holding a trailing bouquet of pale pink roses and accompanied by the evocative music from the solo violinist. The wedding officiant smiled at Angie and then began the ceremony, which included the vows Angie and her groom had written themselves.

Tam stood back and smiled. It was perfect, everything was perfect. She glanced over at Maddie who gave her a nod of approval. The wedding was tiny and yet sublimely beautiful.

Lix was taking endless photos of the couple and there was a cheer when they were pronounced husband and wife. Inside the summer house, Gray and Lucy had laid out a buffet which consisted of local produce, including cured meats, olives, cheeses and wine. Sitting in the middle of the table on a pedestal was a small two-tiered cake. It was vanilla and rose flavoured and was decorated with pink roses that matched Angie's bouquet.

Angie raced up and hugged Tam. 'Thank you so much. This is so beautiful. And the fact that you even had little Rori be my flower girl, I can't thank you enough.'

Tam hugged her back. 'I'm so happy that you're happy,' she said with a smile.

'It's so much more than I imagined it would be. I was so upset when we had to cancel the big wedding but now I don't care because it wouldn't have compared to this,' Angie said with a gesture which encompassed the whole room. 'I feel like a princess.'

Tam grinned. 'You look like a princess,' she said. 'Enjoy the rest of the night and congratulations.'

'Thank you again,' Angie started to turn away but she stopped and looked down at her bouquet. 'Here, I want you to have this in appreciation.'

Tam held up her hands in front of her. 'Oh, you don't have to . . .'

'I know but I want to,' Angie said as she put the flowers in Tam's hands.

Tam gave her a nod. 'Thank you—they're lovely.'

Angie gave her a smile and then walked over to her new husband.

Taking the flowers, Tam walked outside towards the edge of the deck. The sun had now dipped beyond the horizon and twilight was beginning to creep over the lake. The fairy lights began to twinkle as Tam held onto the bouquet and looked out over the water. For the hundredth time that day, she thought of Dylan and wondered how he was going.

The sound of a clicking camera shook her out of her thoughts. She turned her head and saw Lix standing not far away. He gave her a smile.

'Wedding bouquets suit you,' he said before heading back to the wedding.

Forty-Six

On Sunday morning, Tam was at the barn cleaning up the remnants of yesterday's wedding. It had been very different from the one she'd hosted on Friday night. Angie's wedding had been small and intimate, yesterday's had been loud and flashy with the eighty guests partying right up to the time when they were kindly encouraged to leave. Because it had been late, Tam had decided that the bulk of the clean-up could wait until the next day.

Tam was up a small step ladder, taking down the decorations when she glanced up at the bright blue, cloudless sky. She frowned as she remembered that Lix said it was meant to storm. Maybe it was forecast for later in the day because at the moment it was a perfect summer morning.

'How's it going?' Maddie asked as she walked out of the barn carrying a garbage bag in one hand and a glittery evening bag in the other.

Tam looked down at her aunt. 'Good,' she responded. 'Another item for lost property?'

'Yep, first one for the year,' Maddie said with a smile. 'I'm starting a new box.'

Guests often forgot things like the jackets they'd slung over the back of a chair or the odd handbag. But every now and again, there'd be some unexpected things left behind; like the night she'd found a sleeping baby in its carrier, although the new parents only made it as far as the front gate before realising their mistake.

'Is there much more to do inside?' Tam asked.

'There's still quite a bit but I think we're on top of it,' Maddie answered. 'Lix and Gray are mopping the floor and I have to take off to pick Rori up from her friend's place, I won't be long though.'

'No worries. I'll see you when you get back,' Tam said with a smile. 'After lunch, I'm going down to the summer house to do the last tidy-up there.'

'I suppose we should get things squared away before the storm hits,' Maddie said.

'Yeah, Lix said something about that.' Tam pointed up to the sky. 'Although, you wouldn't think it at the moment.'

'True. I'll see you soon,' Maddie said as she started to turn away.

'See ya,' Tam called back before she looked back to the swathes of cream fabric and silk flowers she was taking down.

* * *

After a late lunch, Tam glanced out the kitchen window as she was putting her plate into the dishwasher. The once blue sky of the morning was gone and replaced with an overcast grey. As she straightened up she noticed that the wind had picked up, as the branches of the lemon tree in the back garden were dancing to and fro. It didn't appear to be raining but the chances of it happening soon looked pretty good.

She still had to go to the summer house but the walk from the house to there took about ten minutes, it wasn't far but who wants to do that while soaking wet? Tam decided that she'd take her bike, at least if the storm broke she could get back to the house in a flash.

About an hour later, Tam was standing in the middle of the summer house. She'd been packing up the decorations from Angie's wedding and the last few props she'd used to create a fairy tale theme. She was thinking about heading back to the house when the heavens opened and the heavy downpour began. Taking a chair she sat by the open French doors and watched the torrent pelt down over the deck and the lake. The wind picked up and tugged at the trees, causing their leaves to shake and the trunks to creak. The rain was so heavy that it drummed against the shingle roof. There was no way she was going to even attempt to get back to the house.

The petrichor of the rain swirled around her; she detected the earthy, almost warm smell as the raindrops hit the ground. As she sat and took in the storm her attention was snagged by a pair of headlights flashing through the windows. Tam stood up as she recognised Dylan's ute.

By the time he slammed the car door shut and made it into the summer house, he was drenched.

'Hi,' he said as he wiped himself off. 'I didn't plan that very well, did I?'

Tam smiled. 'Not at all.'

He straightened up and blew out a sigh. 'You didn't answer my messages.'

'I know.'

He looked at her.

'I wasn't meaning to be harsh,' Tam continued. 'I just didn't know what to say. I thought that maybe we needed some time alone to think things out.'

'Well, if you'd let me in on that, I wouldn't have driven through the rain to see you,' he answered with a slight smile.

'I should have said something. Even if it was only a text,' Tam replied. 'So why did you come over?'

Dylan took a step closer to her. 'To see if you were okay and if you'd changed your mind about us.'

'I don't know what I think,' Tam confessed. 'Part of me wants to be with you but I'm still worried that if we stay together you'll eventually resent it. And I couldn't bear that.'

'I told you that would never happen. You're borrowing trouble and getting worried about stuff that may never happen.' He closed the distance between them and placed his hands on her shoulders.

'But, Dylan, what happens if I can't give you the life you want?'

'Then maybe what I want has changed,' he said. 'I've thought about this for days—I love you, I want you and I'm willing to take whatever you can give me. If it's marriage and kids—great. But if not, then that's okay too. I've been in love with you for so long . . . it's like breathing; I can't stop it.'

'Dylan, I . . .' Tam began to say.

'If you want time, you've got it. I'll do whatever I have to do to make it work and make you happy.'

The thunder rumbled overhead as the torrent became a deluge, the day darkened even further and their view from the French doors was overpainted with layers of grey and indigo watercolour.

Tam flinched as lightning crackled overhead and illuminated the dullness of the day.

'I'm not sure if I can do this,' she admitted.

'We can do it together,' Dylan replied.

She was silent for a moment, trying to make sense of the turmoil inside her. She did love him, and because of that she needed to let him go. There was something broken inside her and, even though she hoped that it could and maybe would be mended, how could she take that chance? What if she hurt him?

'I can't,' she said as she broke away from his arms and took a step back. 'I'm doing this for you, you're better off finding someone else—you deserve someone who can love you with their whole heart.'

Dylan stood unmoving as he stared at her. For the first time ever, he looked almost defeated. 'No, babe, you're doing this for you,' he said quietly. 'You're scared to be happy because you think you don't deserve it. And you think you don't deserve it because you still blame yourself for your parents' death.'

Another rumble of thunder sounded overhead as the storm intensified. Tam jumped at a loud crack as a large branch crashed off one of the gums near the water's edge.

'Maybe that's true,' she whispered, 'and that's why we can't be together because I don't know if I can ever break away from the guilt.'

'Your parents wouldn't want you to blame yourself, they'd want you to be happy.'

'I know, but at the end of the day, there's always a piece of me that holds back, like a missing piece, and until I can find it—I can't love you the way I should.'

'Then I'll wait,' he said earnestly.

'It could take forever.'

'Maybe it won't though.' Dylan's eyes pleaded with hers. 'You're talking like it's set in stone, but you've got the power to change it. I'm not saying it'll be easy but you're not by yourself; you're surrounded by people who love you and only want your happiness.'

'And maybe you'll waste your life waiting for a woman who can't commit to you,' Tam said.

She didn't want this, couldn't he see it? It was so hard to push him away and Tam braced herself to stay strong and follow through.

Dylan stood there as if he was absorbing her words. 'Okay,' he said flatly as he took a step back towards the door. 'Okay, I understand. There's nothing that I can say to make you change your mind, so I'll go.'

'Just wait a little while until the worst of this storm blows over.' Tam looked past him to the French doors. 'It's really wild out there.'

He shook his head. 'No, it'll be fine.'

Tam reached out and caught his arm. 'You can't go out there, it's dangerous.'

Dylan put his hand on hers and gently pushed it away. 'I can't stay here, Tam—there's nothing left for me.' He walked out the doors, across the new deck and then ran to his car.

Tam ran to the open door, the rain lashed at her face. 'Dylan, come back,' she called out but the storm snatched her words away. He paused once he was in the car and put his head on the steering wheel. She watched him, thinking that maybe he'd changed his mind but then he started the car and reversed back.

'Dylan!' she called out again but he looked straight ahead and drove away, without giving her a second glance.

Forty-Seven

Tam stared out into the storm. She could just make out the tail-lights from Dylan's ute as he drove away. His words replayed in her mind.

I can't stay here, Tam—there's nothing left for me.

Hot tears ran down her cheeks as she recalled the defeat and sadness in his eyes. *What have I done and how the hell am I going to fix it?* She reached for the little gold compass around her neck. As she touched the pendant, the bail broke and the compass fell onto the ground. Horrified, Tam watched as it rolled across the floor and came to rest just in front of the French doors. She ran across the room and when she bent down to pick it up, she noticed that the tiny arrow was pointing north, as it always did, but this time it was in the direction that Dylan had gone. Tam took it as a sign. She scooped up her pendant and grabbed her helmet.

She fired up the bike and rode after Dylan. She had to slow the bike on the dirt road as the rain had made it slippery and soft in places. Ahead she could see the tail-lights of Dylan's car every now and again. She desperately wanted to speed up but she held back at least until she made it to the main bitumen road. Even then she had to be careful, a patch of oil becoming slippery after the rain was not uncommon.

The storm whipped about her as she negotiated the winding track through the rain-drenched bush. In the distance she saw

Dylan's car pause before it turned onto the road. Hoping for the best, she pushed her bike and her luck a little more and sped up. Soon she made it to the road and, once she'd turned to follow Dylan, she hit the accelerator. He was still quite a way in front of her but the rain had eased a little and now she was able to make out the shape of the ute. Did she have a plan? No, all she knew was that she couldn't let him go.

The turnoff to Dylan's place was not that far away. The road rose up into a gentle hill and there was a steep gully off to the left that ran parallel with it. Beyond that a small road branched off which eventually led to Dylan's cottage.

Tam was watching the road intently when she saw that Dylan's ute had started to climb up the hill. He was still a fair way ahead and she'd have to slow down again once the turnoff changed back into a dirt track so she probably wouldn't catch up to him until the cottage.

But then out of nowhere Dylan's car slid out of control. There was a screech of brakes as the car snaked across the road. Tam's heart raced as she looked on in horror as it skidded to the left, took out a white post and barrelled towards the gully. Time seemed to slow down, and even though she was speeding towards him it felt as if she was in slow motion. This couldn't be happening again; she would not lose him like this.

Tam brought the bike to a halt at the side of the road and ripped off her helmet. From what she could make out the ute had gone over the edge and fallen side-first into a large gum tree. She pulled out her phone and rang triple zero as she ran forward, trying to find a way down.

'This is triple zero, what's your emergency?' the operator asked.

'A car's run off the road and into a gully,' Tam said and then explained where they were.

'Is anyone hurt?'

'I think so, I'm going to check.' Tam felt a small flare of relief when the operator said that help was on the way. She ended the call, shoved her phone back into her pocket and scrambled down the muddy side of the gully towards the car. The ground was slippery from all the rain and she lost her footing more than once. As the car came fully into view she realised with horror that the gully it lay in was now a gushing torrent of water, fed by the run-off from the road, and from the hill above it. Dylan's ute was already partly submerged in the flow, and she could see the rising water level was quickly engulfing the front of the vehicle and the driver's seat.

'Dylan!' she screamed as she clambered down the embankment and into the water. By the time she reached the car, the rushing flood was already halfway up her legs, and the force of the flow was almost too much for her to fight. She grabbed onto the edge of the car roof and pulled herself against the wreck to steady herself.

She looked through the driver's-side window, the rain against the glass gave very little visibility, but she could just make out the shape of Dylan's head, slumped over the steering wheel. She tried to open the door, but it wouldn't budge, so she banged loudly on the window.

'Dylan!' she called desperately. 'You've got to get out!'

He was unresponsive. *Oh God, please don't let him be dead.*

She started to beat on the window. 'Dylan, wake up! Wake up! Wake up!' she shouted. Once again she tried the door, and could not move it. 'I won't lose you too!' she screamed, and with every ounce of strength in her body, she pulled on the door handle, almost slipping into the water around her. Just as her feet started to lose grip in the mud, she felt the door give, and it sent her onto her back as the gushing waters pulled it open.

'Dylan!' she called out as she fought her way back to the car. 'Dylan, answer me!'

Fear gripped her when he didn't answer. For a moment she was dragged back to her parents' accident and she had to fight the searing panic that threatened to overwhelm her.

'No!' she said out loud as she brushed a strand of her dark hair away from her face. Last time she was too late and couldn't do anything but that wasn't going to happen again. She wasn't going to lose him, she loved him too much. To hell with what the future might bring. She'd be happy if he was safe and she could tell him what he really meant to her.

Tam focused her mind, and fought the panic. Time was running out. She knew what she needed to do. Without another thought, she reached into the flooded car, then pushed Dylan's limp body back so that she could reach the seatbelt. Her cold, numb fingers fumbled with the catch, and she grunted in exasperation as the release eluded her. Finally it gave and she felt his body slump down. His head was under the water.

'Damn you, Dylan, you've gotta help me,' she cried. With a super-human effort, she lifted his body out of the seat, and inch by inch, dragged him out of the car and onto the bank.

Tam moved her hand to his neck to find a pulse and let out a sigh of relief when she felt a strong beat against the tips of her fingers.

'Come on,' she said. 'You're scaring the hell out of me. Dylan, wake up.' He had a bloody mark on his forehead, like it had hit the steering wheel, and his left arm appeared to be at a weird angle.

All of a sudden he groaned and coughed, and a burst of relief and gratitude flooded through her body as his eyes began to flutter.

'It's all right, you're going to be all right,' Tam assured him.

His eyes cracked open. 'What happened?' he whispered.

'I don't know, you lost control of the car and ended up in the gully,' Tam replied. 'Maybe it was an oil patch. Help's on the way, just stay calm and everything will be all right.'

Dylan focused on her. 'Babe, you're getting wet.'

Tam laughed, out of relief more than anything. 'Yeah, I am.'

He went to move but then hissed with pain.

'What's wrong?' Tam asked with a frown.

'My arm, might be broken,' Dylan said as he tried not to move.

Tam looked at the angle of his arm and nodded. 'Hang in there, the ambulance is coming.'

'How are you even here?'

'I followed you.'

'Why?'

'Because I realised that I was wrong. I can't be without you even if you'd be better off without me.' Tam gave his good hand a squeeze. 'I love you and that's all that matters.'

'I love you too, babe,' Dylan said, as the falling rain streamed down his bruised face, and dripped off his nose. 'Whatever problems crop up, we'll face them together.'

'Yes, we will,' Tam replied with a smile as her eyes misted with tears.

'Hey, don't cry,' he said.

'I'm not,' she lied. 'It's just raining.'

'Liar,' he said with a slight smile. 'So what made you change your mind?'

Tam was quiet for a moment as she tried to find the right words.

'Let's just say that I was shown the way,' she answered.

Through the rain, Tam could hear the distant ambulance siren.

'Hold on, I'm going to go back to the road so the ambulance can find us.'

'Okay.' He closed his eyes but as she turned to go he touched her arm. 'You'll come back, won't you?'

'Don't worry, I'm not going anywhere,' she said with a smile. 'I love you and you're stuck with me now.'

'I couldn't think of anything better than that,' Dylan said.

Forty-Eight

Summer had faded and been replaced with the golden tones of autumn. The weather was still great but Tam noted there was a crispness to the morning air. Life was good, better than it had been in a long time, at least from her perspective. On a professional level, things were pretty good with a nice selection of weddings, gatherings and events that kept her busy and Carrington Farm humming along.

On a personal level, Tam couldn't wish for more. She'd been going to therapy in Bendigo, her doctor was really nice and easy to talk to and she felt better for it. Her family was doing well, although she did miss her baby brother as Gray had gone back to uni. And her and Seb . . . well, that had been the biggest change of all. Their relationship had improved immensely; oh there were times when they'd still butt heads and she'd call him a jerk but they were few and far between. He'd even accompanied her to therapy a couple of times. Seb seemed to have relaxed a bit and started acting more like a brother, with everyone. And the biggest revelation was that he and Gemma could actually be in the same room together without it all going south and them falling into an argument. So maybe miracles did happen.

Tam was still suggesting that Maddie go out more and maybe even find someone to go out with. But as far as she knew, Maddie still resisted . . . she could be so stubborn at times. And as for her favourite brother, Lix had been spending a bit of time at the old Darcell place working on a series of photographs for an exhibition he was planning. He'd shown her some of the images and they were brilliant, each and every one of them telling a story and drawing an emotion.

Tam was about to head off on her bike when she realised she'd forgotten her phone.

'Are you off somewhere?' Seb called out with a grin as he walked up the path to the back door.

'Yeah, I have to take Dylan to the hospital to get the cast off.'

'On the bike?'

'No,' she said with an eye roll. 'We're taking his car, I'm just going over to his place.'

'I bet he's happy. He's been complaining about that cast constantly over the past couple of weeks,' Seb said with a laugh. 'It's the only time he's been grouchier than me.'

'Let's just say he's been really looking forward to today,' Tam answered as she stowed a stuffed backpack on her bike. She caught Seb looking but he didn't say anything. 'Okay, I'd better take off.'

She was about to put her helmet on when Maddie appeared at the door.

'Tam, I was thinking that since we have a cancellation next Sunday, maybe we could do a family barbecue or something. What do you think?' she asked. 'Gray's coming up and I thought Dylan could join us as well.'

'That's a good idea,' Seb said. 'We could have a cricket match. Maybe I can redeem myself from the Christmas one.'

Tam grinned. 'Sounds great, count us in. I'd better go,' she said. 'Bye.'

* * *

About three and a half hours later, Tam and Dylan walked back inside his cottage. He bent his left arm up and down a couple of times as they stepped into the kitchen.

'I'm so happy to have that damn cast off,' he said.

'I bet.' Tam went to the fridge and took out a bottle of juice. 'You want one?' she asked as she went to grab a couple of glasses.

'Please.' Dylan walked over to Tam and put his arms around her waist.

'Thanks for going with me today,' he said as he kissed the side of her neck.

Tam was silent for a moment as the familiar warmth began to spark inside her. 'That's okay,' she said as she leant against him, the juice forgotten.

He spun her around in his arms until they were standing face to face. She recognised the heat in his eyes, especially as it reflected her own.

'I don't ever want to be without you,' he whispered as he rested his forehead against hers.

Tam wrapped her arms around him. 'You won't be.' She tilted her head and kissed him on the mouth.

The kiss bound them together. In it, Tam tried to convey everything she felt. She wasn't afraid of the future anymore because she knew that she deserved to be happy. It was her right and the one thing her parents had always wished for her. Tam held him tight, his body heat enveloped her and she knew she was where she belonged.

He picked her up and she wound her legs around his hips as they moved towards the bedroom. Dylan sucked in a breath when she kissed his neck as they reached the bedroom door. He put her on the bed and they kissed as they tugged at each other's clothes. When all she was wearing was the little gold compass between her breasts, they fell together on the bed. He left trails of fire as his fingers skimmed over her body. She wanted him in every sense. She held him close and felt the beat of his heart against her skin. They came together, both holding, wanting and needing each other. His fingers intertwined with hers as their tempo increased. There were no lies or fear between them anymore only love.

'I love you, Dylan,' Tam whispered as she looked into his eyes before they chased each other into the void.

* * *

Later Tam raised herself up on her elbow and gave Dylan a quick kiss on the mouth before she went to get out of the bed.

'Hey, where are you going?' he asked as he tried to catch her but missed.

She stepped out of his reach, grabbed his discarded shirt and put it on. 'I'll be back in a minute,' she said as she headed for the door.

'Oh no, wait . . . Tam, come back,' he called after her.

'Just a tick,' she replied over her shoulder.

A couple of minutes later Tam came back carrying an overstuffed backpack.

Dylan gave her a curious look. 'What's that about?' he asked with a frown.

Tam smiled and chucked it on the bed next to him. 'Step one,' she said.

'What does that mean?' Dylan sat up and glanced at the backpack before looking back to her.

Tam touched the compass around her neck. 'It means that you'll have to share a bit of your wardrobe space,' she said as she looked over to the tiny walk-in wardrobe in the corner.

A slow smile began to bloom on Dylan's face. 'Does this mean what I think it does?'

Tam nodded. 'It's just a few things to start with,' she explained. 'I thought we'd ease into it slowly.'

Dylan let out a whoop, pulled her on top of him and kissed her on the lips. 'Do you really mean it?'

She nodded again and smiled. 'Yes, I finally realise where I belong.'